SONS OF DESTINY

THE SAGA OF DARREN SHAN
BOOK 12

Other titles by

DARREN SHAN

THE DEMONATA

THE SAGA OF DARREN SHAN

DARREN SHAN

SONS OF DESTINY

THE SAGA OF DARREN SHAN

BOOK 12

Harper*Trophy*Canada™
An imprint of HarperCollins*PublishersLtd*

Discover your Destiny with Darren Shan
on the web at

www.darrenshan.com

Sons of Destiny
© Darren Shan 2004
All rights reserved.

Published by Harper*Trophy*Canada™, an imprint of
HarperCollins Publishers Ltd.

Harper*Trophy*Canada™ is a trademark of HarperCollins Publishers.

First published in Great Britain by HarperCollins *Children's Books*: 2004.
This Harper*Trophy*Canada edition: 2007

HarperCollins books may be purchased for educational, business, or sales promotional use
through our Special Markets Department.

HarperCollins Publishers Ltd
2 Bloor Street East, 20th Floor
Toronto, Ontario, Canada
M4W 1A8

www.harpercollins.ca

Library and Archives Canada Cataloguing in Publication

Shan, Darren
Sons of destiny / Darren Shan.

(Cirque du freak ; #12)
ISBN-13 978-1-55468-058-0   ISBN-10: 1-55468-058-1

I. Vampires—Juvenile fiction. I. Title. II. Series: Shan, Darren
Cirque du Freak ; #12.

PZ7.S52823So 2007   j823'.92   C2007-903194-3

HC 9 8 7 6 5 4 3 2 1

Printed and bound in the United States

For:

Bas, Biddy and Liam — my three pillars

OBE's
(Order of the Bloody Entrails) to:

"Lucky" Aleta Moriarty

A and Bo — Bangkok's best banshees
Emily "Lilliputian" Chuang
Jennifer "Stacey" Abbots

Saga Editors:
Domenica De Rosa, Gillie Russell, Zoë Clarke and
Julia Bruce — you done good, girls!!!

Bloody Brilliant Buccaneers:
The Christopher Little Cutthroats

And an extra special thank you to all of my Shansters,
especially those who have kept me company on Shanville.
Even in death may you all be triumphant!

PROLOGUE

If my life was a fairy tale and I was writing a book about it, I'd start with, "Once upon a time there were two boys called Darren and Steve…" But my life's a horror story, so if I were to write about it, I'd have to begin with something like this instead:

Evil has a name — Steve Leopard.

He was born Steve Leonard, but to his friends (yes — he had friends once!) he was always Steve Leopard. He was never happy at home, didn't have a dad, didn't like his mum. He dreamt of power and glory. He yearned for strength and respect, and time in which to enjoy it. He wanted to be a vampire.

His chance came when he spotted a creature of the night, Larten Crepsley, performing in the wondrous magical show, the Cirque Du Freak. He asked Mr Crepsley to blood him. The vampire refused — he said Steve had bad blood. Steve hated him for that and vowed to track him down and kill him when he grew up.

Some years later, as Steve was preparing for his life as a vampire hunter, he learnt about the purple-skinned, red-eyed vampaneze. In legends, vampires are wicked killers who suck humans dry. That's hysterical rubbish — they only take small amounts of blood when they feed, causing no harm. But the vampaneze are different. They broke away from the vampire clan six hundred years ago. They live by laws of their own. They believe it's shameful to drink from a human without killing. They always murder when they feed. Steve's sort of people!

Steve went in search of the vampaneze, certain they'd accept him. He probably thought they were as twisted as he was. But he got it wrong. Although the vampaneze were killers, they weren't inherently evil. They didn't torture humans and they tried not to interfere with vampires. They went about their business quietly and calmly, keeping a lower-than-low profile.

I don't know this for sure, but I'm guessing the vampaneze rejected Steve, just like Mr Crepsley did. The vampaneze live by even stricter, more traditional rules than vampires. I can't see them accepting a human into their ranks if they knew he was going to turn out bad.

But Steve found a way in, thanks to that eternal agent of chaos — Desmond Tiny. Most just call him Mr Tiny, but if you shorten his first name and put it with his surname, you get Mr *Destiny*. He's the most powerful person in the world, immortal as far as anyone knows, a meddler of the highest order. He gave the vampaneze a present many centuries earlier, a coffin which filled with fire whenever a person lay within it, burning them to ash within seconds. But he said that one night someone would lie in the coffin and emerge unharmed. That person would be the Lord of the Vampaneze and had to be obeyed by every member of the clan. If they accepted this Lord, they'd gain more power than they'd ever imagined. Otherwise they'd be destroyed.

The promise of such power proved too much for Steve to ignore. He decided to take the test. He probably figured he had nothing to lose. He entered the coffin, the flames engulfed him, and a minute later he stepped out unburnt. Suddenly, everything changed. He had an army of vampaneze at his command, willing to give their lives for him and do anything he asked. He no longer had to settle for killing Mr Crepsley — he could wipe out the entire vampire clan!

But Mr Tiny didn't want the vampaneze to crush the vampires too easily. He thrives on suffering and conflict. A quick, assured victory wouldn't provide him with enough entertainment. So he gave the vampires a get-out clause. Three of them had the ability to kill the Vampaneze Lord before he came fully into his powers. They'd have four chances. If they were successful and killed him, the vampires would win the War of the Scars (that's what the battle between the vampires and vampaneze was known as). If they failed, two would die during the hunt, while the third would survive to witness the downfall of the clan.

Mr Crepsley was one of the hunters. A Vampire Prince, Vancha March, was another. The last was also a Prince, the youngest ever, a half-vampire called Darren Shan — and that's where *I* come in.

I was Steve's best friend when we were kids. We went to the Cirque Du Freak together, and through Steve I learnt of the existence of vampires and was sucked into their world. I was blooded by Mr Crepsley and served as his assistant. Under his guidance I studied the ways of vampires and travelled to Vampire Mountain. There I undertook my Trials of Initiation — and failed. Fearing death, I fled, but during my escape I uncovered a plot to destroy the clan. Later I exposed it, and as a reward I was not only accepted into the fold, but made a Vampire Prince.

After six years in Vampire Mountain, Mr Tiny set me on the trail of the Lord of the Vampaneze, along with Mr Crepsley and Vancha. One of Mr Tiny's Little People travelled with us. His name was Harkat Mulds. Little People are grey-skinned, stitched-together, short, with large green eyes, no nose, and ears sewn beneath the flesh of their heads. They're created from the remains of dead people. Harkat didn't know who he used to be, but we later found out he was Kurda Smahlt in his previous life — the vampire who'd betrayed the clan in the hope of preventing the War of the Scars.

Not knowing who the Vampaneze Lord was, we missed our first chance to kill him when Vancha let him escape, because he was under the protection of Vancha's vampaneze brother, Gannen Harst. Later, in the city of Mr Crepsley's youth, I ran into Steve again. He told me he was a vampaneze hunter and, fool that I was, I believed him. The others did too, although Mr Crepsley was suspicious. He sensed something wrong, but I convinced him to grant Steve the benefit of the doubt. I've made some terrible mistakes in my life, but that was certainly the worst.

When Steve revealed his true colours, we fought, and twice we had the power to kill him. The first time we let him live because we wanted to trade his life for Debbie Hemlock's — my human girlfriend. The second time, Mr Crepsley fought Steve, Gannen Harst and an impostor, who was pretending to be the Lord of the Vampaneze. Mr Crepsley killed the impostor, but then was knocked into a pit of stakes by Steve. He could have taken Steve down with him, but let him live so that Gannen and the other vampaneze would spare the lives of his friends. It was only afterwards that Steve revealed the truth about himself, and made the bitter loss of Mr Crepsley all the more unbearable.

There was a long gap between that and our next encounter. I went with Harkat to find out the truth about his past, to a waste world full of monsters and mutants, which we later discovered was Earth in the future. Upon my return I spent a couple of years travelling with the Cirque Du Freak, waiting for destiny (or Des Tiny) to pit Steve and me together again for one final clash.

Our paths finally crossed in our old home town. I'd returned with the Cirque Du Freak. It was strange revisiting the past, walking the streets of the town where I'd grown up. I saw my sister Annie, now a grown woman with a child of her own, and I ran into an old friend, Tommy Jones, who'd become a professional footballer. I went to watch Tommy play in an important cup game. His team won, but their celebrations were cut short when two of Steve's henchmen invaded the pitch and killed a lot of people, including Tommy.

I chased after the murderous pair, straight into a trap. I faced Steve again. He had a child called Darius with him — his son. Darius shot me. Steve could have finished me off, but didn't. It wasn't the destined time. My end (or his) would only come when I faced him with Vancha by my side.

Crawling through the streets, I was rescued by a pair of tramps. They'd been recruited by Debbie and an ex-police inspector, Alice Burgess, who were building a human army to help the vampires. Vancha March linked up with me while I was recovering. With the ladies and Harkat, we returned to the Cirque Du Freak. We discussed the future with Mr Tall, the owner of the circus. He told us that no matter who won the war, an evil dictator known as the Lord of the Shadows would rise to rule and destroy the world.

As we were trying to come to terms with the shocking news, two of Steve's crazed followers struck — R.V. and Morgan James, the pair who'd killed Tommy. With the help of Darius, they slaughtered Mr Tall and took a hostage — a young boy called Shancus. Half human, half snake, he was the son of one of my best friends, Evra Von.

As Mr Tall lay dying, Mr Tiny and a witch called Evanna mysteriously appeared out of nowhere. It turned out that Mr Tiny was Mr Tall's father, and Evanna his sister. Mr Tiny stayed to mourn the death of his son, while Evanna followed us as we chased after her brother's killers. We managed to kill Morgan James and capture Darius. As the others hurried after R.V. and Shancus, I stole a few words with Evanna. The witch had the ability to see into the future and she revealed that if I killed Steve, I would take his place as the dreaded Lord of the Shadows. I'd become a monster, murder Vancha and anybody else who got in my way, and destroy not just the vampaneze, but humanity as well.

As shocked as I was, there was no time to brood. With my allies, we tracked R.V. to the old cinema where Steve and I had first met Mr Crepsley. Steve was waiting for us, safe on the stage, separated from us by a pit which he'd had dug and filled with stakes. He mocked us for a while, then agreed to trade Shancus's life for Darius's. But he lied. Instead of releasing the snake-boy, he killed him brutally. I still had hold of Darius. In a blind, cold rage, I prepared to murder him for revenge. But just before I stabbed the boy, Steve stopped me with his cruellest revelation yet — Darius's mother was my sister, Annie. If I murdered Steve's son, I'd be killing my own nephew.

And with that he departed, cackling like the demon he was, leaving me to the madness of the blood-drenched night.

PART ONE

CHAPTER ONE

Sitting on the stage. Gazing around the theatre. Remembering the thrilling show I saw the first time I came. Comparing it to tonight's warped 'entertainment'. Feeling very small and lonely.

Vancha didn't lose his head, even when Steve played his trump card. He kept going, picked his way through the pit of stakes to the stage, then raced down the tunnel which Steve, Gannen and R.V. had fled by. It led to the streets at the rear of the theatre. No way of telling which way they'd gone. He returned, cursing with fury. When he saw Shancus, lying dead on the stage like a bird with a broken neck, he stopped and sank to his knees.

Evra was next across, following Vancha's route through the stakes, crying out Shancus's name, screaming for him not to die, even though he must have known it was too late, that his son was already dead. We should have held him back — he fell and pierced himself several times, and could easily have perished — but we were frozen with shock and horror.

Fortunately Evra made it to the stage without injuring himself too severely. Once there, he slumped beside Shancus, desperately checked for signs of life, then howled with loss. Sobbing and moaning with grief, he cradled the dead boy's head in his lap, tears dripping on to his son's motionless face. The rest of us watched from a distance. We were all crying bitterly, even the normally steel-faced Alice Burgess.

In time, Harkat also climbed through the stakes. There was a long plank on the stage. He and Vancha extended it over the pit, so that the rest of us could join them. I don't think anybody really wanted to go up there. For a long moment none of us moved. Then Debbie, sobbing with deep, wracking gulps, stumbled to the plank and hauled herself up.

Alice crossed the pit next. I brought up the rear. I was shaking uncontrollably. I wanted to turn and run. Earlier, I thought I knew how I'd feel if our gamble backfired and Steve killed Shancus. But I'd known nothing. I never truly expected Steve to murder the snake-boy. I'd let R.V. march the boy into Steve's den, certain no harm would come to my honorary godson.

Now that Steve had made a fool of me (yet again) and slaughtered Shancus, all I wanted was to be dead. I couldn't feel pain if I was dead. No shame. No guilt. I wouldn't have to look Evra in the eye, knowing I was responsible for his son's needless, shocking death.

We'd forgotten about Darius. I hadn't killed him — how

could I kill my own nephew? Following Steve's triumphant revelation, the hatred and anger which had filled me like a fire, drained away from me in an instant. I released Darius, having lost my murderous interest in him, and just left him on the far side of the pit.

Evanna was standing near the boy, idly picking at one of the ropes which encircled her body — she preferred ropes to ordinary clothes. It was clear from the witch's stance that she wouldn't interfere if Darius made a break for freedom. It would have been the simplest thing in the world for him to escape. But he didn't. He stood, sentry-like, trembling, waiting for us to summon him.

Finally Alice stumbled over to me, wiping tears from her face. "We should take them back to the Cirque Du Freak," she said, nodding at Evra and Shancus.

"In a while," I agreed, dreading the moment I'd have to face Evra. And what about Merla, Shancus's mother? Would *I* have to break the terrible news to her?

"No — now," Alice said firmly. "Harkat and Debbie can take them. We need to straighten some things out before we leave." She nodded at Darius, tiny and vulnerable under the glare of the lights.

"I don't want to talk about this," I groaned.

"I know," she said. "But we must. The boy might know where Steve is staying. If he does, this is the time to strike. They won't expect —"

"How can you even think about such things?" I hissed angrily. "Shancus is dead! Don't you care?"

She slapped my face. I blinked, stunned. "You're not a child, Darren, so don't act like one," she said coldly. "Of course I care. But we can't bring him back, and we'll achieve nothing by standing around, moping. We need to act. Only in swift revenge can we maybe find a small sliver of comfort."

She was right. Self-pity was a waste. Revenge was essential. As hard as it was, I dug myself out of my misery and set about sending Shancus's body home. Harkat didn't want to leave with Evra and Debbie. He wanted to stay and chase Steve with us. But somebody had to help carry Shancus. He accepted his task reluctantly, but made me promise we wouldn't face Steve without him. "I've come too far with you to ... miss out now. I want to be there when you ... cut the demon down."

Debbie threw her arms around me before leaving. "How could he do it?" she cried. "Even a monster couldn't ... wouldn't..."

"Steve's more than a monster," I replied numbly. I wanted to return her embrace, but my arms wouldn't work. Alice pried her away from me. She gave Debbie a handkerchief and whispered something to her. Debbie sniffed miserably, nodded, gave Alice a hug, then went to stand beside Evra.

I wanted to talk with Evra before he left, but I could think of nothing to say. If he'd confronted me, maybe I'd have responded, but he had eyes only for his lifeless son. Dead people often look like they're sleeping. Shancus didn't. He'd been a vibrant, buzzing, active child. All that vitality was lost now. Nobody could have looked upon him and thought he was anything but dead.

I remained standing until Evra, Debbie and Harkat had departed, Harkat carrying Shancus's body tenderly in his thick, grey arms. Then I slid to the floor and sat there for ages, staring around in a daze, thinking about the past and my first visit here, using the theatre and my memories as a barrier between me and my grief.

Eventually Vancha and Alice approached. I don't know how long the pair had been talking together, but when they came to stand before me they'd wiped their faces clean of tears and looked ready for business.

"Will I talk to the boy or do you want to?" Vancha asked gruffly.

"I don't care," I sighed. Then, glancing at Darius, who still stood alone with Evanna in the vastness of the auditorium, I said, "I'll do it."

"Darius," Alice called. His head rose immediately. "Come here."

Darius went straight to the plank, climbed up and walked across. He had an excellent sense of balance. I found myself thinking that was probably a by-product of his vampaneze blood — Steve had pumped some of his own blood into his son, turning him into a half-vampaneze. Thinking that, I began to hate the boy again. My fingers twitched in anticipation of grabbing him by the throat and...

But then I recalled his face when he'd learnt he was my nephew — shock, terror, confusion, pain, remorse — and my hatred for the boy died away.

Darius walked directly up to us. If he was afraid — and he must have been — he masked it bravely. Stopping, he stared at Vancha, then at Alice, finally at me. Now that I studied him closely, I saw a certain family resemblance. Thinking about that, I frowned.

"You're not the boy I saw before," I said. Darius looked at me uncertainly. "I went to my old home when we first came to town," I explained. "I watched from behind the fence. I saw Annie. She was bringing in laundry. Then you arrived and came out to help her. Except it wasn't *you*. It was a chubby boy with fair hair."

"Oggy Bas," Darius said after a second's thought. "My friend. I remember that day. He came home with me. I sent him out to help Mum while I was taking my shoes off. Oggy always does what I tell him." Then, licking his lips nervously, he looked around at all of us again and said, "I didn't know." It wasn't an apology, just a statement of fact. "Dad told me vampires were evil. He said you were the worst of the lot. 'Darren the cruel, Darren the mad, Darren the baby-killer.' But he never mentioned your surname."

Evanna had crossed the plank after Darius and was circling us, studying us as if we were chess pieces. I ignored her — there'd be time for the witch later.

"What did Steve tell you about the vampaneze?" I asked Darius.

"That they wanted to stop vampires killing humans. They broke away from the clan several hundred years ago and had battled to stop the slaughter of humans ever since. They drank only small amounts of blood when they fed, just enough to survive."

"You believed him?" Vancha snorted.

"He was my dad," Darius answered. "He was always kind to me. I never saw him like I saw him tonight. I'd no reason to doubt him."

"But you doubt him now," Alice noted wryly.

"Yes. He's evil." As soon as he said it, Darius burst into tears, his brave front collapsing. It can't have been easy for a child to admit his father was evil. Even in the midst of my grief and fury, I felt pity for the boy.

"What about Annie?" I asked when Darius had recovered enough to speak again. "Did Steve feed her the same sort of lies?"

"She doesn't know," Darius said. "They haven't spoken since before I was born. I never told her I was meeting him."

I breathed a small sigh of relief. I'd had a sudden, terrifying flash of Annie as Steve's consort, having grown up as bitter and twisted as him. It was good to know she wasn't part of this dark insanity.

"Do you want to tell him the truth about vampires and vampaneze, or will I?" Vancha asked.

"First things first," Alice interrupted. "Does he know where his father is?"

"No," Darius said sadly. "I always met him here. This is

where he was based. If he has another hideout, I don't know about it."

"Damn!" Alice snarled.

"No ideas at all?" I asked. Darius thought for a moment, then shook his head. I glanced at Vancha. "Will you set him straight?"

"Sure." Vancha quickly filled Darius in on the truth. He told him that the vampaneze were the ones who killed when they drank, though he was careful to describe their ways in detail — they kept part of a person's spirit alive within themselves when they drained a human dry, so they didn't look upon it as murder. They were noble. They never lied. They weren't deliberately evil.

"Then your father came along," Vancha said, and explained about the Lord of the Vampaneze, the War of the Scars, Mr Tiny's prediction and our part in it.

"I don't understand," Darius said at the end, forehead creased. "If the vampaneze don't lie, how come Dad lied all the time? And he taught me how to use an arrow-gun, but you said they can't use such weapons."

"They're not supposed to," Vancha said. "I haven't seen or heard of any others breaking those rules. But their Lord's above such laws. They worship him so much — or fear what will happen if they disobey him — that they don't care what he does, as long as he leads them to victory over the vampires."

Darius thought about that in silence for a long time. He was only ten years old, but he had the expression and manner of someone much older.

"I wouldn't have helped if I'd known," he said in the end. "I grew up thinking vampires were evil, like in the movies. When Dad came to me a few years ago and said he was on a mission to stop them, I thought it was a great adventure. I thought he was a hero. I was proud to be his son. I'd have done anything for him. I *did*..."

He looked like he was about to cry again. But then his jaw firmed and he stared at me. "But how did *you* get involved in this?" he asked. "Mum told me you died. She said you broke your neck."

"I faked my death," I said, and gave him a very brief rundown of my early life as a vampire's assistant, sacrificing everything I held dear to save Steve's life.

"But why does he hate you if you saved him?" Darius shouted. "That's crazy!"

"Steve sees things differently," I shrugged. "He believes it was his destiny to become a vampire. He thinks I stole his rightful place. He's determined to make me pay."

Darius shook his head, confused. "I can't understand that," he said.

"You're young." I smiled sadly. "You've a lot to learn about people and how they operate." I fell silent, thinking that those were some of the many things poor Shancus would never learn.

"So," Darius said a while later, breaking the silence. "What happens now?"

"Go home," I sighed. "Forget about this. Put it behind you."

"But what about the vampaneze?" Darius cried. "Dad's still out there. I want to help you find him."

"Really?" I looked at him icily. "You want to help us kill him? You'd lead us to your own father and watch while we cut his rotten heart out?"

Darius shifted uneasily. "He's evil," he whispered.

"Yes," I agreed. "But he's still your father. You're better off out of this."

"And Mum?" Darius asked. "What do I tell her?"

"Nothing," I said. "She thinks I'm dead. Let her go on thinking that. Say nothing of this. The world I live in isn't a fit world for children — and as a child who's lived in it, I should know! Take back your ordinary life. Try not to dwell on what's happened. In time you might be able to dismiss all this as a horrible dream." I placed my hands on his shoulders and smiled warmly. "Go home, Darius. Be good to Annie. Make her happy."

Darius wasn't pleased, but I could see him making up his mind to accept my advice. Then Vancha spoke. "It's not that easy."

"What?" I frowned.

"He's in. He can't opt out."

"Of course he can!" I snapped.

Vancha shook his head stubbornly. "He was blooded. The vampaneze blood is thin in him, but it will thicken. He won't age like normal children, and in a few decades the purge will strike and he'll become a full-vampaneze." Vancha sighed. "But his real problems will start long before then."

"What do you mean?" I croaked, though I sensed what he was getting at.

"*Feeding*," Vancha said. He turned his gaze on Darius. "You'll need to drink blood to survive."

Darius stiffened, then grinned shakily. "So I'll drink like you guys," he said. "A drop here, a drop there. I don't mind. It'll be kind of cool, in a way. Maybe I'll drink from my teachers and — "

"No," Vancha growled. "You can't drink like us. In the beginning, vampaneze were the same as vampires, except in their customs. But they've changed. The centuries have altered them physically. Now a vampaneze *must* kill when he feeds. They're driven to it. They have no choice or control. I was once a half-vampaneze, so I know what I'm speaking about."

Vancha drew himself up straight and spoke sadly but firmly. "In a few months the hunger will grow within you. You won't be able to resist. You'll drink blood because you have to, and when you drink, because you're a half-vampaneze — you'll *kill!*"

CHAPTER TWO

We marched in silence, in single file, Darius leading the way like Oliver Twist at the head of a funeral procession. Following the massacre at the stadium after the football match, a series of road blocks had been set in place around the town. But there weren't many in this area, so we made good time, having to take only a couple of short detours. I was at the back of the line, a few metres behind the others, worrying about the meeting to come. I'd agreed to it easily enough in the theatre, but now that we were getting closer, I was having second thoughts.

While I was running through my words, thinking of all the things I could and should say, Evanna slipped back to walk along beside me. "If it helps, the snake-boy's soul has flown straight to Paradise," she said.

"I never thought otherwise," I replied stiffly, glaring at her hatefully.

"Why such a dark look?" she asked, genuine surprise in her mismatched green and brown eyes.

"You knew it was coming," I growled. "You could have warned us and saved Shancus."

"No," she snapped, irritated. "Why do you people level the same accusations at me over and over? You know I have the power to see into the future, but not the power to directly influence it. I cannot act to change that which is to be. Nor could my brother."

"Why not?" I snarled. "You always say that terrible things will happen if you do, but what are they? What could be worse than letting an innocent child die at the hands of a monster?"

Evanna was quiet a moment, then spoke softly, so that only I could hear. "There are worse monsters than Steve Leonard, and worse even than the Lord of the Shadows — be he Steve or you. These other monsters wait in the timeless wings around the stage of the world, never seen by man, but always seeing, always hungering, always eager to break through.

"I am bound by laws older than mankind. So was my brother and so, to a large extent, is my father. If I took advantage of the present, and tried to change the course of a future I knew about, I'd break the laws of the universe. The monsters I speak of would then be free to cross into this world, and it would become a cauldron of endless, bloody savagery."

"It seems that way already," I said sourly.

"For you, perhaps," she agreed. "But for billions of others it is not. Would you have everyone suffer as you have — and worse?"

"Of course not," I muttered. "But you told me they were going to suffer anyway, that the Lord of the Shadows will destroy mankind."

"He will bring it to its knees," she said. "But he will not crush it entirely. Hope will remain. One day, far in the future, humans might rise again. If I interfered and unleashed the real monsters, hope would become a word without meaning."

I didn't know what to think about these other monsters of Evanna's — it was the first time she'd ever spoken of such creatures — so I brought the conversation back to centre on the monster I knew all too much about. "You're wrong when you say I can become the Lord of the Shadows," I said, trying to change my destiny by denying it. "I'm not a monster."

"You would have killed Darius if Steve hadn't said he was your nephew," Evanna reminded me.

I recalled the hateful fury which had flared to life inside me when I saw Shancus die. In that moment I became like Steve. I didn't care about right or wrong. I only wanted to hurt my enemy by killing his son. I'd seen a glimpse of my future then, the beast I could become, but I didn't want to believe it was real.

"That would have been in revenge for Shancus," I said bitterly, trying to hide from the truth. "It wouldn't have been the act of an out-of-control beast. I wouldn't become a monster just because of a single executioning."

"No?" Evanna challenged me. "There was a time when you thought differently. Do you remember when you killed your first vampaneze, in the caves of Vampire Mountain? You wept afterwards. You thought killing was wrong. You believed there were ways to resolve differences other than through violence."

"I still do," I said, but my words sounded hollow, even to me.

"You would not have tried to take the life of a child if you did," Evanna said, stroking the hairs of her beard. "You have changed, Darren. You're not evil like Steve, but you carry the seeds of evil within you. Your intentions are good, but time and circumstance will see you become that which you despise. This world will warp you and, despite your noble wishes, the monster within you will grow. Friends will become enemies. Truths will become lies. Beliefs will become sick jokes.

"The path of revenge is always lined with danger. By following the ways of those you hate, you risk turning into them. This is your destiny, Darren Shan. You cannot avoid it. Unless Steve kills you and he becomes the Lord of the Shadows instead."

"What about Vancha?" I hissed. "What if he kills Steve? Can't *he* become your bloody Lord of the Shadows?"

"No," she said calmly. "Vancha has the power to kill Steve and decide the fate of the War of the Scars. But moving beyond that, it's either you or Steve. There is no other. Death or monstrosity. Those are your options."

She moved ahead of me then, leaving me with my troubled, frantic thoughts. Was there truly no hope for me or the world? And if not, if I was trapped between death at the hands of Steve or replacing him as the Lord of the Shadows, which was preferable? Was it better to live and terrorize the world — or die now, while I was still halfway human?

I couldn't decide on an answer. There didn't seem to be one. And so I trudged along miserably and let my thoughts return to the more pressing issue — what to say to my grown-up sister who'd buried me as a child.

Twenty minutes later, Darius opened the back door and held it ajar. I paused, staring at the house, filled with a sense of foreboding. Vancha and Alice were behind me, and Evanna further behind them. I looked back at my friends pleadingly. "Do I really have to do this?" I croaked.

"Yes," Vancha said. "It would be wrong to risk his life without informing his mother first. She must decide."

"OK," I sighed. "You'll wait out here till I call?"

"Aye."

I gulped, then stepped over the threshold into the house where I'd lived as a boy. After eighteen long years of wandering, I'd finally come home.

Darius guided me to the living room, though I could have found my way blindfolded. Much had changed within the house — new wallpaper and carpets, furniture and light fittings — but it felt the same, warm and comfy, layered with memories of the distant past. It was like walking through a ghost house — except the house was real and I was the ghost.

Darius pushed the living-room door open. And there was Annie, her brown hair tied up in a bun, sitting in a chair in front of the TV, sipping hot chocolate, watching the news. "Decided to come home at last, did you?" she said to Darius, catching sight of him out of the corner of her eye. She laid the cup of hot chocolate down. "I was worried. Have you seen the news? There's —"

She saw me entering the room after Darius. "Is this one of your friends?" she asked. I could see her thinking I looked too old to be his friend. She was instantly suspicious of me.

"Hello, Annie," I said, smiling nervously, advancing into the light.

"Have we met before?" she asked, frowning, not recognizing me.

"In a way," I chuckled drily.

"Mum, it's —" Darius started to say.

"No," I interrupted. "Let her see for herself. Don't tell her."

"Tell me what?" Annie snapped. She was squinting at me now, uneasy.

"Look closer, Annie," I said softly, walking across the room, stopping less than a metre away from her. "Look at my eyes. They say the eyes never really change, even if everything else does."

"Your voice," she muttered. "There's something about..."

She stood — she was the same height as me — and gazed steadily into my eyes. I smiled.

"You look like somebody I knew a long time ago," Annie said. "But I don't remember who..."

"You did know me a long time ago," I whispered. "Eighteen years ago."

"Nonsense!" Annie snorted. "You'd have only been a baby."

"No," I said. "I've aged slowly. I was slightly older than Darius when you last saw me."

"Is this a joke?" she half laughed.

"Look at him, Mum," Darius said intently. "Really *look* at him."

And she did. And this time I saw something in her expression and realized she'd known who I was the second she saw me — she just hadn't admitted it to herself yet.

"Listen to your instincts, Annie," I said. "You always had good instincts. If I'd had your nose for trouble, maybe I wouldn't have gotten into this mess. Maybe I'd have had more sense than to steal a poisonous spider..."

Annie's eyes widened. "No!" she gasped.

"Yes," I said.

"You can't be!"

"I am."

"But ... *No!*" she growled, firmly this time. "I don't know who put you up to this, or what you think you'll achieve by it, but if you don't get out quick, I'll —"

"I bet you never told anyone about Madam Octa," I cut

her off. She trembled at mention of the spider's name. "I bet you kept that secret all these years. You must have guessed she had something to do with my 'death'. Maybe you asked Steve about it, since he was the one she bit, but I bet you never told Mum or —"

"*Darren?*" she wheezed, confused tears springing to her eyes.

"Hi, sis," I grinned. "Long time no see."

She stared at me, appalled, and then did something I thought only happened in corny old movies — her eyes rolled up, her legs gave way, and she fainted!

Annie sat in her chair, a fresh mug of hot chocolate cupped between her hands. I sat opposite her in a chair I'd dragged over from the other side of the room. Darius stood by the TV, which he'd turned off shortly after Annie fainted. Annie hadn't said much since recovering. Once she'd come to, she'd pressed back into her chair, gazed at me, torn between horror and hope, and simply gasped, "*How?*"

I'd spent the time since then filling her in. I spoke quietly and rapidly, starting with Mr Crepsley and Madam Octa, explaining the deal I'd struck to save Steve's life, giving her a quick rundown of the years since then; my existence as a vampire, the vampaneze, the War of the Scars, tracking the Vampaneze Lord. I didn't tell her Steve was the Lord or involved with the vampaneze — I wanted to see how she reacted to the rest of the story before hitting her with that one.

Her eyes didn't betray her feelings. It was impossible to guess what she was thinking. When I got to the part of the story involving Darius, her gaze slid from me to her son, and she leant forward slightly as I described how he'd been tricked into aiding the vampaneze, again being careful not to refer to Steve by name. I finished with my return to the old cinema theatre, Shancus's death, and the Vampaneze Lord's revelation that Darius was my nephew.

"Once Darius knew the truth, he was horrified," I said. "But I told him he mustn't blame himself. Lots of older and wiser people than him have been fooled by the Lord of the Vampaneze."

I stopped and awaited her reaction. It wasn't long coming.

"You're insane," she said coldly. "If you *are* my brother — and I'm not a hundred per cent convinced — then whatever disease stunted your growth also affected your brain. Vampires? Vampaneze? My son in league with a killer?" She sneered. "You're a madman."

"But it's true!" Darius exclaimed. "He can prove it! He's stronger and faster than any human. He can —"

"Be quiet!" Annie roared with such venom that Darius shut up instantly. She glared at me furiously. "Get out of my house," she snarled. "Stay away from my son. Don't ever come back."

"But —" I began.

"No!" she screamed. "You're not my brother! Even if you are, you're not! We buried Darren eighteen years ago. He's dead and that's the way I want him to stay. I don't care if you're him or not. I want you out of my life — *our* lives — immediately." She stood and pointed at the door. "*Go!*"

I didn't move. I wanted to. If it hadn't been for Darius, I would have slunk out like a kicked dog. But she had to know what her son had become. I couldn't leave without convincing her of the danger he was in.

While Annie stood, pointing at the door, hand trembling wildly, face twisted with rage, Darius stepped away from the TV. "Mum," he said quietly. "Don't you want to know how I fell in with the vampaneze and why I helped them?"

"There are no vampaneze!" she yelled. "This maniac has filled your imagination with lies and —"

"Steve Leonard's the Lord of the Vampaneze," Darius said, and Annie stopped dead. "He came to me a few years ago," Darius went on, edging slowly towards her. "At first we just went for walks together, he took me to the cinema and for meals, stuff like that. He told me not to say anything to you. He said you wouldn't like it, that you'd make him go away."

He stopped in front of her, reached up, took hold of her pointing hand and gently bent her arm down. She was staring at him wordlessly. "He's my dad," Darius said sadly. "I trusted him because I thought he loved me. That's why I believed him when he told me about vampires. He said he was telling me for my protection, that he was worried about me — and *you*. He wanted to protect us. That's where it began. Then I got more involved. He taught me how to use a knife, how to shoot, how to kill."

Annie sank back into her chair, unable to respond.

"It was Steve," Darius said. "Steve who got me into trouble, who killed the snake-boy, who made Darren come back to see you. Darren didn't want to — he knew he'd hurt you — but Steve left him with no choice. It's true, Mum, everything he said. You've got to believe us, because it was Steve, and I think he might come back — come after *you* — and if we aren't ready ... if you don't believe..."

He ground to a halt, running out of words. But he'd said enough. When Annie looked at me again, there was fear and doubt in her eyes, but no scorn. "*Steve?*" she moaned. I nodded unhappily and her face hardened. "What did I tell you about him?" she screamed at Darius, grabbing the boy and shaking him angrily. "I told you never to go near him! That if you ever saw him, you had to run and tell me! I said he was dangerous!"

"I didn't believe you!" Darius cried. "I thought you hated him just because he ran away, that you were lying! He was my dad!" He tore himself away from her and collapsed on the floor, weeping. "He was my dad," he sobbed again. "I loved him."

Annie stared at Darius crying. Then she stared at me. And then she also started to cry, and her sobs were even deeper and more painful than her son's.

I didn't cry. I was saving my tears. I knew the worst was yet to come.

CHAPTER THREE

Later. After the tears. Sitting around the living room. Annie had recovered from the worst of the shock. All three of us were drinking hot chocolate. I hadn't called the others in yet — I wanted some personal time with Annie before I dumped the full fallout from the War of the Scars upon her.

Annie made me tell her more about my life. She wanted to hear about the countries I'd visited, the people I'd met, the adventures I'd had. I told her some of the highlights, leaving out the darker aspects. She listened, dazed, touching me every few minutes to make sure I was real. When she heard I was a Prince, she laughed with delight. "Does that make me a princess?" she smiled.

"Afraid not," I chuckled.

In return, Annie told me what her life had been like. The hard months after I'd 'died'. Slowly returning to normal. She was young, so she recovered, but Mum and Dad never really got over it. She raised the question of whether or not they should be told I was alive. Then, before I could speak, she said, "No. They're happy now. It's too late to change the past. Best not to drag it up again."

I paid close attention when she spoke about Steve. "I was a teenager," she said angrily, "mixed-up and unsure of myself. I had some friends but not many. And no serious boyfriend. Then Steve came back. He was only a few years older than me, but he looked and acted grown-up. And he was interested in me. He wanted to talk to me. He treated me like an equal."

They spent a lot of time together. Steve put on a good act — kind, generous, loving. Annie thought he cared for her, that they had a future together. She fell in love with him, and gave her love to him. Then she found out she was expecting a baby.

"His face lit up when he heard," she said, shivering from the memory. Darius was by her side, solemn, silent, listening intently. "He made me believe he was delighted, that we'd get married and have lots of children together. He told me not to tell anyone — he wanted to keep it secret until we were husband and wife. He went away again. He said it was to earn money, to pay for our wedding and the baby's upkeep. He stayed away a long time. He returned late one night, while I was sleeping. Woke me up. Before I could say anything, he clamped a hand over my mouth and laughed. 'Too late to stop it now!' he mocked me. He said other things, horrible things. Then he left. I haven't heard from him since."

She had to tell Mum and Dad about the baby then. They were furious — not with her, but with Steve. Dad would have killed Steve if he'd found him. But nobody knew where Steve was. He'd vanished.

"Raising Darius was hard," she smiled, ruffling his hair, "but I wouldn't give up a day of it. Steve was wicked, but he gave me the most marvellous gift anyone could have ever given me."

"Soppy old cow," Darius grunted, fighting hard not to smile.

I was quiet a long time after that. I wondered if Steve had meant to use Darius against me even then. This was back before he met the vampaneze and learnt of his abominable destiny. But I bet he was already planning my downfall, one way or the other. Did he deliberately get Annie pregnant, so he could use his nephew or niece to hurt me? Knowing Steve as I did, I guessed those were his exact intentions.

Annie started telling me about her life with Darius, from how Mum and Dad helped rear him until they moved away, how the pair were managing now on their own. She worried about him not having a father, but her experience with Steve had made her wary of men, and she found it hard to trust anyone. I could have listened to Annie talk all night, telling tales about Mum, Dad and Darius. I was catching up on all those missed years. I felt like part of the family again. I didn't want it to stop.

But we were in the middle of a crisis. I'd delayed the moment of truth, but now I had to tell her about it. The night was drawing on, and I was keen to conclude the business I'd come about. I let her finish the story she was telling — about

Darius's first week in school — then asked if I could introduce her to some of my friends.

Annie wasn't sure what to make of Vancha, Alice and Evanna. Alice dressed normally, but Vancha in his animal hides, with his straps of throwing stars and green hair, and the hirsute, deliriously ugly Evanna draped in ropes ... They would have stuck out like a couple of gargoyles anywhere!

But they were my friends (well, Vancha and Alice were, whatever about the witch), so Annie welcomed them — though I could tell she didn't entirely trust the trio. And I knew she sensed they weren't here just to make up the numbers. She guessed that something bad was coming.

We made small talk for a while. Alice told Annie about her years on the police force, Vancha described some of his Princely duties and Evanna gave her tips on how to breed frogs (not that Annie had any interest in that!). Then Darius yawned. Vancha looked at me meaningfully — it was time.

"Annie," I started hesitantly, "I told you Darius pledged himself to the vampaneze. But I didn't tell you what precisely that means."

"Go on," Annie said when I stalled.

"Steve blooded him," I said. "He transferred some of his vampaneze blood to Darius. The blood isn't very strong within him, but it will strengthen. The cells will multiply and take over."

"You're saying he'll become like you?" Annie's face was ashen. "He won't age normally? He'll need to drink blood to survive?"

"Yes." Her face crumpled — she thought that was the worst, the part I'd been holding back. I wished I could spare her the truth, but I couldn't. "There's more," I said, and she stiffened. "Vampires can control their feeding habits. It isn't easy — it requires training — but we can. Vampaneze can't. Their blood forces them to kill every time they feed."

"No!" Annie moaned. "Darius isn't a killer! He wouldn't!"

"He would," Vancha grunted. "He'd have no choice. Once a vampaneze gets the taste of blood, his urges consume him. He goes into a kind of trance and feeds until he's drained the source dry. He can't stop."

"But there must be some way to help him!" Annie insisted. "Doctors ... surgery ... medicine..."

"No," Vancha said. "This isn't a human disease. Your doctors could study him, and restrain him while he was feeding — but do you want your son to spend his life imprisoned?"

"Also," I said, "they couldn't stop him when he was older. As he comes into his full powers, he'll grow incredibly strong. They'd have to keep him comatose to control him."

"No!" Annie shouted, her face dark with stubborn rage. "I won't allow this! There must be a way to save him!"

"There is," I said, and she relaxed slightly. "But it's dangerous. And it won't restore his humanity — it will merely drive him towards a different corner of the night."

"Don't talk in riddles!" Annie snapped. "What does he have to do?"

"Become a vampire," I said.

Annie stared at me in disbelief.

"It's not as bad as it sounds," I went on quickly. "Yes, he'd age slowly, but that's something you and he could learn to cope with. And yes, he'd have to drink blood, but he wouldn't harm when he drank. We'd teach him to master his urges."

"No," Annie said. "There must be another way."

"There isn't," Vancha huffed. "And even this way isn't certain. Nor is it safe."

"I'll have to trade blood with him," I explained. "Pump my vampire cells into his body, and accept his vampaneze cells into mine. The vampire and vampaneze cells will attack each other. If all goes well, Darius will become a half-vampire and I'll carry on as before."

"But if it fails, you'll become a half-vampaneze and Darius won't change?" Annie guessed, trembling at the thought of such a horrible fate.

"No," I said. "It's worse than that. If it fails, I'll die — and so will Darius."

And then I sat back numbly and awaited her decision.

CHAPTER FOUR

Annie didn't like it — nobody did! — but we eventually convinced her that there was no other solution. She wanted to wait, think it over and discuss it with her doctor, but I told her it was now or never. "Vancha and I have a mission to complete," I reminded her. "We might not be able to come back later."

When we'd first discussed the transfusion, Vancha had volunteered. He didn't think it was safe for me to try. I was in the middle of the purge — my vampire cells were taking over, turning me into a full-vampire, and my body was in a state of flux. But when I pressed him, he admitted there was no real reason for thinking that the purge would have any affect on the procedure. It might even work in our favour — since my vampire cells were hyperactive, they might stand a better chance of destroying the vampaneze cells.

We'd tried to quiz Evanna about the dangers. She could look into the future and tell us whether it would succeed or not. But she refused to be drawn. "This has nothing to do with me," she'd said. "I will not comment on it."

"But it must be safe," I'd pressed, hoping for reassurance. "We're destined to meet Steve again. We can't do that if I die."

"Your final encounter with Steve Leonard is by no means set in stone," she'd replied. "If you die beforehand, he will become the Lord of the Shadows by default and the war will swing the way of the vampaneze. Do not think you are immune to danger because of your destiny, Darren — you *can* and perhaps *will* die if you attempt this."

But Darius was my nephew. Vancha didn't approve — he would have preferred to overlook Darius for the time being, and focus on Steve — but I couldn't leave the boy this way, with such a threat hanging over him. If I could save him, I must.

We could have handled the blood transfer with syringes, but Darius insisted on the traditional fingertips method. He was excited, despite the danger, and wanted to do it the old way. "If I'm going to be a vampire, I want to be a real one," he growled. "I don't want to hide my marks. It's all or nothing."

"But it'll be painful," I warned him.

"I don't care," he sniffed.

Annie's doubts remained, but in the end she agreed to the plan. She might not have if Darius had wavered, but he stuck to his guns with grim determination. I hated to admit it — and I didn't say it out loud — but he had his father's sense of commitment. Steve was insanely evil, but he always did what he set out to do, and nothing could change his mind once he'd made it up. Darius was the same.

"I can't believe this is happening," Annie sighed as I sat opposite Darius and prepared to drive my nails into the tips of his fingers. "Earlier tonight I was only thinking about doing the shopping tomorrow, and being here to let Darius in when he got home from school. Then my brother walks back into my life and tells me he's a vampire! And now, as I'm just getting used to that, I might lose him as swiftly as I found him — and my son too!"

She almost called it off then, but Alice stepped up behind her and said softly, "Would you rather lose him when he's human, or when he's a killer like his father?" It was a cruel thing to say, but it steadied Annie's nerves and reminded her of what was at stake. Trembling fiercely, weeping quietly, she stepped away and let me proceed.

Without any warning, I dug my nails into the soft flesh at the tips of Darius's fingers. He yelped painfully and jerked back in his chair. "Don't," I said as he raised his fingers to his mouth to suck them. "Let them bleed."

Darius lowered his hands. Gritting my teeth, I dug my right-hand nails into my left-hand fingertips, then did it the other way round. Blood welled up from ten fleshy springs. I pressed my fingers against Darius's and held them there while my blood flowed into his body, and his into mine.

We remained locked for twenty seconds ... thirty ... more. I could feel the vampaneze cells as soon as his blood entered my veins, itching, burning, sizzling. I ignored the pain. I could see that Darius was also aware of the change, and that it was hurting him more than me. I pressed closer against him, so it was impossible for him to break away.

Vancha stood guard, observing us, calculating. When he thought the time was right, he grabbed my arms and pulled my hands away. I gasped out loud, stood, half smiled, then fell to the floor, writhing in agony. I hadn't expected the cells to kick in so soon, and was unprepared for the brutal speed of the reaction.

During my convulsions, I saw Darius twisting sharply in his chair, eyes bulging, making choking noises, arms and legs thrashing wildly. Annie hurried towards him but Vancha knocked her aside. "Don't interfere!" he barked. "Nature must take its course. We can't get in its way."

For several minutes I jackknifed wildly on the floor. It felt like I was on fire inside my skin. I'd experienced blinding headaches and loads of discomfort during the purge, but this took me to new heights of pain. Pressure built at the back of my eyes, as though my brain was going to bulge out through my eye sockets. I dug the heels of my hands hard into my eyes, then into the sides of my head. I don't know if I was roaring or wheezing — I could hear nothing.

I vomited, then dry-heaved. I crashed into something hard — the TV. I rolled away from it and smashed into a wall. I dug my nails into the plaster and brick, trying to make the pain go away.

Finally the pressure subsided. My limbs relaxed. I stopped dry-heaving. Sight and sound returned, though my fierce headache remained. I looked around, dazed. Vancha was crouching over me, wiping my face clean, smiling. "You've come through it," he said. You'll be OK — with the luck of the vampires."

"Darius?" I gasped.

Vancha raised my head and pointed. Darius was lying on the couch, eyes closed, perfectly still, Annie and Alice kneeling beside him. Evanna sat in a corner, head bowed. For a horrifying moment I thought Darius was dead. Then I saw his chest lift softly and fall, and I knew he was just asleep.

"He'll be fine," Vancha said. "We'll have to keep a close eye on the two of you for a few nights. You'll probably have further fits, less severe than this one. But most who attempt this die of the first seizure. Having survived that, the odds are good for both of you."

I sat up wearily. Vancha took my fingers and spat on them, rubbing his spit in to help close the wounds.

"I feel awful," I moaned.

"You won't improve any time soon," Vancha said. "When I turned from vampanizm to vampirism it took my system a month to settle down, and almost a year to get back to normal. And you've got the purge to contend with too." He chuckled wryly. "You're in for some rough nights, Sire!"

Vancha helped me back to my chair. Alice asked if I'd like water or milk to drink. Vancha said blood would be better for me. Without blinking, Alice used a knife to cut herself and let me feed directly from the wound. Vancha closed the cut with his spit when I was finished. He beamed up at Alice. "You're some woman, Miss Burgess."

"The best," Alice replied dryly.

I leant back, eyes half closed. "I could sleep for a week," I sighed.

"Why don't you?" Vancha said. "You've only recently recovered from a life-threatening wound. You're in the middle of the purge. You've pulled off the most dangerous blood transfusion known to vampires. By the black blood of Harnon Oan, you've earned a rest!"

"But Steve..." I muttered.

"Leonard can wait," Vancha grunted. "We'll send Annie and Darius out of town — Alice will escort them — then get you settled in at the Cirque. A week in your hammock will do you the world of good."

"I guess," I said unhappily. I was thinking about Evra and Merla, and what I could find to say to them. There was Mr Tall to consider too — everyone at the Cirque Du Freak had loved him. Like Shancus, he was dead because of his association with me. Would the people there hate me because of that?

"Who do you think will take over from Mr Tall?" I asked.

"I've no idea," Vancha said. "I don't think anybody ever expected him to die, certainly not in such sudden circumstances."

"Maybe they'll break up," I mused. "Go their own ways, back to whatever they did before they joined. Some might have left the stadium already. I hope —"

"What was that about a stadium?" Annie interrupted. She was still tending to Darius — he was snoring lightly — but she'd overheard us talking.

"The Cirque Du Freak's camped in the old football stadium," I explained. "We're going back there when you leave, but I was saying to Vancha that —"

"The news," Annie interrupted again. "You didn't see tonight's news?"

"No."

"I was watching it when you came in," she said, eyes filling with fresh worry. "I didn't know that's where you were based, so I didn't connect it with you."

"Connect what?" I asked edgily.

"Police have surrounded the stadium," Annie said. "They say the people who killed Tom Jones and the others at the football match are there. I should have put it together earlier, when you were telling me about Tommy, but..." She shook her head angrily, then continued. "They're not letting anyone in or out. When I was watching the news, they hadn't moved in yet. But they said that when they did, they'd go in with full, lethal force. One of the reporters —" She stopped.

"Go on," I said hoarsely.

"He said he'd never seen so many armed police before. He..." She gulped and finished in a whisper. "He said they meant to go in as hard as they could. He said it looked like they planned to kill everyone inside."

CHAPTER FIVE

First things first — make sure Annie and Darius got away safely. I couldn't concentrate on helping my friends trapped inside the stadium if I was worrying about my sister and nephew. Once they were free of Steve's influence, safe somewhere he couldn't find them, I could focus on business entirely. Until that time I would only be a distracted liability.

Annie didn't want to go. This was her home and she wanted to fight to protect it. When, after telling her about some of the atrocities Steve had committed over the years, I convinced her they had to leave, she insisted I go with them. For years she'd believed I was dead. Now she knew otherwise, she didn't want to lose me again so quickly.

"I can't come," I sighed. "Not while my friends are in danger. Later, when it's over, I'll find you."

"Not if Steve kills you!" Annie cried. I had no answer for

that one. "What about Darius?" she pressed. "You said he needs training. What will he do without you?"

"Give us your mobile number," I said. "Alice will contact her people before we go to the stadium. In the worst case scenario, somebody will get in touch. A vampire will link up with you and instruct Darius, or guide him to Vampire Mountain, where Seba or Vanez can look after him."

"Who?" she asked.

"Old friends," I smiled. "They can teach him everything he'll ever need to know about being a vampire."

Annie kept trying to change my mind, telling me my place was with her and Darius, that I was her brother before I became a vampire and I should think of her first. But she was wrong. I left the human world behind when I became a Vampire Prince. I still cared for Annie and loved her, but my first loyalty was to the clan.

When she realized she couldn't win me round, Annie bundled Darius into the back of their car — he was still sound asleep — and tearfully went to gather some personal belongings. I told her to take as much as she could, and not to come back. If we defeated Steve, she and Darius could return. If not, somebody would fetch the rest of her stuff. The house would have to be sold, and they'd remain in hiding under the protection of the vampire clan, for as long as the clan was capable of looking after them. (I didn't say "Until the clan falls," but that's what I was thinking.) It wouldn't be an ideal life — but it would be better than winding up in the hands of Steve Leopard.

Annie hugged me with all her strength before getting into the car. "It's not fair," she wept. "There's so much you haven't told me, so much I want to know, so much I want to say."

"Me too," I said, blinking away tears. It was a weird feeling. Everything was happening at ten times the speed it should. It had only been a few hours since we returned to the Cirque Du Freak to chat with Mr Tall, but it felt like weeks had passed. His death, the chase, Morgan James's beheading, the theatre, Shancus being slaughtered by Steve, finding out about Darius, coming to see my sister ... I wanted to put my foot down on the brake, take time out, make sense of all that was going on. But life makes its own rules and sets its own pace. Sometimes you can rein it in and slow it down — other times you can't.

"You really can't come with us?" Annie tried one last time.

"No," I said. "I want to ... but no."

"Then I wish you all the luck in the world, Darren," she moaned. She kissed me, began to say something else, then broke down in tears. Hurling herself into the car, she checked on Darius, then started the engine and roared away, disappearing into the night, leaving me standing outside my old home — heartbroken.

"Are you all right?" Alice asked, creeping up behind me.

"I will be," I replied, wiping tears from my eyes. "I wish I'd been able to say goodbye to Darius."

"It's not goodbye," Alice said. "Just *au revoir*."

"Hopefully," I sighed, though I didn't really believe it. Win or lose, I had a sick feeling in my stomach that tonight was the last time I'd ever see Annie and Darius. I paused a moment to wish them a silent farewell, then turned around, put them from my thoughts, and let all my emotions and energies centre on the problems to hand and the dangers faced by my friends at the Cirque Du Freak.

Inside the house, we discussed our next move. Alice was for getting out of town as quickly as possible, abandoning our friends and allies. "Three of us can't make a difference if there are hordes of police stationed around the stadium," she argued. "Steve Leonard remains the priority. The others will have to fend for themselves."

"But they're our friends," I muttered. "We can't just abandon them."

"We must," she insisted. "It doesn't matter how much it hurts. We can't do anything for them now, not without placing our own lives in jeopardy."

"But Evra ... Harkat ... *Debbie*."

"I know," she said, her eyes sad but hard. "But like I said, it doesn't matter how much it hurts. We have to leave them."

"I don't agree," I said. "I think..." I stopped, reluctant to voice my belief.

"Go on," Vancha encouraged me.

"I can't explain it," I said slowly, eyes flicking to Evanna, "but I think Steve's there. At the stadium. Waiting for us. He set the police on us before — when Alice was one of them — and I can't see him pulling the same trick twice. It would be boring the second time round. He craves originality and new thrills. I think the police outside are just for cover."

"He could have set a trap in the cinema theatre," Vancha mused, taking up my train of thought. "But that wouldn't have been as elaborate a setting as where we fought him before — in the Cavern of Retribution."

"Exactly," I said. "This is our big showdown. He'll want to go out on a high, with something outlandish. He's as much of a performer as anyone at the Cirque Du Freak. He loves theatrics. He'd relish the idea of a stadium setting. It would be like the ancient gladiator duels in the Colosseum."

"We're in trouble if you're wrong," Alice said uneasily.

"Nothing new about that," Vancha huffed. He cocked an eyebrow at Evanna. "Care to drop us a hint?"

To our astonishment, the witch nodded soberly. "Darren is right. You either go to the stadium now and face your destiny, or flee and hand victory to the vampaneze."

"I thought you couldn't tell us stuff like that," Vancha said, startled.

"The endgame has commenced," Evanna answered cryptically. "I can speak more openly about certain matters now, without altering the future."

"It'd alter it if we turned tail and ran like hell for the hills," Vancha grunted.

"No," Evanna smiled. "It wouldn't. As I said, that would simply mean the vampaneze win. Besides," she added, her smile widening, "you aren't going to run, are you?"

"Not in a million years!" Vancha said, spitting against the wall for added emphasis. "But we won't be fools about this either. I say we check out the stadium. If it looks like

Leonard's in residence, we'll force a way in and chop the fiend's head off. If not, we'll search elsewhere and the circus folk will have to make their own luck. No point risking our lives for them at this stage, aye, Darren?"

I thought of my freakish friends — Evra, Merla, Hans Hands and the rest. I thought of Harkat and Debbie, and what might happen to them. And then I thought of my people — the vampires — and what *would* happen to the clan if we threw our lives away trying to save our non-vampire allies.

"Aye," I said miserably, and though I knew I was doing the right thing, I felt like a traitor.

Alice and Vancha checked their weapons while I armed myself with some sharp kitchen knives. Alice made a few phone calls, arranging protection for Annie and Darius. Then, with Evanna in tow, we pulled out and I left my childhood home for the second time in my life, certain in my heart that I'd never again return.

CHAPTER SIX

The journey across town passed without incident. All the police seemed to have been sent or drawn to the stadium. We didn't run into any road blocks or foot patrols. In fact we met hardly anyone. It was eerily quiet. People were in their homes or in pubs, watching the siege on TV, waiting for the action to kick off. It was a silence I knew from the past, the silence that usually comes before battle and death.

Dozens of police cars and vans were parked in a ring around the stadium when we arrived, and armed guards stood watch at every possible entry or exit point. Barriers had been erected to keep back the public and media. Ultra-bright spotlights were trained on the walls of the stadium. My eyes watered from the glare of the lights, even from a long way off, and I had to stop to tie a strip of thick cloth around them.

"Are you sure you're up to this?" Alice asked, studying me doubtfully.

"I'll do what I have to," I growled, although I wasn't as convinced of my vow as I pretended to be. I was in rough shape, the roughest I'd been since my trip down the stream and through the stomach of Vampire Mountain when I'd failed my Trials of Initiation. The purge, my shoulder wound, overall exhaustion and the blood transfer had sapped me of most of my energy. I wanted only to sleep, not face a fight to the death. But in life we don't usually get to choose the time of our defining moments. We just have to stand and face them when they come, no matter what sort of a state we're in.

A large crowd had gathered around the barriers. We mingled among them, unnoticed by the police in the darkness and crush of people — even the weirdly dressed Vancha and Evanna failed to draw attention. As we gradually pushed our way to the front, we saw thick clouds of smoke rising from within the stadium, and heard the occasional gun report.

"What's happening?" Alice asked the people nearest the barrier. "Have the police moved in?"

"Not yet," a burly man in a hunter's cap informed her. "But a small advance team went in an hour ago. Must be some new crack unit. Most of them had shaved heads and were dressed in brown shirts and black trousers."

"Their eyes were painted red!" a young boy gasped. "I think it was blood!"

"Don't be ridiculous," his mother laughed. "That was just paint, so the glare of the lights wouldn't blind them."

We withdrew, troubled by this new information. As we were leaving, I heard the boy say, "Mummy, one of those women was dressed in ropes!"

His mother responded with a sharp, "Stop making up stories!"

"Sounds like you were right," Alice said when we were at a safe distance. "The vampets are here, and they generally don't go anywhere without their masters."

"But why did the police let them in?" I asked. "They can't be working for the vampaneze — can they?"

We looked at each other uncertainly. Vampires and vampaneze had always kept their battles private, out of the gaze of humanity. Although both sides were in the process of putting together an army of select human helpers, they'd kept the war secret from humans in general. If the vampaneze had broken that age-old custom and were working with regular human forces, it signalled a worrying new twist in the War of the Scars.

"I can still pass for a police officer," Alice said. "Wait here. I'll try to find out more about this."

She slipped forward, through the crowd and past the barrier. She was immediately challenged by a policeman, but following a quick, hushed conversation, she was led away to talk to whoever was in command.

Vancha and I waited anxiously, Evanna standing calmly nearby. I took the time to analyse my situation. I was weak, dangerously so, and my senses were going haywire. My head was pounding and my limbs were trembling. I'd told Alice I was up for a fight, but in all honesty I couldn't say whether or not I'd be able to fend for myself. It would have been wiser to retreat and recover. But Steve had forced this battle. He was calling the shots. I'd have to struggle along as best I could and pray to the gods of the vampires for strength.

I started thinking about Evanna's prophecy again as I waited. If Vancha and I faced Steve this night, one of the three of us would die. If it was Vancha or me, Steve would become the Lord of the Shadows and the vampaneze would rule the night, as well as the world of mankind. But if Steve died, I'd become the Lord instead of him, turn on Vancha and destroy the world.

There must be some way to change that. But how? Try to make peace with Steve? Impossible! I wouldn't even if I could, not after what he'd done to Mr Crepsley, Tommy, Shancus and so many others. Peace wasn't an option.

But what other way was there? I couldn't accept the fact that the world was damned. I didn't care what Evanna said. There must be a way to stop the Lord of the Shadows from rising. There *must*...

Alice returned ten minutes later, her features dark. "They're dancing to a vampaneze tune," she said shortly. "I pretended I was an out-of-town chief inspector. I offered my assistance. The ranking officer said they had everything under control. I asked about the brown-shirted soldiers and he told me they were a special government force. He didn't say as much, but I got the feeling he's taking orders from them. I don't know if they've bribed or threatened him, but they're pulling his strings, no doubt about it."

"So you couldn't persuade him to let us in?" Vancha asked.

"I didn't have to," Alice said. "A way's already open. One rear entrance has been left unblocked. The approaching path is being kept clear. The police around that point aren't to interfere with anyone going in."

"He told you that?" I asked, surprised.

"He was under orders to tell anyone who asked," Alice said. She spat on the ground with disgust. "Traitor!"

Vancha looked at me with a thin smile. "Leonard's in there, isn't he?"

"No doubt about it," I nodded. "He wouldn't miss something like this."

Vancha cocked a thumb at the walls of the stadium. "He's laid this on for our benefit. We're the guests of honour. Be a shame to disappoint him."

"We probably won't come out of there alive if we go in," I noted.

"That's negative thinking," Vancha tutted.

"Then we're going to proceed?" Alice asked. "We're going to push on, even though we're outnumbered and outgunned?"

"Aye," Vancha said after a moment's thought. "I'm too long in the tooth to start bothering with wisdom now!"

I grinned at my fellow Prince. Alice shrugged. Evanna remained as blank-faced as ever. Then, without discussing it any further, we slipped around back to the unguarded entrance.

*　*　*

The lights weren't as bright at the rear of the stadium, and there weren't many people. Lots of police were about, but they deliberately ignored us, as they'd been told to. As we were about to advance through the gap in the ranks of police, Alice stopped us. "I've had an idea," she said hesitantly. "If we all go in, they can close the net around us and we won't be able to punch our way out. But if we attack from two fronts at once…"

She quickly outlined her plan. It made sense to Vancha and me, so we held back while she made several phone calls. Then we waited an impatient hour, taking it easy, preparing ourselves mentally and physically. As we watched, the smoke thickened from the fires inside the stadium, and the crowd around the barriers grew. Many of the newcomers were tramps and homeless people. They mixed with the others and slowly pushed forwards, where they waited close to the barriers, quiet, unnoticed.

When all was as it should be, Alice handed me a pistol and we bade her farewell. The three of us joined hands and wished each other luck. Then Vancha and I set our sights on the unguarded door. With Evanna following us like a ghost, we boldly walked past the ranks of armed police. They averted their eyes or turned their backs on us as we passed. Moments later we left the brightness outside for the darkness of the stadium tunnels and our date with destiny.

We had entered the leopard's den.

CHAPTER SEVEN

The tunnel twisted a lot, but ran directly under the stands to the open interior of the stadium. Vancha and I walked side by side in absolute silence. If Steve was waiting, and the night went against us, one of us would die within the next few hours. There wasn't much to say in a situation like that. Vancha was probably making his peace with the vampire gods. I was worrying about what would happen after the fight, fixed on the idea that there must be some way to stop the coming of the Lord of the Shadows.

There were no traps along the way and we saw nobody. When we left the confines of the tunnel, we stood by the exit for a minute, numbly absorbing the chaos which Steve's troops had created. Evanna moved away slightly to our left, and she studied the carnage too.

The big top of the Cirque Du Freak, along with most of the vans and tents, had been set ablaze — the source of the banks of smoke which clogged the air overhead. The performers and circus crew had been herded together about twenty metres ahead of the tunnel, clear of the stands. Harkat stood among them, near Evra and Merla. I'd never seen his grey face filled with such rage. They were surrounded by eight armed vampets, and spotlights which had been taken from inside the big top were trained upon them. Several dead bodies lay nearby. Most were backstage crew, but one was a long-serving star of the show — the skinny, supple, musical Alexander Ribs would never take to the stage again.

Ripping the piece of cloth away from my eyes, I let my sight adjust, then looked for Debbie among the survivors — there was no sign of her. In a panic, I examined the faces and forms of the corpses again, for fear she was lying among them — but I couldn't see her.

Several vampaneze and vampets patrolled the stadium, circling the burning tents and vans, controlling the flames. As I watched, Mr Tiny strolled out of the burning pyre of the big top, through a wall of fire, rubbing his hands together. He was wearing a red top hat and gloves — Mr Tall's. I understood instinctively that he'd left Mr Tall's body inside the tent, using it as a makeshift funeral pyre. Mr Tiny didn't look upset, but I could tell by his donning of the hat and gloves that, on some level, he'd been in some way affected by his son's death.

Between the burning tent and the surviving members of the Cirque Du Freak stood a new addition — a hastily constructed gallows. Several nooses hung from the crossbeam, but only one was filled — with the poor, thin neck of the snake-boy, Shancus Von.

I cried aloud when I spotted Shancus and made to rush towards him. Vancha gripped my left wrist and jerked me back. "We can't help him now," he growled.

"But —" I started to argue.

"Lower your gaze," he said quietly.

When I did, I saw that a band of vampaneze was grouped beneath the crossbeam and knotted ropes. All were armed with swords or battle-axes. Behind them, standing on something that raised him above them, and smirking evilly, stood their master, the Lord of the Vampaneze — Steve Leopard. He hadn't seen us yet.

"Easy," Vancha said as I stiffened. "No need to rush." His eyes were sliding slowly left and right. "How many vampaneze and vampets are here? Are there more hiding in the stands or behind the burning vans and tents? Let's work out exactly what we have to deal with before we go barging ahead."

Breathing deeply, I forced myself to think calmly, then studied the lie of the land. I counted fourteen vampaneze — nine grouped around Steve — and more than thirty vampets. I didn't see Gannen Harst, but guessed he would be close by Steve, hidden by the group of circus folk between us and the gallows.

"I make it a dozen-plus vampaneze and three times that amount of vampets, aye?" Vancha said.

"More or less," I agreed.

Vancha looked sideways at me and winked. "The odds are in our favour, Sire."

"You think so?"

"Most definitely," he said with fake enthusiasm — we both knew it didn't look good. We were vastly outnumbered by enemies with superior weapons. Our only ace card was that the vampaneze and vampets couldn't kill us. Mr Tiny had predicted doom for them if anybody other than their Lord murdered the hunters.

Without saying anything, we started forward at the exact same moment. I was carrying two knives, one in either hand. Vancha had drawn a couple of throwing stars but was otherwise unarmed — he believed in fighting with his bare hands at close quarters. Evanna moved when we did, shadowing our every footstep.

The vampets surrounding the imprisoned Cirque Du Freak troupe saw us coming but didn't react, except to close a little more tightly around the people they were guarding. They didn't even warn the others that we were here. Then I saw that they didn't need to — Steve and his cronies had already spotted us. Steve was standing on a box, or something, staring happily at us, while the vampaneze in front of him bunched defensively, weapons at the ready.

We had to pass the circus prisoners to get to Steve. I stopped as we drew level with Evra, Merla and Harkat. Evra and Merla's eyes were wet with tears. Harkat's green globes were shining with fury, and he'd pulled down his mask to bare his sharp grey teeth (he could survive up to half a day without the mask).

I gazed sorrowfully at Evra and Merla, then at the body of their son, dangling from the gallows further ahead. The vampets guarding my friends watched me cautiously but made no move against me.

"Come on," Vancha said, tugging at my elbow.

"I'm sorry," I croaked to Evra and Merla, unable to continue without saying something. "I wouldn't ... I didn't ... if I could..." I stopped, unable to think of anything else to say.

Evra and Merla said nothing for a moment. Then, with a screech, Merla smashed through the guards around her and threw herself at me. "I hate you!" she screamed, scratching my face, spitting with rage. "My son's dead because of you!"

I couldn't react. I felt sick with shame. Merla dragged me to the ground, yelling and crying, beating me with her fists. The vampets moved forward to pull her off, but Steve shouted, "No! Leave them alone! This is fun!"

We rolled away from the vampets, Merla driving me back. I didn't even raise my hands to defend myself as she called me every name under the moon. I just wanted the earth to open and swallow me whole.

And then, as Merla lowered her face as though to bite me, she whispered in my ear, "Steve has Debbie." I gawped at her. She roared more insults, then whispered again, "We didn't fight. They think we're gutless, but we were waiting for *you*. Harkat said you'd come and lead us."

Merla cuffed me about the head, then locked gazes with me. "It wasn't your fault," she said, smiling ever so slightly through her tears. "We don't hate you. Steve's the evil one — not you."

"But ... if I hadn't ... if I'd told Vancha to kill R.V ..."

"Don't think that way," she snarled. "You're not to blame. Now help us kill the savages who *are*! Give us a signal when you're ready and we'll answer the call. We'll fight to the death, every last one of us."

She screamed at me again, grabbed me by the neck to strangle me, then fell off and punched the ground, sobbing pitifully. Evra pushed forward, collected his wife and led her back to the pack. He glanced at me once, fleetingly, and I saw the same thing in his expression that I'd seen in Merla's — sorrow for the loss of their son, hatred for Steve and his gang, but only pity for me.

I still felt at fault for what had happened to Shancus and the others. But Evra and Merla's sympathy gave me the strength to carry on. If they'd hated me, I doubt I could have continued. But now that they'd given me their backing, I not only felt able to push on — I felt that I had to. For their sakes, if not my own.

I got to my feet, acting shaken. As Vancha came to help me, I spoke quickly and quietly. "They're with us. They'll fight when we do."

He paused, then carried forward as though I hadn't spoken, checking my face where Merla had scratched me, loudly asking if she'd harmed me, if I was OK, if I wanted to rest a while.

"I'm fine," I grunted, pushing past him, showing my circus friends a stiff back, as if they'd insulted me. "Merla said Steve has Debbie," I hissed to Vancha out of the side of my mouth, barely moving my lips.

"We might not be able to save her," he whispered back.

"I know," I said stonily. "But we'll try?"

A short pause. Then, "Aye," he replied.

With that, we quickened our pace and made a beeline for the gallows and the grinning, demonic, half-vampaneze beast waiting underneath, face half hidden by the shadow of the dangling Shancus Von.

CHAPTER EIGHT

"Halt!" one of the nine vampaneze in front of Steve shouted when we were about five metres away. We stopped. This close, I saw that Steve was actually standing on the body of one of the circus crew — Pasta O'Malley, a man who used to sleepwalk and even sleep-read. I could also see Gannen Harst now, just to Steve's right, sword undrawn, watching us intently.

"Drop your throwing stars," the vampaneze said to Vancha. When he didn't respond, two of the vampaneze raised spears and pointed them at him. With a shrug, Vancha slid the shurikens back into their holders and lowered his hands.

I glanced up at Shancus, swinging in the light breeze. The crossbeam creaked. The sound was louder than normal for me because of the purge — like the squeal of a wild boar.

"Get him down," I snarled at Steve.

"I don't think so," Steve replied lightly. "I like the sight of him up there. Maybe I'll hang his parents beside him. His brother and sister too. Keep the whole family together. What do you think?"

"Why do you go along with this madman?" Vancha asked Gannen Harst. "I don't care what Des Tiny says about him — this lunatic can bring nothing but shame upon the vampaneze. You should have killed him years ago."

"He is of our blood," Gannen Harst replied quietly. "I don't agree with his ways — he knows that — but we don't kill our kin."

"You do if they break your laws," Vancha grunted. "Leonard lies and uses guns. Any normal vampaneze would be executed if they did that."

"But he isn't normal," Gannen said. "He is our Lord. Desmond Tiny said we would perish if we did not follow him and obey. Whether I like it or not, Steve has the power to bend our laws, or even ignore them completely. I'd rather he didn't, but it's not my place to chastise him when he does."

"You can't approve of his actions," Vancha pushed.

"No," Gannen admitted. "But he has been accepted by the clan, and I am only a servant of my people. History can judge Steve. I'm content to serve and protect, in line with the wishes of those who appointed me."

Vancha glared at his brother, trying to stare him down, but Gannen only gazed back blankly. Then Steve laughed. "Aren't family get-togethers a joy?" he said. "I was hoping you'd bring Annie and Darius along. Imagine the fun all six of us could have had!"

"They're far away from here by now," I said. I wanted to dive for him and rip his throat open with my bare hands and teeth, but his guards would have cut me down before I struck. I had to be patient and pray for a chance to present itself.

"How's my son?" Steve asked. "Did you kill him?"

"Of course not," I snorted. "I didn't have to. When he saw you murder Shancus he realized you were a monster. I filled him in on your past *glories*. Annie told him some old stories too. He'll never listen to you again. You've lost him. He's your son no more."

I hoped to wound Steve with my words but he just laughed them off. "Oh well, I was never that fond of him anyway. A scrawny, moody kid. No taste for blood. Although," he chuckled, "I guess he'll develop one soon!"

"I wouldn't be too sure of that," I retorted.

"I blooded him," Steve boasted. "He's half-vampaneze."

"No," I smiled. "He's a half-vampire. Like me."

Steve stared at me uncertainly. "You re-blooded him?"

"Yes. He's one of us now. He won't need to kill when he feeds. Like I said, he's no longer your son — in any way whatsoever."

Steve's features darkened. "You shouldn't have done that," he growled. "The boy was mine."

"He was never yours, not in spirit," I said. "You merely tricked him into believing he was."

Steve started to reply, then scowled and shook his head

gruffly. "Never mind," he muttered. "The child's not important. I'll deal with him — and his mother — later. Let's get down to the good stuff. We all know the prophecy." He nodded at Mr Tiny, who was wandering around the burning tents and vans, paying no apparent interest to us. "Darren or Vancha will kill me, or I'll kill one of you, and that will decide the fate of the War of the Scars."

"If Tiny's right, or telling the truth, aye," Vancha sniffed.

"You don't believe him?" Steve frowned.

"Not entirely," Vancha said. "Tiny and his daughter —" He glared at Evanna. "— have agendas of their own. I accept most of what they predict but I don't treat their predictions as absolute facts."

"Then why are you here?" Steve challenged him.

"In case they *are* correct."

Steve looked confused. "How can you not believe them? Desmond Tiny is the voice of destiny. He sees the future. He knows all that has been and will be."

"We make our own futures," Vancha said. "Regardless of what happens tonight, I believe my people will defeat yours. But I'll kill you anyway," he added with a wicked grin. "Just to be on the safe side."

"You're an ignorant fool," Steve said, shaking with outrage. Then his gaze settled on me. "I bet *you* believe the prophecy."

"Maybe," I replied.

"Of course you do," Steve smiled. "And you know it's you or me, don't you? Vancha's a red herring. You and I are the sons of destiny, the ruler and slave, the victor and vanquished. Leave Vancha behind, step up here alone, and I swear it will be a fair fight. You and me, man to man, one winner, one loser. A Vampaneze Lord to rule the night — or a Vampire Prince."

"How can I trust you?" I asked. "You're a liar. You'll spring a trap."

"No," Steve barked. "You have my word."

"Like that means anything," I jeered, but I could see an eagerness in Steve's expression. His offer was genuine. I glanced sideways at Vancha. "What do you think?"

"No," Vancha said. "We're in this together. We'll take him on as a team."

"But if he's prepared to fight me fairly..."

"That demon knows nothing about fairness," Vancha said. "He'd cheat — that's his nature. We'll do nothing the way he wants."

"Very well." I faced Steve again. "Stuff your offer. What next?"

I thought Steve was going to leap over the ranks of vampaneze and attack me. He gnashed his teeth, hands twisted together, shivering furiously. Gannen Harst saw it too, but to my surprise, rather than step in to calm Steve down, he took a half-step back. It was as if he wanted Steve to leap, like he'd had enough of his insane, evil Lord, and wanted this matter settled, one way or the other.

But just when it seemed as if the moment of final confrontation had come, Steve relaxed and his smile returned. "I do my best," he sighed. "I try to make it easy for everybody, but some people are determined not to play ball. Very well. Here's 'what next'."

Steve put his fingers to his lips and whistled sharply. From behind the gallows, R.V. stepped out. The bearded, ex-eco-warrior was holding a rope between three lonely-looking hooks (Mr Tall had snapped the other hooks off before he died). When he tugged on the rope, a bound woman shuffled out after him — Debbie.

I'd been expecting this, so I didn't panic. R.V. walked Debbie forwards a few paces, but stopped a long way short of Steve. The one-time campaigner for peace and the protection of mother nature didn't look very happy. He was twitchy, head jerking, eyes unfocused, nervously chewing at his lower lip, which was bleeding from where he'd bitten through the flesh. R.V. had been a proud, earnest, dedicated man when I first met him, fighting to save the world from pollution. Then he'd become a mad beast, intent only on gaining revenge for the loss of his hands. Now he was neither — just a ragged, sorry mess.

Steve didn't notice R.V.'s confusion. He had eyes only for Debbie. "Isn't she beautiful?" he mocked me. "Like an angel. More warrior-like than the last time we met, but all the lovelier because of it." He looked at me slyly. "Be a shame if I had to tell R.V. to gut her like a rabid dog."

"You can't use her against me," I said softly, gazing at Steve without blinking. "She knows who you are and what's at stake. I love her, but my first duty is to my clan. She understands that."

"You mean you'll stand there and let her die?" Steve shrieked.

"Yes!" Debbie shouted before I could reply.

"You people," Steve groaned. "You're determined to annoy me. I try to be fair, but you toss it back in my face and..." He hopped off of Pasta O'Malley's back and ranted and raved, striding up and down behind his guards. I kept a close watch on him. If he stepped out too far, I'd strike. But even in his rage he was careful not to expose himself.

All of a sudden Steve stopped. "So be it!" he snarled. "R.V. — kill her!"

R.V. didn't respond. He was gazing miserably down at the ground.

"R.V.!" Steve shouted. "Didn't you hear me? Kill her!"

"Don't want to," R.V. mumbled. His eyes came up and I saw pain and doubt in them. "You shouldn't have killed the kid, Steve. He did nothing to hurt us. It was wrong. Kids are the future, man."

"I did what I had to," Steve replied tightly. "Now you'll do the same."

"But she's not a vampire..."

"She works for them!" Steve shouted.

"I know," R.V. moaned. "But why do we have to kill her? Why did you kill the kid? It was Darren we were meant to kill. *He's* the enemy, man. He's the one who cost me my hands."

"Don't betray me now," Steve growled, stepping towards the bearded vampaneze. "You've killed people too, the innocent as well as the guilty. Don't get moralistic on me. It doesn't become you."

"But ... but ... but..."

"Stop stuttering and kill her!" Steve screamed. He took another step forward and moved clear of his guards without being aware of it. I steeled myself to make a dash at him, but Vancha was one move ahead of me.

"*Now!*" Vancha roared, leaping forward, drawing a shuriken and launching it at Steve. He would have killed him, except the guard at the end of the line saw the danger just in time and threw himself into the path of the deadly throwing star, sacrificing himself to save his Lord.

As the other guards surged sideways to block Vancha's path to their Lord, I sheathed my knives, drew the pistol I'd borrowed from Alice before entering the stadium, aimed it at the sky and pulled the trigger three times — the signal for all-out riot!

CHAPTER NINE

Even before the echoes of the report of my third shot faded, the air outside the stadium filled with answering gunfire, as Alice and her band of vampirites opened fire on the police standing guard. She'd summoned the homeless people before Vancha and I entered the tunnel, and positioned them around the barrier outside the stadium. After years of surviving on the scraps other people threw away, this was their time to rise. They had only a small amount of training and basic weapons, but they had passion and anger on their side, and the desire to prove themselves. So now, at my signal, they leapt the barriers around the stadium and attacked as a unified force, throwing themselves upon the startled police, sacrificing themselves where necessary, fighting and dying not just for their own lives, but for the lives of those who considered them trash.

We weren't sure of the intentions of the police. Steve might have told them to remain outside regardless of what happened within, in which case the attack by the vampirites would serve no purpose at all. But if they were there to support the vampaneze and vampets, to come to their aid if summoned, the vampirites could divert them and buy those of us inside the stadium a bit more space and time.

Most of the vampaneze guarding Steve moved to stop Vancha when he charged, but two lunged at me as I fired the pistol. They tackled me to the ground, knocking the gun from my hand. I struck out at them but they simply lay on top of me, pinning me down. They would have held me there, helpless, while their colleagues dealt with Vancha. Except...

The stars and crew of the Cirque Du Freak had also rallied to my signal. At the same time that the vampirites attacked the police, the prisoners inside the stadium turned on the vampets holding them captive. They attacked with their bare hands, driving the vampets back by sheer force of numbers. The vampets fired into the crowd and hacked wildly with their swords and axes. Several people fell, dead or wounded. But the group pushed on regardless, screaming, punching, kicking, biting — no force on Earth could hold them back.

While the bulk of the Cirque Du Freak troupe grappled with the vampets, Harkat led a small band towards the gallows. He'd grabbed an axe from a dead vampet and with one smooth swing he cut down a vampaneze who tried to intercept them, rushing past without breaking his stride.

Vancha was still locked in a struggle with Steve's guards, doing his best to break through to their Lord. He'd downed two of them but the others were standing firm. He was cut in many places, knife and spear wounds, but none fatal. Looking around, I saw Gannen Harst push Steve away from the threat. Steve was arguing with him — he wanted to take Vancha on.

Behind Steve and Gannen Harst, R.V. had let go of Debbie's rope and was backing away from her, shaking his head, hooks crossed behind his back, wanting no part of this. Debbie was tugging at her bonds, trying to wriggle free.

The two vampaneze holding me down saw Harkat and the others racing towards them. Cursing, they abandoned me and lashed out at their attackers. They were too swift for the ordinary circus folk — three died quickly — but Truska was part of the group, and she wasn't so easily despatched. She'd let her beard grow while she'd been waiting to fight — the unnatural blonde hair now trailed down past her feet. Standing back, she made the beard rise — she could control the hairs as though they were snakes — then directed the twisting strands towards one of the vampaneze. The beard parted into two prongs, then curled around the startled vampaneze's throat and tightened. He sliced at the hair and at Truska, but she had him too firmly in her grip. He fell to his knees, purple features darkening even further as he choked.

Harkat took on the other vampaneze, chopping at him with his axe. The Little Person lacked the speed of a vampaneze, but he was very powerful and his round green eyes were alert to his opponent's swift moves. He could fight as an equal, as he had many times in the past.

I circled around the vampaneze struggling with Vancha. I meant to go after Steve, but he and Gannen had linked up with three of the vampaneze who'd been roaming the grounds of the stadium. I didn't fancy the five-to-one odds, so I went to cut Debbie free instead.

"They surrounded the stadium shortly after Harkat and I arrived," she cried as I sliced through the ropes binding her arms. "I tried phoning, but it wouldn't work. It was Mr Tiny. He blocked my signal. I saw his watch glowing, and he was laughing."

"It's OK," I said. "We'd have come anyway. We had to."

"Is that Alice outside?" Debbie asked — the gunfire was deafening now.

"Yes," I said. "The vampirites seem to be enjoying their first taste of action."

Vancha lurched over to us, streaming blood. The vampaneze had given up on him and retreated, teaming up with the vampets and picking fights with the circus folk. "Where's Leonard?" Vancha bellowed.

I peered around the stadium but it was almost impossible to pick out any individuals in the press of bodies. "I had him in my sights a minute ago," I said. "He must be here somewhere."

"Not if Gannen flitted with him!" Vancha roared. He wiped blood clear of his eyes and looked for Steve and Gannen again.

"Are you badly wounded?" Debbie asked him.

"Scratches!" Vancha grunted. Then he shouted, "There! Behind the fat man!"

He rushed forward, bellowing madly. Squinting, I caught a glimpse of Steve. He was close to the enormous Rhamus Twobellies, warily backing away from him. Rhamus was literally falling on his opponents, squashing them lifeless.

Debbie darted away from me, picked the bodies of the dead vampaneze clean of their weapons, and returned with an array of knives and two swords. She gave one of the swords to me and hefted the other herself. It was too large for her, but she held it steady, face set. "You go get Steve," she said. "I'll help the others."

"Be —" I began, but she'd already raced out of earshot, "— careful," I finished softly. I shook my head, smiled briefly, then set off after Steve.

Around me the battle was raging. The circus folk were locked in bloody combat with the vampets and vampaneze, fighting clumsily but effectively, blind fury compensating for lack of military training. The gifted freaks were a huge help. Truska was causing havoc with her beard. Rhamus was an immovable foe. Gertha Teeth was biting off fingers, noses, sword tips. Hans Hands had tucked his legs behind his neck and was dodging between the enemy forces on his hands, too low for them to easily strike, tripping them up and dividing them.

Vancha had come to a halt, held up by the fighting. He started firing shurikens at those enemies ahead of him, to clear a path. Jekkus Flang stepped up beside him and added his throwing knives to Vancha's stars. A deadly, efficient combination. I couldn't help thinking what a great show they could have put on if we'd been playing to an audience tonight instead of fighting for our lives.

Mr Tiny was picking his way through the mass of warring bodies, beaming merrily, admiring the corpses of the dead, studying the dying with polite interest, applauding those locked in especially vicious duels. Evanna was edging towards her father, disinterested in the carnage, bare feet and lower ropes stained with blood.

Gannen and Steve were still backing away from the massive Rhamus Twobellies, using him as a shield — it was hard for anybody else to get at them with Rhamus in the way. I tracked them like a hound, closing in. I was almost at the mouth of the tunnel through which we'd entered the stadium when fresh bodies burst through it. My insides tightened — I thought the police had come to the aid of their companions, meaning almost certain defeat for us. But then, to my astonished delight, I realized it was Alice Burgess and a dozen or so vampirites. Declan and Little Kenny — the pair who'd rescued me from the street when Darius shot me — were among them.

"Still alive?" Alice shouted as her troops laid into the vampaneze and vampets, faces twisted with excitement and battle lust.

"How'd you get in?" I yelled in reply. The plan had been for her to cause a diversion outside the stadium, to hold up the police — not invade with a force of her own.

"We attacked at the front, as planned," she said. "The police rushed to that point, to battle *en masse* — they lack discipline. Most of my troops fled with the crowd after a few minutes — you should have seen the chaos! — but I slipped around the back with a few volunteers. The entrance to the tunnel is completely unguarded now. We —"

A vampet attacked her and she had to wheel aside to deal with him. I did a very quick head count. With the addition of the vampirites, we seriously outnumbered the vampaneze and vampets. Although the fighting was brutal and disorganized, we had the upper hand. Unless the police outside recovered swiftly and rushed in, we'd win this battle! But that would mean nothing if Steve escaped, so I put all thoughts of victory on hold and went in pursuit of him again.

I didn't get very far. R.V. had backed away from the fighting. He was heading for the tunnel, but I was standing almost directly in his path. When he saw me, he stopped. I wasn't sure what to do — fight or let him escape so that I could go after Steve? While I was making up my mind, Cormac Limbs stepped in between us.

"Come on, hairy!" he roared at R.V., slapping his face with his left hand, jabbing at him with a knife held in his right. "Let's be having you!"

"No!" R.V. moaned. "I don't want to fight."

"The devil you don't, you big, bearded, bug-eyed baboon!" Cormac shouted, slapping R.V. again. This time R.V. lashed out at Cormac's hand with his hooks. He cut two of the fingers off, but they immediately grew back. "You'll have to do better than that, stink-breath!" Cormac taunted him.

"Then I will!" R.V. shouted, losing his cool. Jumping forwards, he knocked Cormac over, knelt on his chest, and before I could do anything, he struck at Cormac's neck with his hooks. He didn't cut it clean off, but sliced about halfway through. Then, with a grunt, he hacked through the rest of it, and tossed Cormac's head aside like a ball.

"You shouldn't have messed with me, man!" R.V. groaned, rising shakily. I was about to attack him, to avenge Cormac's death, but then I saw that he was sobbing. "I didn't want to kill you!" R.V. howled. "I didn't want to kill anybody! I wanted to help people. I wanted to save the world. I…"

He ground to a halt, eyes widening with disbelief. Glancing down, I also came to a stunned stop. Where Cormac's head had been, two new heads were growing, shooting out on a pair of thin necks. They were slightly smaller than his old head, but otherwise identical. When they stopped growing, there was a short pause. Then Cormac's eyes fluttered open and he spat blood out of both mouths. His eyes came into focus. He looked at R.V. with one set and at me with the other. Then his heads turned and he stared at himself.

"So that's what happens when I cut my head off!" he exclaimed through both mouths at the same time. "I always wondered about that!"

"Madness!" R.V. screamed. "The world's gone mad! *Mad!*"

Spinning crazily, he rushed past Cormac, then past me, gibbering insanely, drooling and falling over. I could have killed him easily — but I chose not to. Standing aside, I let the wretch pass, and watched sadly as he staggered down the tunnel, out of sight. R.V. had never been right in the head since losing his hands, and now he'd lost his senses completely. I couldn't bring myself to punish this pathetic shadow of a man.

And now, at last — Steve. He and Gannen were part of a small band of vampaneze and vampets. They'd been forced towards the centre of the stadium by the freaks, circus helpers and vampirites. Lots of smaller fights were still being waged around the stadium, but this was their last big stand. If this unit fell, they were all doomed.

Vancha was closing in on the group. I joined him. There was no sign of Jekkus Flang — I didn't know whether he'd fallen to the enemy or run out of knives, and this wasn't the time to make enquiries. Vancha paused when he saw me. "Ready?" he asked.

"Ready," I said.

"I don't care which of us kills him," Vancha said, "but let me go first. If —" He stopped, face twisting with fear. "No!" he roared.

Following the direction of his eyes, I saw that Steve had tripped. Evra stood over him, a long knife held in both hands, determined to take the life of the man who'd killed his son. If he struck, the Lord of the Vampaneze would die by the hand of one who wasn't destined to kill him. If Mr Tiny's prophecy was true, that would have dire results for the vampire clan.

As we watched, unable to prevent it, Evra stopped abruptly. He shook his head, blinked dumbly — then stepped over Steve and left him lying on the ground, unharmed. Steve sat up, bleary-eyed, not sure what had happened. Gannen Harst stooped and helped him to his feet. The two men stood, alone in the crush, totally ignored by everyone around them.

"Over there," I whispered, touching Vancha's shoulder. Far off to our right, Mr Tiny stood, eyes on Steve and Gannen. He was holding his heart-shaped watch in his right hand. It was glowing redly. Evanna was standing beside him, her face illuminated by the glow of her father's watch.

I don't know if Steve and Gannen saw Mr Tiny and realized that he was protecting them. But they were alert enough to seize their chance and run for the freedom of the tunnel.

Mr Tiny watched the pair race free of danger. Then he looked at Vancha and me, and smiled. The glow of his watch faded and his lips moved softly. Even though we were a long way off, we heard him clearly, as if he was standing next to us. "It's time, boys!"

"Harkat!" I shouted, wanting him to come with us, to be there at the end, as he'd been by my side for so much of the hunt. But he didn't hear me. Nobody did. I glanced around the stadium at Harkat, Alice, Evra, Debbie. All of my friends were locked in battle with the vampaneze and vampets. None of them knew what was happening with Steve and Gannen Harst. They weren't part of this. It was just me and Vancha now.

"To the death, Sire?" Vancha murmured.

"To the death," I agreed miserably. I ran my eyes over the faces of my friends for what might be the final time, bidding silent farewells to the scaly Evra Von, the grey-skinned Harkat Mulds, the steely Alice Burgess and my beloved Debbie Hemlock, more beautiful than ever as she tore into her foes like an Amazonian warrior of old. Perhaps it was for the best that I couldn't bid them a proper farewell. There was so much to say, I don't know where I would have begun.

Then Vancha and I jogged after Steve and Gannen Harst, not rushing, sure that they wouldn't flit, not this time, not until we'd satisfied the terms of Mr Tiny's prophecy and Steve or one of us lay dead. Behind us, Mr Tiny and Evanna followed like ghosts. They alone would bear witness to the final battle, the death of one of the hunters or Steve — and the birth of the Lord of the Shadows, destroyer of the present and all-ruling monster of the future.

CHAPTER TEN

We followed Steve and Gannen down the hill at the rear of the stadium. They were fleeing towards the river, but they weren't racing at top speed. Either one of them was injured or, like ourselves, they'd simply accepted the fact that we had to fight, an evenly matched contest, to the bitter, bloody end.

As we jogged down the hill, leaving the stadium, lights and noises behind, my headache lessened. I would have been glad of that, except now that I was able to focus, I realized how physically drained I was. I'd been operating on reserve energy for a long time and had just about run dry. Even the simplest movement was a huge chore. All I could do was carry on as long as possible and hope I got an adrenaline burst when we caught up with our prey.

As we reached level ground at the bottom of the hill, I stumbled and almost fell. Luckily Vancha had been keeping an eye on me. He caught and steadied me. "Feel bad?" he asked.

"Awful," I groaned.

"Maybe you're not meant to go any further," he said. "Perhaps you should rest here and —"

"Save your breath," I stopped him. "I'm going on, even if I have to crawl."

Vancha laughed, then tilted my head back and examined my face, his small eyes unusually dark. "You'll make a fine vampire," he said. "I hope I'm around to celebrate your coming of age."

"You're not getting defeatist on me, are you?" I grunted.

"No." He smiled weakly. "We'll win. Of course we will. I just..."

He stopped, slapped my back and urged me on. Wearily, every step an effort, I threw myself after Steve and Gannen Harst again. I did my best to match Vancha's pace, swinging my legs as evenly as I could, keeping the rest of my body limp, relaxed, saving energy.

Steve and Gannen reached the river and turned right, jogging along the bank. As they came to the arch of a bridge spanning the river, they stopped. It looked like they were having an argument. Gannen was trying to pick Steve up — I assumed he meant to flit, with Steve on his back, as they'd escaped from us once before. Steve was having none of it. He slapped his protector's hands away, gesturing furiously. Then, as we closed upon them, Gannen's shoulders sagged and he nodded wearily. The pair turned away from the pass beneath the bridge, drew their weapons and stood waiting for us.

We slowed and walked the rest of the way. I could hear Mr Tiny and Evanna close behind — they'd caught up to us within the last few seconds — but I didn't turn to look back.

"You could use your shurikens," I whispered to Vancha as we came within range of Steve and Gannen Harst.

"That would be dishonourable," Vancha replied. "They've faced us openly, in expectation of a fair fight. We must confront them."

He was right. Killing mercilessly wasn't the vampire way. But I half wished he'd put his principles aside, for once, and fire his throwing stars at them until they dropped. It would be much simpler and surer that way.

We drew to a halt a couple of metres short of Steve and Gannen. Steve's eyes were alight with excitement and a slight shade of fear — he knew there were no guarantees now, no more opportunities for dirty tricks or games. It was a plain, fair fight to the death, and that was something he couldn't control.

"Greetings, brother," Gannen Harst said, bowing his head.

"Greetings," Vancha replied stiffly. "I'm glad you face us like true creatures of the night at last. Perhaps in death you can find again the honour which you abandoned during life."

"Honour will be shared by all here tonight," Gannen said, "both the living and the dead."

"They don't half go on a lot," Steve sighed. He squared up to me. "Ready to die, Shan?"

I stepped forward. "If that's what fate has in store for me — yes," I answered. "But I'm also ready to kill." With that I raised my sword and struck the first blow of the fight which would decide the outcome of the War of the Scars.

Steve stood his ground, brought his own sword up — it was shorter and easier to handle than mine — and turned my blow aside. Gannen Harst stabbed at me with his long, straight sword. Vancha slapped the blade wide of its target and pulled me out of immediate range of his brother.

Vancha only gave me a relatively gentle tug, but in my weakened state I staggered backwards and wound up in an untidy mess on the ground, close to Mr Tiny and Evanna. By the time I struggled to my feet, Vancha was locked in combat with Steve and Gannen Harst, hands a blur as he defended himself against their swords with his bare palms.

"He's a fierce creature, isn't he?" Mr Tiny remarked to his daughter. "Quite the beast of nature. I like him."

Evanna didn't reply. All her senses were focused on the battle, and there was worry and uncertainty in her eyes. I knew in that moment that she'd told the truth and really didn't know which way this would go.

I turned away from the onlookers and caught quick flashes of the fight which was unfolding at superhuman speed. Steve nicked Vancha's left arm near the top — Vancha kicked him in the chest in return. Gannen's sword scraped down Vancha's left side, slicing a thin gouge from breast to waist — Vancha replied by grabbing his brother's sword hand and wrenching it back, snapping the bones of his wrist. Gannen gasped with pain as he dropped the sword, then ducked for it and grabbed it with his left hand. As he came to his feet again, Vancha struck his head with his right knee. Gannen fell away with a heavy grunt.

Vancha spun round to deal with Steve, but Steve was already upon him, making short sweeps with his sword, keeping Vancha at bay. Vancha tried to grab the sword, but only succeeded in having the flesh of his palms cut open. I staggered up beside him. I wasn't of much use right then — I could barely raise my sword, and my legs dragged like dead weights — but at least it provided Steve with a double threat. If I could distract him, Vancha might be able to penetrate his defences and strike.

As I drew level with Vancha, panting and sweating, Gannen swung back into battle, dazed but determined, chopping angrily at Vancha, forcing him to retreat. I stabbed at Gannen, but Steve diverted my sword with his, then let go of the handle with one hand and punched me between the eyes. I dropped back, startled, and Steve drove the tip of his sword at my face.

If he'd had both hands on the sword, he'd have thrust it through me. But one-handed, he wasn't able to direct it as powerfully as he wished. I managed to knock it aside with my left arm. A deep cut opened up just below my elbow and I felt all the strength leave the fingers of that hand.

Steve stabbed at me again. I raised my sword to protect myself. Too late I realized he'd only feinted. Wheeling around, he threw himself into me, right shoulder first. He struck me heavily in the chest and I fell back, winded losing hold of my sword. There was a yell behind me and I crashed into Vancha. Both of us went down, Vancha taken by surprise, arms and legs entangled with mine.

It took Vancha no more than a second to free himself — but that second was all Gannen Harst required. Darting forward, almost too fast for me to see, he stuck the tip of his sword into the small of Vancha's back — then shoved it all the way through and out the front of Vancha's stomach!

Vancha's eyes and mouth shot wide open. Gannen stood behind him a moment. Then he stepped away and pulled his sword free. Blood gushed out of Vancha, both in front and behind, and he collapsed in agony, face twisted, limbs thrashing.

"May your gods forgive me, brother," Gannen whispered, his face haggard, eyes haunted. "Though I fear I'll never forgive myself."

I scrabbled away from the downed Prince, chasing my sword. Steve stood close by, laughing. With an effort, Gannen regained control and set about securing victory. Hurrying over to me, he stood on my sword so that I couldn't lift it, sheathed his own blade and grabbed my head with his good left hand. "Hurry!" he barked at Steve. "Kill him quick!"

"What's the rush?" Steve muttered.

"If Vancha dies of the wound I gave him, we'll have broken the rules of Mr Tiny's prophecy!" Gannen shouted.

Steve pulled a face. "Bloody prophecies," he grumbled. "Maybe I'll let him die and see what happens. Maybe I don't care about Tiny or..." He stopped and rolled his eyes. "Oh, how *silly* we are! The answer's obvious — *I'll* kill Vancha before he dies of your wound. That way we'll fulfil the requirements of the stupid prophecy *and* I'll get to hang on to Darren, so I can torture him later."

"Clever boy," I heard Mr Tiny murmur.

"Have it any way you wish!" Gannen roared. "But if you're going to kill him, kill him now, so that —"

"*No!*" someone screamed. Before anyone could react, a large shape shot out of the underpass beneath the bridge and hurled itself at Gannen, knocking him off me, almost toppling him into the river. Sitting up, I got a shocked fix on my most unlikely of rescuers — *R. V.!*

"Not gonna let you do it, man!" R.V. screamed, pounding Gannen Harst with his hooks. "You're evil!"

Gannen had been taken completely unawares, but he swiftly recovered, fumbled his sword free of its scabbard, and dug at R.V. with it. R.V. caught the sword with his gold right-handed hooks and smashed it against the ground, snapping it in two. With a roar of triumph, he slammed his silver left-handed hook into the side of Gannen's head. There was a crack and Gannen's eyes went blank. He slumped beneath R.V., unconscious. R.V. howled with joy, then drew both arms back to bring them down sharply and finish Gannen off.

Before R.V. could strike, Steve stepped up behind him and forced a knife up beneath his bushy beard, deep into his throat. R.V. shuddered and bowled Steve over. R.V. stood, spinning crazily, grabbing for the handle of the knife with his hooks. After missing it several times, he fell down, landing on his knees, head thrown back.

R.V. knelt there a moment, swaying sickeningly. Then his arms slowly rose. He gazed at the gold and silver hooks, his face glowing with wonder. "My hands," he said softly, and although his voice was gurgly with blood, his words were clear. "I can see them. My hands. They're back. Everything's OK now. I'm normal again, man." Then his arms dropped, his smile and pale red eyes froze in place, and his soul passed quietly on to the next world.

CHAPTER ELEVEN

I gazed at R.V.'s peaceful expression as he knelt in his death pose. He'd left his pain behind at last, for ever. I was glad for him. If he'd lived, he'd have had to carry around the memory of the evil he'd committed while in league with the vampaneze. Maybe he was better off this way.

"And now there's two — just me and you," Steve trilled, breaking my train of thought. I glanced up and saw him standing a few metres away from R.V., smiling. Gannen Harst was still out for the count, and although Vancha was alive, he was lying motionless, wheezing fitfully, unable to defend himself or attack.

"Yes," I agreed, standing and picking up my sword. My left hand wouldn't work and my system was maybe a minute or two away from complete shutdown. But I'd enough strength left for one last fight. First though — Vancha. I paused over him and studied at his wound. It was seeping blood and his face was creased with pain. He tried to speak but words wouldn't form.

As I hovered uncertainly by the side of my fellow Prince, unwilling to leave him like this, Evanna crossed to his side, knelt and examined him. Her eyes were grave when she looked up. "It is not fatal," she said softly. "He will live."

"Thank you," I muttered.

"Save your thanks," Mr Tiny said. He was standing directly behind me. "She didn't tell you to cheer you up, silly boy. It was a warning. Vancha won't die for the time being, but he's out of the fight. You're alone. The final hunter. Unless you turn tail and run, it's down to you and Steve now. If Steve doesn't die, death will come within the next few minutes for *you*."

I looked over my shoulder at the small man in the yellow suit and green wellington boots. His face was bright with bloodthirsty glee. "If death comes," I said shortly, "it will be a far more welcome companion than you."

Mr Tiny chuckled, then stepped away to my left. Rising, Evanna took up position on my right. Both waited for me to move, so that they could follow. I spared Vancha one final glance — he grinned painfully at me and winked — then faced Steve.

He backed away from me casually, entering the shadows beneath the bridge. I trailed after him, sword by my side, taking deep breaths, clearing my mind, focusing on the death-struggle to come. Although this could have been Vancha's battle, a part of me had known all along that it would come down to this.

Steve and I were opposite sides of a coin, linked since childhood, first by friendship, then hatred. It was only fitting that the final confrontation should fall to the two of us.

I entered the cool darkness of the underpass. It took my eyes a few seconds to adjust. When they did, I saw Steve waiting, right eye twitching nervously. The river gurgled softly beside us, the only noise except for our panting and chattering teeth.

"There is where we settle matters, once and for all, in the dark," Steve said.

"As good a place as any," I replied.

Steve raised his left palm. I could vaguely make out the shape of the pink cross he'd carved into his flesh eighteen years before. "Remember when I did this?" he asked. "That night, I swore I'd kill you and Creepy Crepsley."

"You're halfway there," I noted dryly. "You must be delighted."

"Not really," he said. "To be honest, I miss old Creepy. The world's not the same without him. I'll miss you even more. You've been the driving force behind everything I've done since I was a child. Without you, I'm not sure I'll have much of an interest in life. If possible, I'd let you go. I enjoy our games — the hunt, the traps, the fights. I'd happily keep doing it, over and over, a new twist here, a fresh shock there."

"But life doesn't work like that," I said. "Everything has to end."

"Yes," Steve said sadly. "That's one thing I can't change." His mood passed and he regarded me with a sneer. "Here's where *you* end, Darren Shan. This is your grand finale. Have you made your peace with the vampire gods?"

"I'll do that later," I snarled, and swung my sword wide, moving forward so that on its return arc he'd be within range. But before it had completed its first arc, the tip of the sword smashed into the wall. It bounced off in a shower of sparks and a shock ran down my arm.

"Silly boy," Steve purred, mimicking Mr Tiny. He raised a knife. "No room here for swords."

Steve leapt forward and jabbed the knife at me. I pulled back and lobbed my sword at him, momentarily halting him. In that second, I drew one of the knives I'd brought from Annie's kitchen. When Steve advanced, I was ready. I caught his thrust with the hilt of my knife and turned his blade aside.

There was no room in the underpass to circle one another, so we had to jab and stab, ducking and weaving to avoid each other's blows. The conditions actually played into my favour — in the open I'd have had to be nimbler on my feet, spinning to keep up with Steve. That would have exhausted me. Here, since we were so cramped, I could stand still and direct my rapidly dwindling strength into my knife hand.

We fought silently, fast, sharp, impulsive. Steve nicked the flesh of my forearm — I nicked his. He opened shallow wounds on my stomach and chest — I repaid the compliment. He almost cut my nose off — I nearly severed his left ear.

Then Steve came at me from the left, taking advantage of

my dead arm. He grabbed the material of my shirt and pulled me towards him, driving his knife hard at my belly with his other hand. I rolled with the force of his pull, throwing myself into him. His knife cut the wall of my stomach, a deep wound, but my momentum carried me forward despite the pain. I drove him down, landing awkwardly on him as he hit the path. His right hand flew out by his side, fingers snapping open. His knife shot free and struck the river with a splash, vanishing from sight in an instant.

Steve brought his empty right hand up, to push me off. I stabbed at it with my knife and hit home, spearing him through his forearm. He screamed. I freed my knife before he could knock it from my grip, raised it to shoulder height and redirected it, so the tip was pointing at Steve's throat. His eyes shot to the gleam of the blade and his breath caught. This was it. I had him. He'd been out-fought and he knew it. One quick thrust of the knife and —

Searing pain. A white flash inside my head. I thought Gannen had recovered and struck me from behind, but he hadn't. It was an aftershock from when I blooded Darius. Vancha had warned me about this. My limbs trembled. A roaring in my ears, drowning out all other sounds. I dry-heaved and fell off Steve, almost tumbling into the river. "No!" I tried to scream. "Not now!" But I couldn't form the words. I was in the grip of immense pain, and could do nothing against it.

Time seemed to collapse. Gripped by panic, I was dimly aware of Steve crawling on top of me. He wrestled my knife from my hand. There was a sharp stabbing sensation in my stomach, followed by another. Steve crowed, "Now I have you! Now you're gonna die!" Something blurry passed in front of my eyes, then back again. Fighting the white light inside my head, I got my eyes to focus. It was the knife. Steve had pulled it out and was waving it in my face, teasing me, sure he'd won, prolonging the moment of triumph.

But Steve had miscalculated. The pain of the stabbing brought me back from the brink of all-out confusion. The agony in my gut worked against the pain in my head, and the world began to swim back into place around me. Steve was perched on top of me, laughing. But I wasn't afraid. Unknown to himself, he was helping me. I was able to think halfway straight now, able to plan, able to act.

My right hand stole to waist of my trousers as Steve continued to mock me. I gripped the handle of a second knife. I caught a glimpse of Mr Tiny peering over Steve's shoulder. He'd seen my hand moving and knew what was coming. He was nodding, though I'm not sure if he was encouraging me or merely bobbing his head up and down with excitement.

I lay still, gathering my very last dredges of energy together, letting Steve torment me with wild promises of what was to come. I was bleeding freely from the stab wounds in my stomach. I wasn't sure if I'd be alive come the dawn, but of one thing I was certain — Steve would die before me.

"— and when I finish with your toes and fingers, I'll move on to your nose and ears!" Steve yelled. "But first I'll cut your eyelids off, so you can see everything that I'm gonna do. After that I'll —"

"Steve," I wheezed, stopping him midflow. "Want to know the secret of winning a fight like this? Less talking — more stabbing."

I lunged at him, using the muscles of my stomach to force my body up. Steve wasn't prepared for it. I knocked him backwards. As he fell, I swung my legs around, then pushed with my knees and feet, so I drove him all the way back with the full weight of my body. He hit the pavement with a grunt, for the second time within the space of a few minutes. This time he managed to hold on to his knife, but that was no use to him. I wasn't going to make the same mistake twice.

No hesitation. No pausing to pick my point. No cynical, memorable last words. I put my trust in the gods of the vampires and blindly thrust my knife forward. I brought it around and down in a savage arc, and by luck or fate drove it into the centre of Steve's left breast — clean through his shrivelled forgery of a heart!

CHAPTER TWELVE

Steve's eyes and mouth popped wide with shock. His expression was comical, but I was in no mood to laugh. There was no recovery from a strike like that. Steve was finished. But he could take me with him if I wasn't careful. So instead of celebrating, I grabbed his left hand, holding it down tight by his side so he couldn't use his knife on me.

Steve's gaze slid to the handle of the knife sticking out of his chest. "Oh," he said tonelessly. Then blood trickled from the sides of his mouth. His chest heaved up and down, the handle rising and falling with it. I wanted to pull the knife out, to end matters — he could maybe go on like this for a minute or two, the knife stopping the gush of blood from his heart — but my left hand was useless and I didn't dare free my right.

Then — applause. My head lifted, and Steve's eyes rolled back in their sockets so that he could look behind him. Mr Tiny was clapping, bright red tears of joy dripping down his cheeks. "What passion!" he exclaimed. "What valour! What a never-say-die spirit! My money was always on you, Darren. It could have gone either way, but if I was a betting man, I'd have bet big on you. I said as much beforehand, didn't I, Evanna?"

"Yes, father," Evanna answered quietly. She was studying me sadly. Her lips moved silently, but even though she uttered no sounds, I was able to make out what she said. "To the victor, the spoils."

"Come, Darren," Mr Tiny said. "Pull out the knife and tend to your wounds. They're not immediately life-threatening, but you should have a doctor see to them. Your friends in the stadium are almost done with their foes. They'll be coming soon. They can take you to a hospital."

I shook my head. I only meant that I couldn't pull the knife out, but Mr Tiny must have thought I didn't want to kill Steve. "Don't be foolish," he snapped. "Steve is the enemy. He deserves no mercy. Finish him, then take your place as the rightful ruler of the night."

"You are the Lord of the Shadows now," Evanna said. "There is no room in your life for mercy. Do as my father bids. The sooner you accept your destiny, the easier it will be for you."

"And do you ... want me to ... kill Vancha now too?" I panted angrily.

"Not yet," Mr Tiny laughed. "That will come in its own time." His laughter faded and his expression hardened.

"Much will come in time. The vampaneze will fall, and so shall the humans. This world will be yours, Darren — rather, *ours*. Together we'll rule. Your hand at the tiller, my voice in your ear. I'll guide and advise you. Not openly — I haven't the power to directly steer you — but on the sly. I'll make suggestions, you'll heed them, and together we'll build a world of chaos and twisted beauty."

"What makes you ... think I'd have anything to do ... with a monster like you?" I snarled.

"He has a point, father," Evanna murmured. "We both know what lies in store for Darren. He will become a ruler of savage, unrelenting power. But he hates you. That hatred will increase over the centuries, not diminish. What makes you think you can rule with him?"

"I know more about the boy than you do," Mr Tiny said smugly. "He will accept me. He was born to." Mr Tiny squatted and looked straight down into Steve's eyes. Then he looked up into mine, his face no more than five or six centimetres away. "I have always been there for you. For both of you," he whispered. "When you competed with your friends for a ticket to the Cirque Du Freak," he said to me, "I whispered in your ear and told you when to grab for it."

My jaw dropped. I *had* heard a voice that day, but I'd thought it was only an inner voice, the voice of instinct.

"And when you," he said to Steve, "noticed something strange about Darren after your meeting with Larten Crepsley, who do you think kept you awake at night, filling your thoughts with doubt and suspicion?"

Mr Tiny pulled back half a metre. His smile had returned, and it now threatened to spread from his face and fill the tunnel. "*I* influenced Crepsley and inspired him to blood Darren. *I* urged Gannen Harst to suggest Steve try the Coffin of Fire. Both of you have enjoyed enormous slices of good fortune in life. You put it down to the luck of the vampires, or the survival instinct of the vampaneze. But it was neither. You owe your nine cat's lives — and quite a few more — to *me.*"

"I don't understand," I said, confused and alarmed. "Why would you go to all that trouble? Why ruin our lives?"

"*Ruin?*" he barked. "With my help you became a Prince and Steve became a Lord. With my backing the two of you have led the creatures of the night to war, and one of you — *you*, Darren! — now stands poised to become the most powerful tyrant in the history of the world. I have *made* your lives, not ruined them!"

"But why us?" I pressed. "We were ordinary kids. Why pick on Steve and me?"

"You were never ordinary," Mr Tiny disagreed. "From birth — no, from conception you were both unique." He stood and looked at Evanna. She was staring at him uncertainly — this was news to her too. "For a long time I wondered what it would be like to father children," Mr Tiny said softly. "When, spurred on by a stubborn vampire, I finally decided to give parenthood a try, I created two offspring in my own mould, beings of magic and great power.

"Evanna and Hibernius fascinated me at first, but in time I

grew tired of their limitations. Because they can see into the future, they — like me — are limited in what they can do in the present. All of us have to abide by laws not of our making. I can interfere in the affairs of mankind more than my children can, but not as much as I'd wish. In many ways my hands are tied. I can influence mortals, and I do, but they're contrary creatures and short-lived. It's difficult to manipulate large groups of humans over a long period of time — especially now that there are billions of them!

"What I longed for was a mortal I could channel my will through, a being not bound by the laws of the universe, nor shackled by the confines of humanity. My ally would have to start as a human, then become a vampire or vampaneze. With my help he would lead his clan to rule over all. Together we could govern the course of the world for hundreds of years to come, and through *his* children I could control it for thousands of years — maybe even the rest of time itself."

"You're mad," I growled. "I don't care if you did help me. I won't work with you or do what you want. I'm not going to link myself to your warped cause. I doubt that Steve would have either, if he'd won."

"But you *will* join me," Mr Tiny insisted, "just as Steve would have. You must. It's in your nature. Like sides with like." He paused, then said proudly and provocatively, "Son sides with sire."

"*What?*" Evanna exploded, leaping to an understanding sooner than I did.

"I required a less powerful heir," Mr Tiny said, his gaze

fixed on me. "One who'd carry my genes and mirror my desires, but who could act freely as a mortal. To weed out any weaknesses, I created a pair, then set them against each other. The weaker would perish and be forgotten. The stronger would go on to claim the world." He stuck his arms out, the gesture both mocking and strangely heartfelt. "Come and give your father a hug, Darren — *my son!*"

CHAPTER THIRTEEN

"You're mad!" I croaked. "I have a father, a real dad. It isn't you!"

"Dermot Shan was not your father," Mr Tiny replied. "You were a cuckoo's child. Steve too. I did my work quietly, unknown to your mothers. But trust me — you're both mine."

"This is outrageous!" Evanna screeched, her body expanding, becoming more that of a wolf than human, until she filled most of the tunnel. "It is forbidden! How dare you!"

"I acted within the confines of the universe's laws!" Mr Tiny snapped. "You'd know if I had not — all would be chaos. I stretched them a bit, but I didn't break them. I am allowed to breed, and my children — if they lack my magical powers — can act the same way as any normal mortal."

"But if Darren and Steve are your sons, then *you* have created the future where one of them becomes the Lord of the Shadows!" Evanna roared. "*You* have cast mankind into the abyss, and twisted the strands of the future to suit your own foul needs!"

"Yes," Mr Tiny chuckled, then pointed a finger at Evanna. "Do not cross me on this, daughter. I would not harm my own flesh and blood, but I could make life very unpleasant if you got on the wrong side of me."

Evanna glared at her father hatefully, then gradually resumed her regular shape and size. "This is unjust," she muttered. "The universe will punish you, perhaps not immediately, but eventually you'll pay a price for your arrogance."

"I doubt it," Mr Tiny smirked. "Mankind was heading towards an all-time boring low. Peace, prosperity, global communication, brotherly love — where's the fun in *that*? Yes, there were still plenty of wars and conflicts to enjoy, but I could see the people of the world moving ever closer together. I did my best, nudged nations along the path to battle, sowed seeds of discontent everywhere I could, even helped get a few tyrants wrongfully elected to some of the most powerful positions on Earth — I was sure those fine specimens would push the world to the brink!

"But no! No matter how tense things got, no matter how much meddling my minions did, I could see peace and understanding gradually winning through. It was time for drastic action, to take the world back to the good old days, when everyone was at everybody else's throat. I've simply restored the natural order of beautiful chaos. The universe won't punish me for that. If anything, I expect —"

"Shut up!" I screamed, surprising both Mr Tiny and Evanna. "It's bull, all of it! You're not my father! You're a monster!"

"And so are you," Mr Tiny beamed. "Or soon will be. But don't worry, son — monsters have all the fun!"

I stared at him, sickened, senses reeling, unable to take it all in. If this was true, everything in my life had been false. I was never the person I thought I was, only a pawn of Mr Tiny's, a time bomb waiting to explode. I'd been blooded simply to extend my life, so I could live longer and do more of Mr Tiny's work. My war with Steve had served only to get rid of the weaker of us, so that the stronger could emerge as a more powerful beast. I'd done nothing for the sake of the vampires or my family and friends — everything had been for Mr Tiny. And now that I'd proved myself worthy, I'd become a dictator and lay low anyone who opposed him. My wishes would count for nothing. It was my destiny.

"Fa-fa-fa…" Steve stammered, spitting blood from his mouth. With his free hand he reached out to Mr Tiny. "Father," he managed to croak. "Help … me."

"Why?" Mr Tiny sniffed.

"I … never … had … a … Dad." Each word was a heart-churning effort, but Steve forced them out. "I … want … to … know … you. I'll … serve … you … and … love … you."

"What on earth would I want with *love?*" Mr Tiny laughed. "Love is one of the most basic human emotions. I'm so pleased I was never cursed with it. Servitude, gratitude, fear, hatred, anger — these I like. Love … you can take your love to the Lake of Souls when you die. Perhaps it will provide you with some comfort there."

"But ... I'm ... your ... son," Steve cried weakly.

"You were," Mr Tiny sneered. "Now you're just a loser, and soon you'll be dead meat. I'll toss your carcass to my Little People to eat — that's how little I feel for you. This is a winner's world. Second place equals second rate. You're nothing to me. Darren's my only son now."

The pain in Steve's eyes was awful to behold. As a child, he'd been crushed when he thought I'd betrayed him. Now he'd been openly mocked and disowned by his father. It destroyed him. His heart had been full of hatred before this, but now that it was down to its last few beats, there was room only for despair.

But in Steve's anguish I found hope. Consumed by smugness, Mr Tiny had revealed too much, too soon. At the back of my brain an idea sparked into life. In a whirl I began to put various pieces together — Mr Tiny's revelation and Evanna's reaction. Evanna said Mr Tiny had created the future in which Steve or I was the Lord of the Shadows. He'd bent the laws he and she lived by, to twist things round and build a chaotic world which he and I could rule over. Evanna and Mr Tall had told me there was no escaping the Lord of the Shadows, that he was part of the world's future. But they were wrong. He was part of *Mr Tiny's* future. Des Tiny might be the most powerful individual in the universe, but he was still only an individual. What one individual could build, another could destroy.

Mr Tiny's eyes were on Steve. He was laughing at him, enjoying Steve's dying misery. Evanna's head was bowed — she'd given in and accepted this. Not me. If I'd inherited Mr Tiny's evil, destructive streak, I'd also inherited his cunning. I'd stop at nothing to deny him his vision of a ruined future.

Slowly, everso slowly, I released Steve's left hand and moved my arm away. He had a free shot at my stomach now, in the perfect position to finish the job he'd started when he stabbed me earlier. But Steve didn't notice. He was wrapped up in his sorrow. I faked a cough and plucked at his left sleeve. If Mr Tiny had seen it, he could have stopped my plan there. But he thought he'd won, that it was all over. He couldn't even imagine the vaguest possibility of a threat.

Steve's gaze flickered down. He realized his hand was free. He saw his chance to kill me. His fingers stiffened on the handle of his knife ... then relaxed. For a terrible moment I thought he'd died, but then I saw that he was still alive. What made him pause was doubt. He'd spent most of his life hating me, but now he'd been told I was his brother. I could see his brain churning. I was a victim of Des Tiny, just as he was. He'd been wrong to hate me — I'd had no choice in what I'd done. In all the world, I was the person he should be closest to, and instead I was the person he'd hurt the most.

What Steve found in those last few moments was what I thought he'd lost for ever — his humanity. He saw the error of his ways, the evil he'd committed, the mistakes he'd made. There was possible salvation in that recognition. Now that he could see himself for what he truly was, perhaps, even at this late stage, he could repent.

But I couldn't afford humanity. Steve's salvation would be my undoing — and the world's. I needed him mad as hell, fire in his gut, filled with fury and hate. Only in that state could he find the power to maybe help me break Des Tiny's hold over the future.

"Steve," I said, forcing a wicked smile. "You were right. I *did* plot with Mr Crepsley to take your place as his assistant. We made a mug of you, and I'm glad. You're a nobody. A nothing. This is what you deserve. If Mr Crepsley was alive, he'd be laughing at you now, just like the rest of us are."

Mr Tiny howled with delight. "That's my boy!" he hooted. He thought I was getting one last dig in before Steve died. But he was wrong.

Steve's eyes refilled with hatred. The human within him vanished in an instant and he was Steve Leopard, vampire killer, again. In one fast, crazed movement he brought his left hand up and drove his knife deep into my stomach. Less than a second later he did it again, then again.

"Stop!" Mr Tiny yelled, seeing the danger too late. He lurched at us, to pull me off, but Evanna slid in front of him and blocked his way.

"No, father!" she snapped. "You cannot interfere in this!"

"Get out of my way!" he bellowed, struggling with her. "The fool's going to let Leonard kill him! We have to stop it!"

"Too late," I giggled, as Steve's blade slid in and sliced through my guts for a fifth time. Mr Tiny stopped and blinked dumbly, at a complete loss for what may well have been the first time in his long, ungodly life. "Destiny ... rejected," I said with my final whole breath. Then I grabbed Steve tight as he lunged at me with his knife again, and rolled to my right, off the edge of the path, into the river.

We went into the water together, wrapped in each other's arms, and sank quickly. Steve tried stabbing me again, but it was too much for him. He went limp and fell away from me, his dead body dropping into the dark depths of the river, disappearing from sight within seconds.

I was barely conscious, hanging sluggishly, limbs being picked at and made to sway by the current of the river. Water rushed down my throat and flooded my lungs. Part of me wanted to strike for the surface, but I fought against it, not wanting to give Mr Tiny even the slightest opportunity to revive me.

I saw faces in the water, or in my thoughts — impossible to tell the difference. Sam Grest, Gavner Purl, Arra Sails, Mr Tall, Shancus, R.V., Mr Crepsley. The dead, come to welcome me.

I stretched my arms out to them, but our fingers didn't touch. I imagined Mr Crepsley waving, and a sad expression crossed his face. Then everything faded. I stopped struggling. The world, the water, the faces faded from sight, then from memory. A roaring which was silence. A darkness which was light. A chill which burnt. One final flutter of my eyelids, barely a movement, impossibly tiring. And then, in the lonely, watery darkness of the river, as all must do when the Grim Reaper calls — I died.

INTERLUDE

Timelessness. Eternal gloom. Drifting in slow, never-ending circles. Surrounded but alone. Aware of other souls, trapped like me, but unable to contact them. No sense of sight, hearing, taste, smell, touch. Only the crushing boredom of the present and painful memories of the past.

✶

I know this place. It's the Lake of Souls, a zone where spirits go when they can't leave Earth's pull. Some people's souls don't move on when they die. They remain trapped in the waters of this putrid lake, condemned to swirl silently in the depths for all eternity.

I'm sad I ended up here, but not surprised. I tried to live a good life, and I sacrificed myself at the end in an effort to save others, so in those respects I was maybe deserving of Paradise. But I was also a killer. Whatever my reasons, I took lives and created unhappiness. I don't know if some higher power has passed judgement on me, or if I'm imprisoned by my own guilt. It doesn't really matter, I guess. I'm here and there's no getting out. This is my lot. For ever.

✶

No sense of time. No days, nights, hours, minutes — not even seconds. Have I been here a week, a year, a century? Can't tell. Does the War of the Scars still rage? Have the vampires or vampaneze fallen? Has another taken my place as the Lord of the Shadows? Did I die for no reason? I don't know. I probably never will. That's part of my sentence. Part of my curse.

If the souls of the dead could speak, they'd scream for
release. Not just release from the Lake, but from their
memories. Memories gnaw away at me relentlessly. I
remember so much of my past, all the times where I failed or
could have done better. With nothing else to do, I'm forced
to review my life, over and over. Even my most minor errors
become supreme lapses of judgement. They torment me
worse than Steve ever did.

I try to hide from the pain of the memories by retreating
further into my past. I remember the young Darren Shan,
human, happy, normal, innocent. I spend years, decades — or
is it just minutes? — reliving the simple, carefree times. I piece
together my entire early life. I recall even the smallest details —
the colours of toy cars, homework assignments, throwaway
conversations. I go through everyday chat a hundred times, until
every word is correct. The longer I think about it, the deeper
into those years I sink, losing myself, human again, almost able
to believe that the memories are reality, and my death and the
Lake of Souls nothing but an unpleasant dream.

But eternity can't be dodged for ever. My later memories
are always hovering, picking away at the boundaries of the
limited reality which I've built. Every so often I flash
ahead to a face or event. Then I lose control and find
myself thrust into the darker, nightmarish world of my life
as a half-vampire. I relive the mistakes, the wrong choices,
the bloodshed.

So many friends lost, so many enemies killed. I feel responsible for all of them. I believed in peace when I first went to Vampire Mountain. Even though Kurda Smahlt betrayed his people, I felt sorry for him. I knew he did it in an effort to avoid war. I couldn't understand why it had come to this. If only the vampires and vampaneze had sat down and talked through their differences, war could have been avoided.

When I first became a Prince, I dreamt of being a peacemonger, taking up where Kurda left off, bringing the vampaneze back into the clan. I lost those dreams somewhere during the six years I spent living within Vampire Mountain. Surviving as a vampire, learning their ways, training with weapons, sending friends out to fight and die ... It all rubbed off on me, and when I finally returned to the world beyond the mountain, I'd changed. I was a warrior, fierce, unmoved by death, intent on killing rather than talking.

I wasn't evil. Sometimes it's necessary to fight. There are occasions when you have to cast aside your nobler ideals and get your hands dirty. But you should always strive for peace, and search to find the peaceful solution to even the most bloody of conflicts. I didn't do that. I embraced the war and went along with the general opinion — that if we killed the Vampaneze Lord, all our problems would be solved and life would be hunky-dory.

We were wrong. The death of one man never solved anything. Steve was just the start. Once you set off down the road of murder, it's hard to take a detour. We couldn't have stopped. The death of one foe wouldn't have been enough. We'd have set about annihilating the vampaneze after Steve, then humanity. We'd have established ourselves as the rulers of the world, crushing all in our path, and I'd have gone along with it. No, more than that — I'd have led, not just followed.

That guilt, not just of what I've done but of what I would have done, eats away at me like a million ravenous rats. It doesn't matter that I'm the son of Desmond Tiny, that wickedness was in my genes. I had the power to break away from the dark designs of my father. I proved that at the end, by letting myself die. But why didn't I do it sooner, before so many people were killed?

I don't know if I could have stopped the war, but I could have said, "No, I don't want any part of this." I could have argued for peace, not fought for it. If I'd failed, at least I maybe wouldn't have wound up here, weighed down by the chains of so many grisly deaths.

✱

Time passes. Faces swim in and out of my thoughts. Memories form, are forgotten, form again. I blank out large parts of my life, recover them, blank them out again. I succumb to madness and forget who I was. But the madness doesn't last. I reluctantly return to my senses.

I think about my friends a lot, especially those who were alive when I died. Did any of them perish in the stadium? If they survived that, what came next? Since Steve and I both died, what happened with the War of the Scars? Could

Mr Tiny replace us with new leaders, men with the same powers as Steve and me? Hard to see how, unless he fathered another couple of children.

Was Harkat alive now, pushing for peace between the vampires and vampaneze, like he had when he was Kurda Smahlt? Had Alice Burgess led her vampirites against the vampets and crushed them? Did Debbie mourn for me? Not knowing was an agony. I'd have sold my soul to the Devil for a few minutes in the world of the living, where I could find answers to my questions. But not even the Devil disturbed the waters of the Lake of Souls. This was the exclusive resting place of the dead and the damned.

Drifting, ghostly, resigned. I fixate on my death, remembering Steve's face as he stabbed me, his hatred, his fear. I count the number of seconds it took me to die, the drops of blood I spilt on the riverbank where he killed me. I feel myself topple into the water of the river a dozen times ... a hundred ... a thousand.

That water was so much more alive than the water of the Lake of Souls. Currents. Fish swam in it. Air bubbles. Cold. The water here is dead, as lifeless as the souls it contains. No fish explore its depths, no insects skim its surface. I'm not sure how I'm aware of these facts, but I am. I sense the awful emptiness of the Lake. It exists solely to hold the spirits of the miserable dead.

I long for the river. I'd meet any asking price if I could go back and experience the rush of flowing water again, the chill as I fell in, the pain as I bled to death. Anything's better than this limbo world. Even a minute of dying is preferable to an eternity of nothingness.

★

One small measure of comfort — as bad as this is for me, it must be much worse for Steve. My guilt is nothing compared to his. I was sucked into Mr Tiny's evil games, but Steve threw himself heart and soul into them. His crimes far outweigh mine, so his suffering must be that much more.

Unless he doesn't accept his guilt. Perhaps eternity means nothing to him. Maybe he's just sore that I beat him. It could be that he doesn't worry about what he did, or realize just how much of a monster he was. He might be content here, reflecting with fondness on all that he achieved.

But I doubt it. I suspect Mr Tiny's admission destroyed a large part of Steve's mad defences. Knowing that he was my brother, and that we were both puppets in our father's hands, must have shaken him up. I think, given the time to reflect — and that's all one can do here — he'll weep for what he did. He'll see himself for what he truly was, and hate himself for it.

I shouldn't take pleasure in that. There, but for the grace of the gods ... But I still despise Steve. I can understand why he acted that way, and I'm sorry for him. But I can't forgive him. I can't stretch that far. Perhaps that's another reason why I'm here.

★

I'm retreating from the painful memories again. Withdrawing from the vampire world, pretending it never happened. I imagine myself as a child, living the same days over and over, refusing to go beyond the afternoon when I won a ticket to the Cirque Du Freak. I build a perfect, sealed-off, comfortable reality. I'm Darren Shan, loving son and brother, not the best behaved boy in the world, but far from the worst. I do chores for Mum and Dad, struggle with homework, watch TV, hang out with my friends. One moment I'm six or seven years old, the next ten or eleven. Continually twisting back upon myself, living the past, ignoring all that I don't want to think about. Steve's my best friend. We read comics, watch horror movies, tell jokes to each other. Annie's a child, always a child — I never think of her as a woman with a son of her own. Vampires are monsters of myth, like werewolves, zombies, mummies, not to be taken seriously.

It's my aim to become the Darren of my memories, to lose myself completely in the past. I don't want to deal with the guilt any more. I've gone mad before and recovered. I want to go mad again, but this time let madness swallow me whole.

I struggle to vanish into the past. Remembering everything, painting the details more precisely every time I revisit a moment. I start to forget about the souls, the Lake, the vampires and vampaneze. I still get occasional flashes of reality, but I clamp down on them quickly. Thinking as a child, remembering as a child, becoming a child.

I'm almost there. The madness waits, arms spread wide, welcoming me. I'll be living a lie, but it will be a peaceful, soothing lie. I long for it. I work hard to make it real. And I'm getting there. I feel myself sliding closer towards it. I reach for the lie with the tendrils of my mind. I feel around it, explore it, start to slip inside it, when all of a sudden — a new sensation...

Pain! Heaviness. Rising. The madness is left behind. The water of the Lake closes around me. Searing pain! Thrashing, coughing, gasping. *But with what?* I have no arms to thrash, no mouth to cough, no lungs to gasp. Is this part of the madness? Am I...

And suddenly my head — an actual, real *head!* — breaks the surface. I'm breathing air. Sunlight blinds me. I spit water out. My arms come clear of the Lake. I'm surrounded, but not by the souls of the dead — by nets! People pulling on them. Coming out of the Lake. Screaming with pain and confusion — but no sounds. Body forming, incredibly heavy after all this weightless time. I land on hard, warm earth. My feet drag out of the water. Amazed, I try to stand. I make it to my knees, then fall. I hit the ground hard. Pain again, fresh and frightening. I curl up into a ball, shivering like a baby. I shut my eyes against the light and dig my fingers into the earth to reassure myself that it's real. And then I sob feebly as the incredible, bewildering, impossible realization sinks in — *I'm alive!*

PART TWO

CHAPTER FOURTEEN

The sun hammered down fiercely upon me but I couldn't stop shivering. Someone threw a blanket around me, hairy and thick. It itched like mad, but the sensation was delicious. Any sensation would have been welcome after the numbness of the Lake of Souls.

The person who'd draped the blanket over me knelt by my side and tilted my head back. I blinked water from my eyes and focused. It took a few seconds, but finally I fixed on my rescuer. It was a Little Person. At first I thought it was Harkat. I opened my mouth to shout his name happily. Then I did a double take and realized this wasn't my old friend, just one of his grey, scarred, green-eyed kind.

The Little Person examined me silently, prodding and poking. Then he stood and stepped aside, leaving me. I wrapped the blanket tighter around myself, trying to stop the shivers. After a while I worked up the strength to look around. I was lying by the rim of the Lake of Souls. The earth around me was hard and dry, like desert. Several Little People stood nearby. A couple were hanging up nets to dry — the nets they'd fished me out with. The others simply stared off into space or at the Lake.

There was a screeching sound high overhead. Looking up, I saw a huge winged beast circling the Lake. From my previous trip here, I knew it was a dragon. My insides clenched with fear. Then I noticed a second dragon. A third. A fourth. Jaw dropping, I realized the sky was full of them, dozens, maybe hundreds. If they caught sight of me...

I started to scrabble weakly for safety, then paused and glanced at the Little People. They knew the dragons were there, but they weren't bothered by the giant flying reptiles. They might have dragged me out of the Lake to feed me to the dragons, but I didn't think so. And even if they had, in my feeble state I could do nothing about it. I couldn't flee or fight, and there was nowhere to hide. So I just lay where I was and waited for events to run their course.

For several minutes the dragons circled and the Little People stood motionless. I was still filled with a great chill, but I wasn't shivering quite as much as when I first came out of the Lake. I was gathering what small amounts of energy I could call on, to try and walk over to the Little People and quiz them about what was going on, when somebody spoke behind me.

"Sorry I'm late."

I looked over my shoulder, expecting Mr Tiny, but it was his daughter, (my half-sister!) Evanna, striding towards me.

She looked no different from how I remembered her, though there was a sparkle in her green and brown eyes which had been absent when last we met.

"Whuh!" I croaked, the only sound I was able to make.

"Easy," Evanna said, reaching me and bending to squeeze my shoulder warmly. "Don't try to speak. It will take a few hours for the effects of the Lake to wear off. I'll build a fire and cook some broth for you. That's why I wasn't here when you were fished out — I was looking for firewood." She pointed to a mound of logs and branches.

I wanted to besiege her with questions, but there was no point taxing my throat when it wasn't ready to work. So I said nothing as she picked me up and carried me to the pile of wood like a baby, then set me down and turned her attention to the kindling.

When the fire was burning nicely, Evanna took a flat circular object out from beneath the ropes she was wearing. I recognized it immediately — a collapsible pot, the same sort that Mr Crepsley had once used. She pressed it in the middle, causing it to pop outwards and assume its natural shape, then filled it with water (not from the Lake, but from a bucket) and some grass and herbs, and hung it from a stick over the flames.

The broth was weak and tasteless, but its warmth was like the fire of the gods to me. I drank deeply, one bowl, another, a third. Evanna smiled as I slurped, then sipped slowly from a bowl of her own. The dragons screeched at regular intervals overhead, the sun burnt brightly, and the scent of the smoke was magical. I felt strangely relaxed, as if this was a lazy summer Sunday afternoon.

I was halfway through my fourth bowl before my stomach growled at me to say, "Enough!" Sighing happily, I laid the bowl down and sat, smiling lightly, thinking only of the good feelings inside. But I couldn't sit silently for ever, so eventually I raised my gaze, looked at Evanna and tested my vocal chords. "Urch," I creaked — I'd meant to say "Thanks."

"It's been a long time since you spoke," Evanna said. "Start simply. Try the alphabet. I will hunt for more wood, to sustain the fire. We won't be staying here much longer, but we may as well have warmth while we are. Practise while I am gone, and we can maybe talk when I return."

I did as the witch advised. At first I struggled to produce sounds anything like they should be, but I stuck with it and gradually my As started to sound like As, my Bs like Bs, and so on. When I'd run through the alphabet several times without making a mistake, I moved on to words, simple stuff to begin with — cat, dog, Mum, Dad, sky, me. I tried names after that, longer words, and finally sentences. It hurt to speak, and I slurred some words, but when Evanna eventually came back, clutching an armful of pitiful twigs, I was able to greet her in a gravelly but semi-normal voice. "Thanks for the broth."

"You're welcome." She threw some of the twigs on to the fire, then sat beside me. "How do you feel?"

"Rough as rust."

"Do you remember your name?"

I squinted at her oddly. "Why shouldn't I?"

"The Lake twists the minds of people," she said. "It can destroy memories. Many of the souls forget who they are. They go mad and lose track of their pasts. You were in there a long time. I feared the worst."

"I came close," I admitted, hunching up closer to the fire, recalling my attempts to go mad and escape the weight of my memories. "It was horrible. Easier to be crazy in there than sane."

"So what is it?" Evanna asked. When I blinked dumbly, she laughed. "Your name?"

"Oh." I smiled. "Darren. Darren Shan. I'm a half-vampire. I remember it all, the War of the Scars, Mr Crepsley, Steve." My features darkened. "I remember my death, and what Mr Tiny said just before it."

"Quite the one for surprises, isn't he — our father?"

She looked at me sideways to see what I'd say about that, but I couldn't think of anything — how do you respond to the news that Des Tiny is your dad, and a centuries-old witch is your half-sister? To avoid the subject, I studied the land around me. "This place looks different," I said. "It was green when I came with Harkat, lots of grass and fresh earth."

"This is further into the future," Evanna explained. "Before, you travelled a mere two hundred or so years ahead of the present. This time you have come hundreds of thousands of years, maybe more. I'm not entirely certain. This is the first time our father has ever allowed me to come here."

"Hundreds of…" My head spun.

"This is the age of dragons," Evanna said. "The age after mankind."

My breath caught in my throat, and I had to clear it twice before I could respond. "You mean humanity has died out?"

"Died out or moved on to other worlds or spheres." Evanna shrugged. "I cannot say for sure. I know only that the world belongs to dragons now. They control it as humans once did, and dinosaurs before them."

"And the War of the Scars?" I asked nervously. "Who won that?"

Evanna was silent a moment. Then she said, "We have much to speak about. Let's not rush." She pointed at the dragons high above us. "Call one of them down."

"What?" I frowned.

"Call them, the way you used to call Madam Octa. You can control dragons like you controlled your pet spider."

"How?" I asked, bewildered.

"I will show you. But first — call." She smiled. "They will not harm us. You have my word."

I wasn't too sure about that, but how cool would it be to control a dragon! Looking up, I studied the creatures in the sky, then fixed on one slightly smaller than the others. (I didn't want to bring a large one down, in case Evanna was wrong and it attacked.) I tracked it with my eyes for a few seconds, then stretched out a hand towards it and whispered, "Come to me. Come down. Come, my beauty."

The dragon executed a backwards somersault, then dropped swiftly. I thought it was going to blast us into a thousand pieces. I panicked and tried to run. Evanna hauled me back into place. "Calmly," she said. "You cannot control it if you break contact, and now that it knows we are here, it would be dangerous to let it have its own way."

I didn't want to play this game, but it was too late to back out now. With my heart beating fiercely, I fixed on the swooping dragon and spoke to it again. "Easy. Pull up. I don't want to hurt you — and I don't want you to hurt us! Just hover above us a bit and..."

The dragon pulled out of its fall and came to a halt several metres overhead. It flapped its leathery wings powerfully. I could hear nothing over the sound, and the force of the air knocked me backwards. As I struggled to right myself, the dragon came to land close beside me. It tucked its wings in, thrust its head down as though it meant to gobble me up, then stopped and just stared.

The beast was much like those I'd seen before. Its wings were a light green colour, it was about six metres long, scaled like a snake, with a bulging chest and thin tail. The scales on its stomach were a dull red and gold colour, while those on top were green with red flecks. It had two long forelegs near the front of its body, and two small hindlegs about a quarter of the way from the rear. Lots of sharp claws. A head like an alligator, long and flat, with bulging yellow eyes and small pointed ears. Its face was dark purple. It also had a long forked tongue and, if it was like the other dragons, it could blow fire.

"It's incredible," Evanna said. "This is the first time I have seen one up so close. Our father excelled himself with this creation."

"Mr Tiny made the dragons?"

Evanna nodded. "He helped human scientists create them. Actually, one of your friends was a key member of the team — Alan Morris. With our father's aid he made a breakthrough which allowed them to be cloned from a combination of dinosaur cells."

"*Alan?*" I snorted. "You're telling me Alan Morris made dragons? That's total and utter..." I stopped short. Tommy had told me Alan was a scientist, and that he'd specialized in cloning. It was hard to believe the foolish boy I'd known had grown up to become a creator of dinosaurs — but then again, it was hard to believe Steve had become the Vampaneze Lord, or myself a Vampire Prince. I suppose all influential men and women must start out as normal, unremarkable children.

"For many centuries, the rulers of this world will keep the dragons in check," Evanna said. "They'll control them. Later, when they lose their hold on power — as all rulers must — the dragons will fly free and multiply, becoming a real menace. In the end they'll outlive or outlast all the humans, vampires and vampaneze, and rule the world in their turn. I'm not sure what comes after them. I've never looked that far ahead."

"Why doesn't it kill us?" I asked, eyeing the dragon uneasily. "Is it tame?"

"Hardly!" Evanna laughed. "Normally the dragons would tear us apart. Our father masks this area from them — they can't see the Lake of Souls or anyone around it."

"This one sees us," I noted.

"Yes, but you're controlling it, so we are safe."

"The last time I was here, I was almost roasted alive by dragons," I said. "How can I control them now when I couldn't before?"

"But you could," Evanna replied. "You had the power — you just didn't know it. The dragons would have obeyed you then, as they do now."

"Why?" I frowned. "What's so special about me?"

"You're Desmond Tiny's son," Evanna reminded me. "Even though he did not pass on his magical powers to you, traces of his influence remain. That is why you were skilled at controlling animals such as spiders and wolves. But there is more to it than that."

Evanna reached out, her hand extending far beyond its natural length, and touched the dragon's head. Its skull glowed beneath the witch's touch. Its purple skin faded, then became translucent, so I could see inside to its brain. The oval, stone-like shape was instantly familiar, though it took me a few seconds to recall what it reminded me of. Then it clicked.

"The Stone of Blood!" I exclaimed. While this was much smaller than the one in the Hall of Princes, it was unmistakably the same type. The Stone of Blood had been a gift to the vampires from Mr Tiny. For seven hundred years the members of the clan had fed their blood to it, and used it to keep track of and communicate with each other. It was an invaluable tool, but dangerous — if it had fallen into the hands of the vampaneze, they could have tracked down and killed almost every living vampire.

"Our father took the brain of a dragon into the past and gave it to the vampires," Evanna said. "He often does that — travels into the past and makes small changes which influence the present and future. Through the Stone of Blood he bound the vampires more tightly to his will. If the vampires win the War of the Scars, they will use the Stone to control the dragons, and through them the skies. I don't think the vampaneze will use it if they win.. They never trusted this gift of Desmond Tiny's — it was one of the reasons they broke away from the rest of the vampire clan. I'm not sure what their relationship with the dragons would be like. Perhaps our father will provide them with some other way of controlling the beasts — or maybe it will please him to let them be enemies."

"The Stone of Blood was supposed to be the clan's last hope," I muttered, unable to take my eyes off the dragon's glowing brain. "There was a legend — if we lost the war with the vampaneze, the Stone of Blood might some night help us rise again."

Evanna nodded and removed her hand from the dragon's head. It stopped glowing and resumed its normal appearance. The dragon didn't seem to have noticed any change. It continued staring at me, awaiting my command.

"Above all else, our father craves chaos," Evanna said. "Stability bores him. He has no interest in seeing any race rule for ever. For a time it pleased him to let humans rule this planet, since they were violent, always at war with one another. But when he saw them heading the way of peace during the latter half of the twentieth century — or thought he did; to be honest, I don't agree with his assessment — he set about overthrowing them. He will do the same with their successors.

"If the vampaneze win the War of the Scars and wipe out the vampires, he'll use the Stone in the future. He will lead humans to it and teach them to extract the blood cells and build a new army of cloned vampires. But they won't be vampires as you know them. Desmond will control the cloning process and meddle with the cells, twisting and re-shaping them. The new creatures will be more savage than the original vampires, with less developed brains, slaves to the whim of our father." Evanna smiled twistedly. "So yes, our father told the truth when he said the Stone of Blood could help the vampires rise again — but he kept a few of the less savoury facts to himself."

"Then neither side can truly win," I said. "He's just setting the victors up for a later fall."

"That has always been Desmond's way," Evanna said. "What he helps create, he later destroys. Many empires — Egyptian, Persian, British — have already learnt that to their cost."

"Egyptian?" I blinked.

"Our father is a great fan of empires," Evanna said. "Cavemen hitting each other with sticks and bones were of very limited interest to him. He prefers to see people killing each other with more effective weapons, and in greater numbers. But for mankind to advance barbarically, it also had to advance in other ways. It had to grow socially, culturally, spiritually, technologically, medically. Only a nation which was great in all aspects could wage war greatly.

"Our father has had his hand in most of the notable architectural, technical or medical breakthroughs of mankind. He could never openly lead, but he influenced slyly. The only area where he had no real power was that of literature. Desmond is not a fictional dreamer. Reality is everything to him. He has no interest in the wonderful stories of mankind. Writers have always been alien to him — he does not read works of fiction, or take any notice of them."

"Never mind that," I grunted, not giving a hoot about Mr Tiny's choice of reading material. "Tell me more about his meddling with mankind, and time-travelling. You say Mr Tiny goes into the past to change the present and future. But what about the time paradox?" I'd seen lots of science fiction movies and TV shows. I knew all about the problems associated with the theory of time travel.

"There is no paradox," Evanna said. "The universe keeps natural order. The key events of the past cannot be changed — only the people involved."

"Huh?" I said.

"Once something important happens in the present — the universe, to give the higher force a name, decides what is important or not — it can never be changed," Evanna explained. "But you can alter the people involved. For instance, now that it has happened, you cannot travel to the past and prevent World War Two — but you *could* go back and kill Adolf Hitler. The universe would immediately create another person to fill his shoes. That person would be born like any normal person, grow up, then do what Hitler did, with precisely the same results. The name would change, but nothing else."

"But Hitler was a monster," I said. "He murdered millions of people. Do you mean, if Mr Tiny went back and killed him, some innocent guy would take his place? All those people would still die?"

"Yes," Evanna said.

"But then that person wouldn't have chosen their fate," I frowned. "They wouldn't be responsible for their actions."

Evanna sniffed. "The universe would have to create a child with the potential for wickedness — a good man cannot be forced to do evil — but once it did, yes, that person would become a victim of destiny. It does not happen often. Our father only occasionally replaces important figures of the past. Most people have free will. But there *are* a few who don't."

"Am I one of them?" I asked quietly, fearing the answer.

"Most definitely not," Evanna smiled. "Your time is the present time, and you are an original creation. Though you were manipulated by our father since birth, the path you trod had not been laid down by anyone before you."

Evanna thought for a few seconds, then tried to explain the situation in a way which I could more easily understand.

"Although our father cannot change the events of the past, he can make minor alterations," she said. "If something happens in the present which is not to his liking, he can return to the past and create a train of events designed to lead to a solution to whatever is troubling him. That's how vampires came to be so numerous and powerful."

"Mr Tiny created vampires?" I shouted — there was a myth that he'd made us, but I'd never believed it.

"No," Evanna said. "Vampires came into being by themselves. But there were never many of them. They were weak and disorganized. Then, in the middle of the twentieth century, our father decided mankind was taking a path towards peace and unity. Disliking it, he travelled to the past and spent a couple of decades trying different approaches to undermine humanity. In the end he settled on vampires. He gave them extra strength and speed, the power to flit and share their thoughts — all the supernatural abilities which you know about. He also provided them with leaders who would knock them into shape and turn them into an army.

"As powerful as the clan became, our father ensured they couldn't be a threat to humans. Originally vampires were able to come out by day — Desmond Tiny made them prisoners of the night, and robbed them of the gift of childbirth. Carefully shackled and maintained this way, the vampires had to live separately to the world of man and remain in the shadows. Since they didn't change anything important in the human history, the universe let them exist, and they eventually become part of the present — which is when our father was free to use them however he wished."

"And the present was my time?" I asked.

"Yes," Evanna said. "Time passes at the same rate, whether our father is in the past, present or future. So, since he spent almost twenty years stuck in the past, trying to find a way to topple humanity, it was late in the twentieth century when he returned to the present."

"And because vampires were now part of that present," I said, my brain hurting as I tried to keep up with all this mind-boggling information, "they were free to influence the future?"

"Correct," Evanna said. "But our father then saw that the clan wouldn't launch an attack on humanity if left to their own devices — they were content to stay out of the affairs of men. So he went back again — just for a few months this time — and engineered the vampaneze breakaway. By then planting the legend of the Lord of the Vampaneze, he edged them towards conflict with the vampires."

"And that led to the War of the Scars, and eventually the downfall of humanity," I growled, sick at the thought of the little man's terrible slyness.

"Well," Evanna smiled, "that was the plan."

"Do you mean —" I began to say excitedly, sensing hope in her smile.

"Hush," Evanna stopped me. "I will reveal all shortly. But now it is time for us to move on." She pointed to where the sun was setting on the horizon. "The nights are colder in this time than in yours. We will be safer underground. Besides," she said, rising, "we have an appointment to keep."

"With who?" I asked.

She looked at me steadily. "Our father."

CHAPTER FIFTEEN

Mr Tiny was the last person in the world — in all of time! — that I wanted to see. I argued with Evanna hotly, wanting to know why I should present myself to him, or what it could achieve. I hated and feared the meddler more than ever now that I knew so much about him.

"I want to be on the opposite side of the world to wherever he is!" I cried. "Or in another universe, if possible!"

"I understand," Evanna said, "but we must go to him regardless."

"Is he forcing you to do this?" I asked. "Is he the one who ordered me fished out of the Lake? Is he making you take me to him, so that he can mess my life up all over again?"

"You will find out when you meet him," Evanna said coolly, and since I didn't really have any option but to follow her lead — she could have had me tossed back into the Lake if I disobeyed — eventually, and with much angry muttering, I reluctantly followed after her as she set off into the arid wilderness.

As we left the warmth of the fire, the dragon flapped its wings and took to the skies. I watched it join the throng of dragons far above me, then lost track of it. When I looked back at Evanna, I saw that she was still staring up at the sky. "I wish we could have gone for a flight," she said, sounding curiously sad.

"On the dragon?" I asked.

"Yes. It has always been a wish of mine to fly on a dragon."

"I could call it back," I suggested.

She shook her head quickly. "This isn't the time for it," she said. "And there are too many of them. The others would see us on its back and attack. I don't think you would be able to control so many, not without more practice. And while I can mask us from them downhere, I couldn't up there."

As we continued to walk, I looked around and backwards, and my gaze settled on the Little People standing motionless by the Lake. "Why are that lot here?" I asked.

"This is the age in which our father fishes for the souls of the dead to create his Little People," Evanna said, without looking back or slowing. "He could take them from any time, but it's easier this way, when there is nobody to interfere. He leaves a small band of his helpers here, to fish when he gives the order." She glanced at me. "He could have rescued you much earlier. In the present, only two years have passed. He had the power to remove you from the Lake then, but he wanted to punish you. Your sacrifice threw his plans into disarray. He hates you for that, even though you are his son. That's why he sent me forward to this point in time to help you. In this future, your soul has suffered for countless generations. He wanted you to feel the pain of near-eternal imprisonment, and perhaps even go mad from it, so that you couldn't be saved."

"Nice," I grunted sarcastically. Then my eyes narrowed. "If that's the way he feels, why rescue me at all?"

"That will soon become clear," Evanna said.

We walked a long way from the Lake. The air was turning cold around us as the sun dipped. Evanna was looking for a specific spot, pausing every few seconds to examine the ground, then moving on. Finally she found what she was searching for. She came to a halt, knelt and breathed softly on the dusty earth. There was a rumbling sound, then the ground split at our feet and the mouth of a tunnel opened up. I could only see a few metres down it, but I sensed danger.

"Don't tell me we have to go down there," I muttered.

"This is the way to our father's stronghold," she said.

"It's dark," I stalled.

"I will provide light," she promised, and I saw that both her hands were glowing softly, casting a dim white light a few metres ahead of her. She looked at me seriously. "Stay by my side down there. Don't stray."

"Will Mr Tiny get me if I do?" I asked.

"Believe it or not, there are worse monsters than our father," she said. "We will be passing some of them. If they get their hands on you, your millennia of torment in the Lake of Souls will seem like a pleasant hour spent on a beach."

I doubted that, but the threat was strong enough to ensure I kept within a hair's breadth of the witch as she started down the tunnel. It sloped at a fairly constant thirty-degree angle. The floor and walls were smooth and made of what looked like solid rock. But there were shapes moving within the rock, twisted, inhuman, elongated shapes, all shadows, claws, teeth and tendrils. The walls bulged outwards as we passed — the *things* trapped within were reaching for us. But none could break through.

"What are they?" I croaked, sweating from fear as much as the dry heat of the tunnel.

"Creatures of universal chaos," Evanna answered. "I told you about them before — they're the monsters I spoke of. They are kin to our father, though he is not as powerful as them. They are imprisoned by a series of temporal and spatial laws — the laws of the universe which our father and I live by. If we ever break the laws, these creatures will be freed. They will turn the universe into a hell of their own making. All will fall beneath them. They'll invade every time zone and torture every mortal being ever born — for ever."

"That's why you were angry when you found out I was Mr Tiny's son," I said. "You thought he'd broken the laws."

"Yes. I was wrong, but it was a close-run thing. I doubt if even he was sure of his plan's success. When he gave birth to Hibernius and me, we knew of the laws, and we obeyed them.

If he was wrong about you — if he'd given you more power than he meant to — you could have unknowingly broken the laws and brought about the ruin of everything we know and love." She looked back at me and grinned. "I bet you never guessed you were that important to the world!"

"No," I said sickly. "And I never wanted to be."

"Don't worry," she said, her smile softening. "You took yourself out of the firing line when you let Steve kill you. You did what Hibernius and I never thought possible — you changed what seemed an inevitable future."

"You mean I prevented the coming of the Lord of the Shadows?" I asked eagerly. "That's why I let him kill me. It was the only way I could see to stop it. I didn't want to be a monster. I couldn't bear the thought of destroying the world. Mr Tiny said one of us had to be the Lord of the Shadows. But I thought, if both of us were dead..."

"You thought right," Evanna said. "Our father had edged the world to a point where there were only two futures. When you killed Steve *and* sacrificed yourself, it opened up dozens of possible futures again. I could not have done it — I would have broken the laws if I'd interfered — but as a human, you were able to."

"So what's happened since I died?" I asked. "You said two years have passed. Did the vampires defeat the vampaneze and win the War of the Scars?"

"No," Evanna said, pursing her lips. "The war still rages. But an end is within sight — an end very much not to our father's liking. Persuasive leaders are pushing for peace, Vancha and Harkat Mulds on the side of the vampires, Gannen Harst for the vampaneze. They are debating a treaty, discussing the guidelines by which both sides can live as one. Others fight against them — there are many in both clans who do not wish for peace — but the voices of reason are winning out."

"Then it worked!" I gasped. "If the vampires and vampaneze make peace, the world will be saved!"

"Perhaps," Evanna hummed. "It's not as clear-cut as that. Under Steve, the vampaneze made contact with human political and military leaders. They promised them long lives and power in exchange for their help. They wanted to create nuclear and chemical warfare, with the aim of bringing the world and its survivors under their direct control. That could still happen."

"Then we've got to stop it!" I shouted. "We can't let —"

"Easy," Evanna hushed me. "We are trying to prevent it. That's why I am here. I cannot meddle too deeply in the affairs of mankind, but I can do more now than before, and your actions have convinced me that I *should* interfere. Hibernius and I always stayed neutral. We did not get involved in the affairs of mortals. Hibernius wished to, but I argued against it, afraid we might break the laws and free the monsters." She sighed. "I was wrong. It's necessary to take risks every now and then. Our father took a risk in his attempt to wreak havoc — and I must now take one in an attempt to secure peace."

"What are you talking about?" I frowned.

"Mankind has been evolving," she said. "It has a destiny of its own, a growth towards something wonderful, which our father is intent on ruining. He used the vampires and vampaneze to throw mankind off course, to reduce the cities of the world to rubble, to drag humans back into the dark ages, so that he could control them again. But his plan failed. The clans of the night now seek to reunite and live separately from mankind, hidden, doing no harm, as they did in the past.

"Because the vampires and vampaneze have become part of the present, our father cannot unmake them. He could return to the past and create another race to combat them, but that would be difficult and time-consuming. Time, for once, is against him. If he cannot divide the clans within the next year or so, it is unlikely that he will be able to bring about the downfall of mankind which he craved. He might — and no doubt will — plot afresh in the future, and seek some other way to break them, but for the time being the world will be safe."

Evanna paused. Her hands were directed towards her face, illuminating her features. I'd never seen her look so thoughtful. "Do you remember the story of how I was created?" she asked.

"Of course," I said. "A vampire — Corza Jarn — wanted vampires to be able to have children. He pursued Mr Tiny until he agreed to grant him his wish, and by mixing Corza Jarn's blood with a pregnant she-wolf, and using his magic on her, he fathered you and Mr Tall."

"That was not his only reason for creating us," Evanna said, "but it was an important one. I can bear a vampire or a vampaneze's children, and they in turn could have children of their own. But any children of mine will be different from their fathers. They will have some of my powers — not all — and they'll be able to live by day. Sunlight won't kill them."

She looked at me intently. "A new breed of creature, an advanced race of vampire or vampaneze. If I gave birth to such children now, it would drive the clans apart. The war-mongers of both sides would use the children to stir up new visions and violence. For instance, if I had a child by a vampire father, those vampires opposed to peace would hail the child as a saviour, and say he was sent to help them wipe out the vampaneze. Even if the wiser vampires prevailed, and talked down the troublemakers, the vampaneze would be afraid of the child and suspicious of the vampire clan's long-term plans. How could they discuss peace terms, knowing they were now inferior to vampires, for ever at risk?

"The War of the Scars promises to end because both sides see that it might go on for ever. When the Lord of the Vampaneze and the vampire hunters were active, everybody knew the war would have a destined end. Now that Steve and you are dead, it might never finish, and neither vampires nor vampaneze want that. So they're willing to talk about peace.

"But my children could change everything. With the renewed promise of victory — either for the vampires or vampaneze, depending on which I chose to be the fathers of my young — the war would continue. As my children grew — and they'd grow quickly, since they'd be creatures of a certain amount of magic — they'd be raised on hatred and fear. In time they'd become warriors and lead their clan to victory over the other — and our father's plan would fall back into place, a little later than anticipated, but otherwise intact."

"Then you mustn't have them!" I exclaimed. "Mr Tiny can't make you, can he?"

"Not directly," she said. "He has threatened and bribed me ever since the night you and Steve died. But he does not have the power to force me to give birth."

"Then it's OK." I smiled weakly. "You won't have any children, and that will be that."

"Oh, but I will," Evanna said, and lowered her hands so that they shone on her stomach. "In fact, I'm pregnant already."

"*What?*" I exploded. "But you just said —"

"I know."

"But if you —"

"I know."

"But —"

"Darren!" she snapped. "I. Know."

"Then why do it?" I cried.

Evanna stopped to explain. As soon as she paused, the shapes in the walls began to press closer towards us, hissing and snarling, claws and tendrils extending, stretching the fabric of the rock. Evanna spotted this and strode forward again, speaking as she walked.

"I asked Desmond to free your spirit. Guilt drove you to the Lake of Souls, and would have kept you there eternally — there is no natural escape from that Lake of the damned. But rescue is possible. Souls can be fished out. Knowing that you were my half-brother, I felt honour-bound to free you."

"What about Steve?" I asked. "He was your half-brother too."

"Steve deserves his imprisonment." Her eyes were hard. "I feel pity for him, since he was to some extent a victim of our father's meddling. But Steve's evil was primarily of his own making. He chose his path and now must suffer the consequences. But you tried to do good. It wasn't fair that you should rot in the Lake of Souls, so I pleaded with our father to help." She chuckled. "Needless to say, he refused.

"He came to me a few months ago," she continued. "He realized his plans were unravelling and he saw me as his only solution. He'd spent most of the time since your death trying to convince me to have children, with no more success than I'd had trying to get him to free you. But this time he took a fresh approach. He said we could help each other. If I had a child, he'd free your soul."

"You agreed to that?" I roared. "You sold out the world just to help me?"

"Of course not," she grunted.

"But you said you were pregnant."

"I am." She looked back at me and smiled shyly. "My first thought was to reject our father's offer. But then I saw a way to use it to our advantage. There is still no guarantee of a peaceful settlement between the vampires and vampaneze. It looks promising but is by no means certain. If talks break down, the war could continue, and that would play into our father's hands. He would have time to go back to the past and create a new leader, one who could pick up where Steve left off.

"I was thinking of this when Desmond put his suggestion to me. I recalled the way you tricked him, and wondered what you would do in my situation. Then, in a flash, I saw it.

"I accepted his proposal but told him I wasn't sure whether I wanted a vampire's child or a vampaneze's. He said it didn't matter. I asked if I could choose. He said yes. So I spent some time with Gannen Harst, then with Vancha March. When I returned to our father, I told him I had chosen and was pregnant. He was so delighted, he didn't even complain when I refused to reveal who the father was — he just quickly arranged to send me here to free you, so that we could move forward without any further distractions."

She stopped talking and rubbed her stomach with her hands. She was still smiling that strange shy smile.

"So whose is it?" I asked. I didn't see what difference it made but I was curious to know the answer.

"Both," she said. "I am having twins — one by Vancha, one by Gannen."

"A vampire child *and* a vampaneze child!" I cried, excited.

"More than that," Evanna said. "I have allowed the three blood lines to mix. Each child is one third vampire, one third vampaneze, and one third me. That's how I've tricked him.

He thought any baby of mine would divide the clans, but instead they will pull them closer together. My children, when they are ready, will breed with other vampires and vampaneze, to give birth to a new, multi-race clan. All divisions will be erased and finally forgotten.

"We're going to create peace, Darren, in spite of our father. That's what you taught me — we don't have to accept destiny, *or* Des Tiny. We can create our own future, all of us. We have the power to rule our lives — we just have to make the choice to use it. You chose when you sacrificed your life. Now I've chosen too — by giving life. Only time will tell what our choices lead to, but I'm sure that whatever future we help usher in, it has to be better than the one our father planned."

"Amen to that!" I muttered, then followed her silently down the tunnel, thinking of the future and all the surprises and twists it might hold. My head was buzzing with thoughts and ideas. I was having to take on board so much, so quickly, that I felt overwhelmed by it all, not sure what to make of everything. But there was one thing I was absolutely sure of — when Mr Tiny found out about Evanna's babies, he'd all but explode with anger!

Thinking of that, and the nasty little meddler's face when he heard the news, I burst out laughing. Evanna laughed too, and the laughter stayed with us for ages, following us down the tunnel like a flock of chuckling birds, acting almost like a protective spell against the banks of walled-in, ever-moving, ever-reaching monsters.

CHAPTER SIXTEEN

About an hour later the tunnel ended and we entered the home of Desmond Tiny. I'd never really thought of him having a home. I just assumed he wandered the world, always on the move, in search of bloodshed and chaos. But, now that I considered it, I realized every monster needs a den to call its own, and Mr Tiny's had to be the strangest of them all.

It was a huge — and I mean HUGE — cave, maybe a couple of miles or so wide, and stretching as far ahead as I could make out. Much of the cave was natural, stalagmites and stalactites, waterfalls, beautifully weird rock colours and formations. But much more of it was incredibly *un*natural.

There were grand old cars from what I guessed must be the 1920s or 1930s floating in the air overhead. At first I thought they were attached to the ceiling by wires, but they were in constant motion, circling, crossing paths, even looping around like planes, and not a wire in sight.

There were mannequins all over the place, dressed in costumes from every century and continent, from a primitive loincloth to the most outrageous modern fashion accessories. Their blank eyes unsettled me — I got the feeling that they were watching me, ready to spring to life at Mr Tiny's command and leap upon me.

There were works of art and sculpture, some so famous that even an art cretin like me recognized them — the *Mona Lisa*, *The Thinker*, *The Last Supper*. Mixed in with them, displayed like art exhibits, were dozens of brains preserved in glass cases. I read a few of the labels — Beethoven, Mozart, Wagner, Mahler. (That one gave me a jump — I'd gone to a school named after Mahler!)

"Our father loves music," Evanna whispered. "Where humans collect sheet music or gramophone records —" She obviously hadn't heard about CDs yet! "— he collects brains of composers. By touching them, he can listen to all the tunes they ever composed, along with many they never completed or shared with the world."

"But where does he get them from?" I asked.

"He travels to the past when they have just died and robs their graves," she said, as though it was the most casual thing in the world. I thought about questioning the right and wrong of something like that, but there were weightier issues to deal with, so I let it slide.

"He likes art too, I take it," I said, nodding at a flowery Van Gogh.

"Immensely," Evanna said. "These are all originals of course — he doesn't bother with copies."

"Nonsense!" I snorted. "These can't be real. I've seen some of the real paintings. Mum and Dad —" I still thought of my human Dad as my real father, and always would. "— took me to see the *Mona Lisa* in the Loo once."

"The Louvre," Evanna corrected me. "That is a copy. Some of our father's Little People are created from the souls of artists. They make perfect copies of pieces he especially admires. Then he slips back to the past and swaps the copy for the original. In most cases even the actual artist cannot tell the difference."

"You're telling me the *Mona Lisa* in Paris is a fake?" I asked sceptically.

"Yes." Evanna laughed at my expression. "Our father is a selfish man. He always keeps the best for himself. What he wants, he takes — and he normally wants the best of everything. Except books." Her voice became pointed, as it had earlier when she'd been talking about his attitude towards books. "Desmond never reads works of fiction. He doesn't collect books or pay any attention to authors. Homer, Chaucer, Shakespeare, Dickens, Tolstoy, Twain — all have passed him by unmarked. He doesn't care what they have to say. He has nothing to do with the world of literature. It's as if it exists in a separate universe from his."

Once again I didn't see her point in telling me this, so I let my interest wander. I'd never been a big art fan, but even I was impressed by this display. It was the ultimate collection, capturing a slice of pretty much all the artistic wonder and imagination mankind had ever conjured into being.

There was far too much for any one person to take in. Weapons, jewellery, toys, tools, albums of stamps, bottles of vintage wine, Fabergé eggs, grandfather clocks, suites of furniture, thrones of kings and queens. A lot of it was precious, but there were plenty of worthless items too, stuff which had simply caught Mr Tiny's fancy, such as bottle tops, oddly shaped balloons, digital watches, a collection of empty ice-cream tubs, thousands of whistles, hundreds of thousands of coins (old ones mixed in with brand new ones), and so on. The treasure cave in *Aladdin* seemed like a bargain bin in comparison.

Even though the cave was packed with all manner of wonders and oddities, it didn't feel cluttered. There was plenty of space to walk about and explore. We wound our way through the various collections and artefacts, Evanna pausing occasionally to point out a particularly interesting piece — the charred stake on which Joan Of Arc was burnt, the pistol which had been used to shoot Lincoln, the very first wheel.

"Historians would go crazy in this place," I noted. "Does Mr Tiny ever bring anybody here?"

"Almost never," Evanna said. "This is his private sanctuary. I've only been here a handful of times myself. The exceptions are those he pulls out of the Lake of Souls. He has to bring them here to turn them into Little People."

I stopped when she said that. I'd had a sudden premonition. "Evanna…" I began, but she shook her head.

"Ask no more questions," she said. "Desmond will explain the rest to you. It won't be long now."

Minutes later we reached what felt like the centre of the cave. There was a small pool of green liquid, a pile of blue robes and, standing beside them, Mr Tiny. He was staring at me sourly through the lenses of his thick glasses.

"Well, well," he drawled, hooking his thumbs behind his braces. "If it isn't the young martyr himself. Meet anyone interesting in the Lake of Souls?"

"Ignore him," Evanna said out of the side of her mouth.

Mr Tiny waddled forward and stopped a few metres shy of me. His eyes seemed to dance with fire this close up. "If I'd known what a nuisance you were going to be, I'd never have spawned you," he hissed.

"Too late now," I jeered.

"No it isn't," he said. "I could go back and erase you from the past, make it so you never lived. The universe would replace you. Somebody else would become the youngest ever Vampire Prince, hunt for the Vampaneze Lord, etc. — but *you* would never have existed. Your soul wouldn't just be destroyed — it would be unmade completely."

"Father," Evanna said warningly, "you know you aren't going to do that."

"But I could!" Mr Tiny insisted.

"Yes," she tutted, "but you won't. We have an agreement. I've upheld my end. Now it's your turn."

Mr Tiny muttered something unpleasant, then forced a fake smile. "Very well. I'm a man of my word. Let's get on with it. Darren, my woebegotten boy, get rid of that blanket and hop into the pool." He nodded at the green liquid.

"Why?" I asked stiffly.

"It's time to recast you."

A few minutes earlier, I wouldn't have known what he was talking about. But Evanna's hint had prepared me for this. "You want to turn me into a Little Person, don't you?" I said.

Mr Tiny's lips twitched. He glared at Evanna, but she shrugged innocently. "A right little know-it-all, aren't you?" he huffed, disgusted that I'd ruined his big surprise.

"How does it work?" I asked.

Mr Tiny crossed to the pool and crouched beside it. "This is the soup of creation," he said, running a finger through the thick green liquid. "It will become your blood, the fuel on which your new body runs. Your bones will be stripped bare when you step in. Your flesh, brain, organs and soul will dissolve. I shall mix the lot up and build a new body out of the mess." He grinned. "Those who've been through it tell me it's a most frightfully painful procedure, the worst they've ever known."

"What makes you think I'm going to do it?" I asked tightly. "I've seen how your Little People live, mindless, speechless, unable to remember their original identities, slaves to your whims, eating the flesh of dead animals — even humans! Why should I place myself under your spell like that?"

"No deal with my daughter if you don't," Mr Tiny said simply.

I shook my head stubbornly. I knew Evanna was trying to out-fox Mr Tiny, but I didn't see why this was necessary. How could I help bring about peace between the vampires and vampaneze by going through a load of pain and becoming a Little Person? It didn't make sense.

As if reading my thoughts, Evanna said softly, "This is for *you*, Darren. It has nothing to do with what is happening in the present, or the War of the Scars. This is your only hope of escaping the pull of the Lake of Souls and going to Paradise. You can live a full life as you are, in this waste world, and return to the Lake when you die. Or you can trust us and place yourself in our father's hands."

"I trust *you*," I said to Evanna, shooting an arch look at Mr Tiny.

"Oh, my boy, if you only knew how much that hurts," Mr Tiny said miserably, then laughed. "Enough of the dawdling. You either do this or you don't. But take heed, daughter — by making the offer, I've fulfilled my end of the bargain. If the boy refuses to accept your advice, on his head be it. I'll expect you to keep your word."

Evanna looked at me questioningly, not placing any pressure on me. I thought about it at length. I hated the idea of becoming a Little Person. It wasn't so much the pain as letting Mr Tiny become my master. And what if Evanna was lying? I'd said I trusted the witch, but thinking back, I realized there was precious little reason to trust her. She'd never betrayed her father before, or worked for the good of any individual. Why start now? What if this was a twisted scheme to ensnare me, and she was in league with Mr Tiny, or had been tricked into doing his bidding? The whole thing stank of a trap.

But what other option had I? Give Evanna the cold shoulder, refuse to enter the pool, walk away? Even assuming Mr Tiny let me leave, and the monsters in the tunnel didn't catch me, what would I have to look forward to? A life lived in a world full of dragons, followed by eternity in the Lake of Souls, wasn't my idea of a good time! In the end I decided it was better to gamble and hope for the best.

"OK," I said reluctantly. "But there's one condition."

"You're in no position to set conditions," Mr Tiny growled.

"Maybe not," I agreed, "but I'm setting one anyway. I'll only do it if you guarantee me a free memory. I don't want to wind up like Harkat, not knowing who I was, obeying your orders because I've no free will of my own. I'm not sure what you have planned for me once I become a Little Person, but if it involves serving as one of your fog-brained slaves..."

"It doesn't," Mr Tiny interrupted. "I admit I quite like the idea of having you toady to me for a few million years or so, but my daughter was very precise when it came to the terms of our agreement. You won't be able to talk but that's the only restriction."

"Why won't I be able to talk?" I frowned.

"Because I'm sick of listening to you!" Mr Tiny barked. "Besides, you won't need to speak. Most of my Little People don't. Muteness hasn't harmed any of the others, and it won't harm you."

"OK," I muttered. I didn't like it, but I could see there was no point arguing. Stepping up to the edge of the pool, I shrugged off the blanket which the Little People had draped around me shortly after I emerged from the Lake of Souls. I stared into the dark green liquid. I couldn't see my reflection in it. "What —" I started to ask.

"No time for questions!" Mr Tiny barked and nudged me hard with an elbow. I teetered on the edge of the pool a moment, arms flailing, then splashed heavily into what felt like the sizzling fires of hell.

CHAPTER SEVENTEEN

Instant agony and burning. My flesh bubbled, then boiled away. I tried to scream but my lips and tongue had already come undone. My eyes and ears melted. No sensation except pain.

The liquid stripped my flesh from my bones, then set to work on the marrow within the bones. Next it burnt through to my inner organs, then ate me up from the inside out. Inside my head my brain sizzled like a knob of butter in a heated frying pan, and melted down just as quickly. My left arm — just bone now — tore loose from my body and floated away. It was soon followed by my lower right leg. Then I came apart completely, limbs, charred organs, tiny strips of flesh, bare pieces of bone. All that stayed constant was the pain, which hadn't lessened in the slightest.

In the midst of my suffering came a moment of spiritual calm. With whatever remained of my brain, I became aware of a separation. There was another presence in the pool with me. At first I was confused, but then I realized it was the flicker of Sam Grest's soul which I'd carried within me since drinking his blood at the time of his death. Sam had passed on to Paradise many years ago, and now this final shard of his spirit was departing this world too. In my mind's eye a face formed in the liquid, young and carefree, smiling in spite of the torment, popping a pickled onion into his mouth. Sam winked at me. A ghostly hand saluted. Then he was gone and I was finally, totally alone.

Eventually the pain ceased. I'd dissolved completely. There were no pain sensors left to transmit feelings, and no brain cells to respond to them. A weird peace descended. I'd become one with the pool. My atoms had mixed with the liquid and the two were now one. I *was* the green liquid. I could sense the hollow bones from my body drifting to the bottom of the pool, where they settled.

Some time later hands — Mr Tiny's — were dunked in the liquid. He wiggled his fingers and a shiver ran up the memory of my spine. He picked up the bones from the floor — being careful to scrape up every single piece — and dumped them on the ground of the cave. The bones were covered in molecules of the liquid — molecules of *me* — and through them I felt Mr Tiny putting the bones together, snapping them into small pieces, melting some down, bending or twisting others, creating a frame entirely different to my previous form.

Mr Tiny worked on the body for hours. When he had all

the bones in place, he packed them full with organs —
brain, heart, liver, kidneys — then covered them with
clammy grey flesh, which he stitched together to hold the
organs and bones in place. I'm not sure where the organs
and flesh came from. Perhaps he grew them himself, but I
think it more likely that he harvested them from other
creatures — probably dead humans.

Mr Tiny finished with the eyes. I could feel him
connecting the orbs up to my brain, fingers working at
lightning-fast speed, with all the precision of the world's
greatest surgeon. It was an incredibly artistic undertaking,
one which even Dr Frankenstein would have struggled to
match.

Once he'd finished with the body, he stuck his fingers back
into the liquid of the pool. The fingers were cold this time,
and grew colder by the second. The liquid began to condense,
becoming thicker. There was no pain. It was just strange, like I
was squeezing in upon myself.

Then, when the liquid was a fraction of the size it had been,
with the texture of a thick milk shake, Mr Tiny removed his
hands and tubes were inserted. There was a brief pause, then
suction from the tubes, and I felt myself flowing through them,
out of the pool and into ... what? ... not tubes like those
which had been stuck into the pool, but similar...

Of course — *veins!* Mr Tiny had told me the liquid would
serve as my fuel — my blood. I was leaving the confines of
the pool for the fleshy limits of my new body.

I felt myself fill the gaps, forcing my way through the

network of veins and arteries, making slow but sure progress. When the liquid hit the brain and gradually seeped into it, absorbed by the cold grey cells, my bodily senses awoke. I became aware of my heartbeat first, slower and heavier than before. A tingle ran through my hands and feet, then up my newly crafted spine. I twitched my fingers and toes. Moved an arm slightly. Shook a leg softly. The limbs didn't respond as quickly as my old limbs had, but maybe that was just because I wasn't used to them yet.

Sound came next, a harsh roaring noise at first, which gradually died away to allow normal sounds through. But the sounds weren't as sharp as before —like all the Little People, my ears had been stitched within the skin of my head. Hearing was soon followed by a dim sense of vision — but no smell or sense or taste, since — again, in common with all of Mr Tiny's creations — I'd been created without a nose.

My vision improved as more and more blood was transferred to my new brain. The world looked different through these eyes. I had a wider field of view than before, since my eyes were rounder and bigger. I could see more, but through a slightly green haze, as though staring through a filter.

The first sight I fixed on was Mr Tiny, still working on my body, monitoring the tubes, applying a few final stitches, testing my reflexes. He had the look of a loving, devoted parent.

Next I saw Evanna, keeping a close eye on her father, making sure he didn't pull any tricks. She handed him needles and string from time to time, like a nurse. Her expression was a mixture of suspicion and pride. Evanna knew all of Mr Tiny's shortcomings, but she was still his daughter, and I could see now that despite her misgivings she loved him — in a way.

Eventually the transfer was complete. Mr Tiny removed the tubes — they'd been stuck in all over, my arms, legs, torso, head — and sealed the holes, stitching them shut. He gave me a final once-over, fixed a spot where I was leaking, did some fine-tuning at the corners of my eyes, checked my heartbeat. Then he stepped back and grunted. "Another perfect creation, even if I do say so myself."

"Sit up, Darren," Evanna said. "But slowly. Don't rush."

I did as she said. A wave of dizziness swept over me when I raised my head, but it soon passed. I pushed up gradually, pausing every time I felt dizzy or sick. Finally I was sitting upright. I was able to study my body from here, its broad hands and feet, thick limbs, dull grey skin. I noted that, like Harkat, I was neither fully male nor female, but something in between. If I could have blushed, I would have!

"Stand," Mr Tiny said, spitting on his hands and rubbing them together, using his spit to wash himself. "Walk about. Test yourself. It won't take you long to get used to your new shape. I design my Little People to go into immediate action."

With Evanna's help I stood. I weaved unsteadily on my feet, but soon found my balance. I was much stouter and heavier than before. As I'd noticed when lying down, my limbs didn't react as quickly as they once did. I had to focus hard to make my fingers curl or to edge a foot forward.

"Easy," Evanna said as I tried to turn and almost fell back into the now empty pool. She caught and held me until I was steady again. "Slowly, one bit at a time. It won't take long — just five or ten minutes." I tried to ask a question but no sound came out. "You cannot speak," Evanna reminded me. "You do not have a tongue."

I slowly raised a chunky grey arm and pointed a finger at my head. I stared at Evanna with my large green eyes, trying to transmit my question mentally. "You want to know if we can communicate telepathically," Evanna said. I nodded my neck-less head. "No. You have not been designed with that ability."

"You're a basic model," Mr Tiny chipped in. "You won't be around very long, so it would have been pointless to kit you out with a bunch of unnecessary features. You can think and move, which is all you need to do."

I spent the next several minutes getting to know my new body. There were no mirrors nearby, but I spotted a large silver tray in which I could study my reflection. Hobbling over to it, I ran a critical green eye over myself. I was maybe four and a half feet tall and three feet wide. My stitches weren't as neat as Harkat's, and my eyes weren't exactly level, but otherwise we didn't look too different. When I opened my mouth I saw that not only did I lack a tongue, but teeth too. I turned carefully and looked at Evanna, pointing to my gums.

"You will not have to eat," she said.

"You won't be alive long enough to bother with food," Mr Tiny added.

My new stomach clenched when he said that. I'd been tricked! It *had* been a trap, and I'd fallen for it! If I could have spoken, I'd have cursed myself for being such a fool.

But then, as I looked for a decent weapon to defend myself with, Evanna smiled positively. "Remember why we did this, Darren — to free your soul. We could have given you a new, full life as a Little Person, but that would have complicated matters. It's easier this way. You have to trust us."

I didn't feel very trusting, but the deed was done. And Evanna didn't look like somebody who'd been tricked, or who was gloating from having tricked me. Putting fears of betrayal and thoughts of fighting aside, I decided to stay calm and see what the pair planned next for me.

Evanna picked up the pile of blue robes which had been lying near to the pool and came over with them. "I prepared these for you earlier," she said. "Let me help you put them on." I was going to signal that I could dress myself, but Evanna flashed me a look which made me stop. Her back was to Mr Tiny, who was examining the remains of the pool. While his attention was diverted, she slipped the robes on over my head and arms. I realized there were several objects inside the robes, stitched into the lining.

Evanna locked gazes with me and a secret understanding passed between us — she was telling me to act as if the objects weren't there. She was up to something which she didn't want Mr Tiny to know about. I'd no idea what she might have hidden in the robes, but it must be important. Once the robes were on I kept my arms out by my sides and tried not to think about the secret packages I was carrying, in case I accidentally tipped off Mr Tiny.

Evanna gave me a final once-over, then called out, "He is ready, father."

Mr Tiny waddled across. He looked me up and down, sniffed snootily, then thrust a small mask at me. "You'd better put that on," he said. "You probably won't need it, but we might as well be safe as sorry."

As I strapped on the mask, Mr Tiny bent and drew a line in the earth of the cave floor. He stepped back from it and clutched his heart-shaped watch. The timepiece began to glow, and soon his hand and face were glowing too. Moments later a doorway grew out of the line in the ground, sliding upwards to its full height. It was an open doorway. The space between the jambs was a grey sheen. I'd been through a portal like this before, when Mr Tiny had sent Harkat and me into what would have been the future (what still might be, if Evanna's plan failed).

When the doorway was complete, Mr Tiny nodded his head at it. "Time to go."

My eyes flicked to Evanna — was she coming with me? "No," she said in answer to my unasked question. "I will return to the present through a separate door. This one goes further back." She stooped so we were at the same height. "This is goodbye, Darren. I don't imagine I'll ever make the journey to Paradise — I don't think it's intended for the likes of me — so we'll probably never see each other again."

"Maybe he won't go to Paradise either," Mr Tiny sneered. "Perhaps his soul is meant for the great fires beneath."

Evanna smiled. "We don't know all the secrets of the beyond, but we've never seen any evidence of a hell. The Lake of Souls seems to be the only place where the damned end up, and if our plan works, you won't go back there. Don't worry — your soul will fly free."

"Come on," Mr Tiny snapped. "I'm bored with him. Time to kick him out of our lives, once and for all." He pushed Evanna aside, grabbed the shoulder of my robes and hauled me to the doorway. "Don't get any smart ideas back there," he growled. "You can't change the past, so don't go trying. Just do what you have to — tough luck if you can't work out what that is — and let the universe take care of the rest."

I turned my face towards him, not sure what he meant, wanting more answers. But Mr Tiny ignored me, raised a wellington-clad foot, then — without a word of farewell, as though I was a stranger who meant nothing to him — booted me clean through the door and back to a date with history.

CHAPTER EIGHTEEN

"Ladies and gentlemen, welcome to the Cirque Du Freak, home of the world's most remarkable human beings."

I had no eyelids, so I couldn't blink, but beneath my mask my jaw dropped a hundred miles. I was in the wings of a large theatre, staring out at a stage and the unmistakable figure of the dead Hibernius Tall. Except he wasn't dead. He was very much alive, and in the middle of introducing one of the fabled Cirque Du Freak performances.

"We present acts both frightening and bizarre, acts you can find nowhere else in the world. Those who are easily scared should leave now. I'm sure there are people who…"

Two beautiful women stepped up next to me and prepared to go on. They were tugging at their glittering costumes, making sure they fit right. I recognized the women — Davina and Shirley. They'd been part of the Cirque Du Freak when I first joined, but had left after a few years to get jobs in the ordinary world. The life of a travelling performer wasn't for everyone.

"... is unique. And none are harmless," Mr Tall finished, then walked off. Davina and Shirley moved forward and I saw where they were heading — the Wolf Man's cage, which stood uncovered in the middle of the stage. As they left, a Little Person took his place by my side. His face was hidden beneath the hood of his blue robes, but his head turned in my direction. There was a moment's pause, then he reached up and pulled my hood further over my face, so that my features were hidden too.

Mr Tall appeared by our side with the speed and silence for which he was once renowned. Without a word he handed each of us a needle and lots of orange string. The other Little Person stuck the needle and string inside his robes, so I did the same, not wanting to appear out of place.

Davina and Shirley had released the Wolf Man from his cage and were walking through the audience with him, letting people stroke the hairy man-beast. I studied the theatre more closely while they paraded the Wolf Man around. This was the old abandoned cinema theatre in my home town, where Steve had murdered Shancus, and where — many years earlier — I had first crossed paths with Mr Crepsley.

I was wondering why I'd been sent back here — I had a pretty good hunch — when there was a loud explosion. The Wolf Man went wild, as he often did at the start of an act — what looked like a mad outburst was actually carefully staged. Leaping upon a screaming woman, he bit one of her hands off. In a flash, Mr Tall had left our side and reappeared next to the Wolf Man. He pulled him off the screaming woman, subdued him, then led him back to his cage, while Davina and Shirley did their best to calm down the crowd.

Mr Tall returned to the screaming woman, picked up her severed hand and whistled loudly. That was the signal for my fellow Little Person and me to advance. We ran over to Mr Tall, careful not to reveal our faces. Mr Tall sat the woman up and whispered to her. When she was quiet he sprinkled a sparkly pink powder on to her bleeding wrist and stuck the hand against it. He nodded to my companion and me. We pulled out our needles and string and started to stitch the hand back on to the wrist.

I felt light-headed while I stitched. This was the greatest sense of déjà vu I'd ever experienced! I knew what was coming next, every second of it. I'd been sent back into my past, to a night which had been etched unforgettably into my memory. All the times I'd prayed for the chance to come back and change the course of my future. And now, in the most unexpected of circumstances, here it was.

We finished stitching and returned backstage. I wanted to stand in the shadows again and watch the show — if I remembered correctly, Alexander Ribs would come on next, followed by Rhamus Twobellies — but my fellow Little Person was having none of it. He nudged me ahead of him, to the rear of the theatre, where a young Jekkus Flang was waiting. In later years Jekkus would become an accomplished knife-thrower, and even take part in the shows. But in this time he'd only recently joined the circus, and was in charge of preparing the interval gift trays.

Jekkus handed each of us a tray packed with items such as rubber dolls of Alexander Ribs, clippings of the Wolf Man's hair, and chocolate nuts and bolts. He also gave us price tags for each item. He didn't speak to us — this was back in the time before Harkat Mulds, when everyone thought Little People were mute, mindless robots.

When Rhamus Twobellies stomped offstage, Jekkus sent us out into the audience to sell the gifts. We moved among the crowd, letting people study our wares and buy if they wished. My fellow Little Person took charge of the rear areas of the theatre, leaving me to handle the front rows. And so, a few minutes later, as I'd come to suspect I would, I came face to face with two young boys, the only children in the entire theatre. One was a wild child, the sort of kid who stole money from his mother and collected horror comics, who dreamt of being a vampire when he grew up. The other was a quiet, but in his own way equally mischievous boy, the kind who wouldn't think twice about stealing a vampire's spider.

"How much is the glass statue?" the impossibly young and innocent Steve Leopard asked, pointing to a statue on my tray which you could eat. Shakily, fighting to keep my hand steady, I showed him the price tag. "I can't read," Steve said. "Will you tell me how much it costs?"

I noted the look of surprise on Darren's — Charna's guts! — on *my* face. Steve had guessed straightaway that there was something strange about the Little People, but I hadn't been so sharp. The young me had no idea why Steve was lying.

I shook my head quickly and moved on, leaving Steve to explain to my younger self why he'd pretended he couldn't read. If I'd been feeling light-headed earlier, I felt positively empty-headed now. It's a remarkable, earth-shattering thing to look into the eyes of a youthful you, to see yourself as you once were, young, foolish, gullible. I don't think anyone ever remembers what they were really like as kids. Adults think they do, but they don't. Photos and videos don't capture the real you, or bring back to life the person you used to be. You have to return to the past to do that.

We finished selling our wares and headed backstage to collect fresh trays full of new items, based on the next set of performers — Truska, Hans Hands, and then, appearing like a phantom out of the shadows of the night, Mr Crepsley and his performing tarantula, Madam Octa.

I couldn't miss Mr Crepsley's act. When Jekkus wasn't looking I crept forward and watched from the wings. My heart leapt into my mouth when my old friend and mentor walked on to the stage, startling in his red cloak with his white skin, orange crop of hair and trademark scar. Seeing him again, I wanted to rush out and throw my arms around him, tell him how much I missed him and how much he'd meant to me. I wanted to say that I loved him, that he'd been a second father to me. I wanted to joke with him about his stiff manner, his stunted sense of humour, his overly precious pride. I wanted to tell him how Steve had tricked him, and gently wind him up for being taken in by the pretence and dying for no reason. I was sure he'd see the funny side of it once he stopped steaming!

But there could be no communication between us. Even if I'd had a tongue, Mr Crepsley wouldn't have known who I was. On this night he hadn't yet met the boy named Darren Shan. I was nobody to him.

So I stood where I was and watched. One final turn from the vampire who'd altered my life in so many ways. One last performance to savour, as he put Madam Octa through her paces and thrilled the crowd. I shivered when he first spoke — I'd forgotten how deep his voice was — then hung on his every word. The minutes passed slowly, but not slowly enough for me — I wanted it to last an age.

A Little Person led a goat on stage for Madam Octa to kill. It wasn't the Little Person who'd been with me in the audience — there were more than two of us here. Madam Octa killed the goat, then performed a series of tricks with Mr Crepsley, crawled over his body and face, pulsed in and out of his mouth, played with tiny cups and saucers. In the crowd, the young Darren Shan was falling in love with the spider — he thought she was amazing. In the wings, the older Darren regarded her sadly. I used to hate Madam Octa — I could trace all my troubles back to the eight-legged beast — but not any longer. None of it was her fault. It was destiny. All along, from the first moment of my being, it had been Des Tiny.

Mr Crepsley concluded his act and left the stage. He had to pass me to get off. As he approached, I thought again about trying to communicate with him. I wasn't able to speak, but I could write. If I grabbed him and took him aside, scribbled a message, warned him to leave immediately, to get out now...

He passed.

I did nothing.

This wasn't the way. Mr Crepsley had no reason to trust me, and explaining the situation would have taken too much time — he was illiterate, so I'd have had to get somebody to read the note for him. It might also have been dangerous. If I'd told him about the Vampaneze Lord and all the rest, he might have tried to change the course of the future, to prevent the War of the Scars. Evanna had said it was impossible to change the past, but if Mr Crepsley — prompted by my warning — somehow managed to do so, he might free those terrible monsters which even Mr Tiny was afraid of. I couldn't take that risk.

"What are you doing here?" someone snapped behind me. It was Jekkus Flang. He poked me hard with a finger and pointed to my tray. "Get out there quick!" he growled.

I did as Jekkus ordered. I wanted to follow the same route as before, so that I could study myself and Steve again, but this time the other Little Person got there before me, so I had to trudge to the rear of the theatre and do the rounds there.

At the end of the interval Gertha Teeth took to the stage, to be followed by Sive and Seersa (the Twisting Twins) and finally Evra and his snake. I retreated to the rear of the theatre, not keen on the idea of seeing Evra again. Although the snake-boy was one of my best friends, I couldn't forget the pain I'd put him through. It would have hurt too much to watch him perform, thinking about the agony and loss he was to later endure.

While the final trio of acts brought the show to a close, I turned my attention to the objects stitched into the lining of my robes. Time to find out what Evanna had sent me back with. Reaching underneath the heavy blue cloth, I found the first of the rectangular items and ripped it loose. When I saw what it was, I broke out into a wide toothless smile.

The sly old witch! I recalled what she'd told me on the way from the Lake of Souls to Mr Tiny's cave — although the past couldn't be changed, the people involved in major events could be replaced. Sending me back to this period in time was enough to free my soul, but Evanna had gone one step further, and made sure I was able to free my old self too. Mr Tiny knew about that. He didn't like it, but he'd accepted it.

However, working on the sly, unknown to her father, Evanna had presented me with something even more precious than personal freedom — something that would drive Des Tiny absolutely cuckoo when he found out how he'd been swindled!

I pulled all the other objects out, set them in order, then checked the most recent addition. I didn't find what I expected, but as I scanned through it, I saw what Evanna had done. I was tempted to flick to the rear and read the last few words, but then decided I'd be better off not knowing.

I heard screams from within the theatre — Evra's snake

must have made its first appearance of the night. I didn't have much time left. I slipped away before Jekkus Flang sought me out and burdened me with another tray. Exiting by the back door, I sneaked around and re-entered the cinema at the front. I walked down the long corridor to where an open door led to a staircase — the way up to the balcony.

I climbed a few steps, then set Evanna's gift down and waited. I thought about what to do with the objects — the *weapons*. Give them to the boy directly? No. If I did, he might use them to try to change the future. That wasn't allowed. But there must be a way to get them to him later, so that he could use them at the right time. Evanna wouldn't have given them to me if there wasn't.

It didn't take me long to figure it out. I was happier when I knew what to do with the gift, because it also meant I knew exactly what to do with young Darren.

The show ended and the audience members poured out of the theatre, eagerly discussing the show and marvelling aloud. Since the boys had been sitting near the front, they were two of the last to leave. I waited in silence, safe in the knowledge of what was to come.

Finally, a frightened young Darren opened the door to the stairway, slipped through, closed it behind him, and stood in the darkness, breathing heavily, heart pounding, waiting for everyone to file out of the theatre. I could see him in spite of the gloom — my large green eyes were almost as strong as a half-vampire's — but he had no idea I was there.

When the last sounds had faded, the boy came sloping up

the stairs. He was heading for the balcony, to keep an eye on his friend Steve and see that he came to no harm. If he made it up there, his fate would be sealed and he'd have to live the tormented life of a half-vampire. I had the power to change that. This, in addition to freedom from the Lake of Souls, was Evanna's gift to me — and the last part of the gift as far as Mr Tiny was aware.

As young Darren drew close, I launched myself at him, picked him up before he knew what was happening, and ran with him down the stairs. I burst through the door into the light of the corridor, then dumped him roughly on the floor. His face was a mask of terror.

"D-d-d-don't kill me!" he squealed, scrabbling backwards.

In answer I tore my hood back, then ripped off my mask, revealing my round, grey, stitched together face and huge gaping maw of a mouth. I thrust my head forward, leered and spread my arms. Darren screamed, lurched to his feet and stumbled for the exit. I pounded after him, making lots of noise, scraping the wall with my fingers. He flew out of the theatre when he got to the door, rolled down the steps, then picked himself up and ran for his life.

I stood on the front door step, watching my younger self flee for safety. I was smiling softly. I'd stand guard here to be certain, but I was sure he wouldn't return. He'd run straight home, leap beneath the bed covers and shiver himself to sleep. In the morning, not having seen what Steve got up to, he'd phone to find out if his friend was OK. Not knowing who Mr Crepsley was, he'd have no reason to fear Steve, and Steve would have no reason to be suspicious of Darren. Their friendship would resume its natural course and, although I was sure they'd talk often about their trip to the Cirque Du Freak, Darren wouldn't go back to steal the spider, and Steve would never reveal the truth about Mr Crepsley.

I retreated from the entrance and climbed the steps up to the balcony. There, I watched as Steve had his showdown with Mr Crepsley. He asked to be the vampire's assistant. Mr Crepsley tested his blood, then rejected him on the grounds that he was evil. Steve left in a rage, swearing revenge on the vampire.

Would Steve still seek out that revenge now that his main nemesis — me — had been removed from the equation? When he grew up, would his path still take him away from normal life and towards the vampaneze? Was he destined to live his life as he had the first time round, only with a different enemy instead of Darren Shan? Or would the universe replace Steve, like me, with somebody else?

I had no way of knowing. Only time would tell, and I wouldn't be around long enough to see the story through to its end. I'd had my innings, and they were just about over. It was time for me to step back, draw a line under my life, and make my final farewell.

But first — one last cunning attempt to wreck the plans of Desmond Tiny!

CHAPTER NINETEEN

The key events of the past can't be changed, but the people in it can. Evanna had told me that if she went back and killed Adolf Hitler, the universe would replace him with somebody else. The major events of World War II would unfold exactly as they were meant to, only with a different figurehead at the helm. This would obviously create a number of temporal discrepancies, but nothing the higher force of the universe couldn't set right.

While I couldn't alter the course of my history, I *could* remove myself from it. Which was what I'd done by scaring off young Darren. The events of my life would unravel the same way they had before. A child would be blooded, travel to Vampire Mountain, unmask Kurda Smahlt, become a Vampire Prince, then hunt for the Vampaneze Lord. But it wouldn't be the boy I'd frightened off tonight. Somebody else — some other child — would have to fill the shoes of Darren Shan.

I felt bad about putting another kid through the tough trials of my life, but at least I knew that in the end — in death — he would be triumphant. The person who replaced me would follow in my footsteps, kill the Vampaneze Lord and die in the battle, and out of that death peace would hopefully grow. Since the child wouldn't be responsible for his actions, his soul should go straight to Paradise when he died — the universe, I hoped, was harsh but fair.

And maybe it wouldn't even be a boy. Perhaps I'd be replaced by a girl! The new Darren Shan didn't have to be an exact replica of the old one. He or she could come from any background or country. All the child needed was a strong sense of curiosity and a slightly disobedient streak. Anyone with the nerve to sneak out late at night and go see the Cirque Du Freak had the potential to take my place as Mr Crepsley's assistant.

Since my part would change, the parts of others could change too. Maybe another girl — or boy — would fill Debbie's role, and somebody else could be Sam Grest. Perhaps Gavner Purl wouldn't be the vampire who was killed by Kurda, and even Steve could be replaced by another. Maybe Mr Crepsley wouldn't be the one to die in the Cavern of Retribution, and would live to be a vampire of ancient years and wisdom, like his mentor, Seba Nile. Many of the parts in the story — the saga — of my life might be up for grabs now that the central character had been changed.

But that was all wild speculation. What I did know for certain was that the boy I'd once been would now lead a normal life. He'd go to school, grow up like anybody else, get a job, maybe raise a family of his own one day. All the things the original Darren Shan had missed out on, the new Darren would enjoy. I'd given him his freedom — his humanity. I could only pray to the gods of the vampires that he made the most of it.

The objects stitched into the lining of my robes were my diaries. I'd kept a diary just about as long as I could remember. I'd recorded everything in it — my trip to the Cirque Du Freak, becoming Mr Crepsley's assistant, my time in Vampire Mountain, the War of the Scars and hunt for the Vampaneze Lord, right up to that final night when I'd had my fatal last run-in with Steve. It was all there, everything important from my life, along with lots of trivial stuff too.

Evanna had brought the diary up to date. She must have taken it from the house where Debbie and Alice were based, then described all that had happened on that blood-drenched night, the showdown with Steve and my death. She'd then briefly outlined my long years of mental suffering in the Lake of Souls, followed by a more detailed account of my rescue and rebirth as a Little Person. She'd even gone beyond that, and told what happened next, my return, the way I'd scared the original Darren away, and...

I don't know what she wrote in the last few pages. I didn't read that far. I'd rather find out for myself what my final actions and thoughts are — not read about them in a book!

* * *

After Steve left and Mr Crepsley retired to the cellar where his coffin was stored, I went in search of Mr Tall. I found him in his van, going over the night's receipts. He used to do that regularly. I think he enjoyed the normality of the simple task. I knocked on the door and waited for him to answer.

"What do you want?" he asked suspiciously when he saw me. Mr Tall wasn't used to being surprised, certainly not by a Little Person.

I held the diaries out to him. He looked at them warily, not touching them.

"Is this a message from Desmond?" he asked. I shook my neck-less head. "Then what...?" His eyes widened. "No!" he gasped. "It can't be!" He pushed my hood back — I'd replaced it after I'd scared off the young me — and studied my features fiercely.

After a while Mr Tall's look of concern was replaced by a smile. "Is this my sister's work?" he enquired. I nodded my chunky head a fraction. "I never thought she'd get involved," he murmured. "I imagine there's more to it than just freeing your soul, but I won't press you for information — better for all concerned if I don't know."

I raised the diaries, wanting him to take them, but Mr Tall still didn't touch them. "I'm not sure I understand," he said.

I pointed to the name — Darren Shan — scrawled across the front of the top copy, then to myself. Opening it, I let him see the date and the first few lines, then flicked forward to where it described my visit to the Cirque Du Freak and what had happened. When he'd read the part where I told about watching Steve from the balcony, I pointed up and shook my head hard.

"Oh," Mr Tall chuckled. "I see. Evanna not only saved your soul — she gave the old you his normal life back."

I smiled, pleased he finally understood. I closed the diary, tapped the cover, then offered the books to him again. This time he took them.

"Your plan is clear to me now," he said softly. "You want the world to know of this, but not yet. You are right — to reveal it now would be to risk unleashing the hounds of chaos. But if it's released later, around the time when you died, it could affect only the present and the future."

Mr Tall's hands moved very swiftly and the diaries disappeared. "I will keep them safe until the time is right," he said. "Then I will send them to ... who? An author? A publisher? The person you have become?"

I nodded quickly when he said that.

"Very well," he said. "I cannot say what he will do with these — he might consider them a hoax, or not understand what you want of him — but I'll do as you request." He started to close the door, then paused. "In this time, of course, I do not know you, and now that you have removed yourself from your original timeline, I never shall. But I sense we were friends." He put out a hand and we shook. Mr Tall only very rarely shook hands. "Good luck to you, friend," he whispered. "Good luck to us all." Then he quickly broke contact and closed the door, leaving me to retire, find a nice quiet spot where I could be alone — and die.

I now know why Evanna commented on Mr Tiny not being a reader. He has nothing to do with books. He doesn't pay attention to novels or other works of fiction. If, many years from now, an adult Darren Shan comes along and publishes a series of books about vampires, Mr Tiny won't know about it. His attention will be focused elsewhere. The books will come out and be read, and even though vampires aren't avid readers, word will surely trickle back to them.

As the War of the Scars comes to a wary pause and leaders on both sides try to forge a new era of peace, my diaries will — with the luck of the vampires — hit book shops around the world. Vampires and vampaneze will be able to read my story (or have it read to them if they're illiterate). They'll discover more about Mr Tiny than they ever imagined. They'll see precisely how much of a meddler he really is, and learn of his plans for a desolate future world. Armed with that knowledge, and united by the birth of Evanna's children, I'm certain they'll band together and do all they can to stop him.

Mr Tall will send my diaries to the grown Darren Shan. I don't imagine he'll add any notes or instructions of his own — he dare not meddle with the past in that way. It's possible the adult me will dismiss the diaries, write them off as a bizarre con job, and do nothing with them. But knowing me the way I do (now *that* sounds weird!), I think, once he's read them, he'll take them at face value. I like to believe I always had an open mind.

If the adult me reads the diaries all the way to the end, and believes they're real, he'll know what to do. Rewrite them, fiddle with the names so as not to draw unwelcome attention to the real people involved, rework the facts into a story, cut out the duller entries, fictionalize it a bit, create an action-packed adventure. And then, when he's done all that — sell it! Find an agent and publisher. Pretend it's a work of fantasy. Get it published. Promote it hard. Sell it to as many countries as he can, to spread the word and increase the chances of the story capturing the attention of vampires and vampaneze.

Am I being realistic? There's a big difference between a diary and a novel. Will the human Darren Shan have the ability to draw readers in and spin a tale which keeps them hooked? Will he be able to write a series of novels strong enough to attract the attention of the children of the night? I don't know. I was pretty good at writing stories when I was younger, but there's no way of knowing what I'll be like when I grow up. Maybe I won't read any more. Maybe I won't want to or be able to write.

But I've got to hope for the best. Freed from his dark destiny, I've got to hope the young me keeps on reading and writing. If the luck of the vampires is really with me (with *us*) maybe that Darren will become a writer even before Mr Tall sends the package to him. That would be perfect, if he was already an author. He could put the story of my life out as just another of his imaginative works, then get on with writing his own stuff, and nobody — except those actually involved in the War of the Scars — would ever know the difference.

Maybe I'm just dreaming. But it *could* happen. I'm proof that stranger things have taken place. So I say: Go for it, Darren! Follow your dreams. Take your ideas and run with them. Work hard. Learn to write well. I'll be waiting for you up ahead if you do, with the weirdest, twistiest story you've ever heard. Words have the power to alter the future and change the world. I think, together, we can find the right words. I can even, now that I think about it, suggest a first line for the book, to start you out on the long and winding road, perhaps something along the lines of, "I've always been fascinated by spiders…"

CHAPTER TWENTY

I'm on the roof of the old cinema, lying on my back, studying the beautiful sky. Dawn is close. Thin clouds drift slowly across the lightening horizon. I can feel myself coming undone. It won't be much longer now.

I'm not one hundred per cent sure how Mr Tiny's resurrection process works, but I think I understand enough of it to know what's going on. Harkat was created from the remains of Kurda Smahlt. Mr Tiny took Kurda's corpse and used it to create a Little Person. He then returned Harkat to the past. Harkat and Kurda shouldn't have been able to exist simultaneously. A soul can't normally share two bodies at the same time. One should have given way for the other. As the original, Kurda had the automatic right to life, so Harkat's body should have started to unravel, as it did when Kurda was fished out of the Lake of Souls all those years later.

But it didn't. Harkat survived for several years in the same time zone as Kurda. That makes me assume that Mr Tiny has the power to protect his Little People, at least for a while, even if he sends them back to a time when their original forms are still alive.

But he didn't bother to protect *me* when he sent me back. So one of the bodies has to go — this one. But I'm not moaning. I'm OK with my brief spell as a Little Person. In fact, the shortness of this life is the whole point! It's how Evanna has freed me.

When Kurda was facing death for the second time, Mr Tiny told him that his spirit wouldn't return to the Lake — it would depart this realm. By dying now, my soul — like Kurda's — will fly immediately to Paradise. I suppose it's a bit like not passing "Go" on a Monopoly board and going straight to jail, except in this case "Go" is the Lake of Souls and "jail" is the afterlife.

I feel exceptionally light, as though I weigh almost nothing. The sensation is increasing by the moment. My body's fading away, dissolving. But not like in the green pool of liquid in Mr Tiny's cave. This is a gentle, painless dissolve, as though some great force is unstitching me, using a pair of magical knitting needles to pick my flesh and bones apart, strand by strand, knot by knot.

What will Paradise be like? I can't answer that one. I can't even hazard a guess. I imagine it's a timeless place, where the dead souls of every age mingle as one, renewing old friendships and making new acquaintances. Space doesn't exist, not even bodies, just thoughts and imagination. But I have no proof of that. It's just what I picture it to be.

I summon what little energy I have left and raise a hand. I can see through the grey flesh now, through the muscles and bones, to the twinkle of the stars beyond. I smile and the corners of my lips continue stretching, off my face, becoming a limitless, endless smile.

My robes sag as the body beneath loses the ability to support them. Atoms rise from me like steam, thin tendrils at first, then a steady stream of shafts which are all the colours of the rainbow, my soul departing from every area of my body at once. The tendrils wrap around one another and shoot upwards, bound for the stars and realms beyond.

There's almost nothing left of me now. The robes collapse in on themselves completely. The last traces of my spirit hover above the robes and the roof. I think of my family, Debbie, Mr Crepsley, Steve, Mr Tiny, all those I've known, loved, feared and hated. My last thought, oddly, is of Madam Octa — I wonder if they have spiders in Paradise?

And now it's over. I'm finished with this world. My final few atoms rise at a speed faster than light, leaving the roof, the theatre, the town, the world, far, far behind. I'm heading for a new universe, new adventures, a new way of being. Farewell world! Goodbye Darren Shan! So long old friends and allies! This is it! The stars draw me towards them. Explosions of space and time. Breaking through the barriers of the old reality. Coming apart, coming together, moving on. A breath on the lips of the universe. All things, all worlds, all lives. Everything at once and never. Mr Crepsley waiting. Laughter in the great beyond. I'm going ... I'm ... going ... I'm ... gone.

THE END

THE SAGA OF DARREN SHAN
MAY 8TH 1997 — MAY 19TH 2004

HOCKEY'S HOTTEST PLAYERS

The On- & Off-Ice Stories of the Superstars

Arpon Basu

OVER
TIME
BOOKS

© 2005 by OverTime Books
First printed in 2005 10 9 8 7 6 5 4 3 2 1
Printed in Canada

The Publisher: OverTime Books is an imprint of Éditions de
             la Montagne Verte

Library and Archives Canada Cataloguing in Publication

Basu, Arpon, 1976–
   Hockey's hottest players : the on- and off-ice stories of
   the superstars / Arpon Basu.

   ISBN-13: 978-0-9737681-3-8
   ISBN-10: 0-9737681-3-4

   1. Hockey players—Biography. 2. National Hockey League—
Biography. I. Title.

GV848.5.A1B38   2005 796.962'092'2   C2005-905013-6

Project Director: Jay Poulton
Project Editor: Kathy van Denderen
Production: Jodene
Cover Design: Valentino
Cover Image: Jarome Iginla. Courtesy of Getty Images / Dave
Sandford (photographer).

PC: P5

Contents

Dedication

To my mother, Nila, and father, Dipak, who made great sacrifices so that I may grow up in the land where hockey is king.

Introduction

The National Hockey League (NHL) is emerging from the darkest period of its long and storied history. Although league commissioner Gary Bettman wanted desperately for the NHL to be first in the hearts and minds of the entire continent's sports fans, becoming the first North American major sports league to lose an entire season to a labour dispute was not really what he had in mind.

So how will the NHL, and by extension the game of hockey, emerge from the year-long lockout to convince fans to spend their hard-earned dollars on a sport that has essentially given them all a collective slap in the face? It will attempt to do so by improving its on-ice product, giving a game that was bogged down by overly defensive strategies a new life with various rule changes meant to increase offence and excitement for the fans who are the league's lifeline.

But the NHL will also need some star power to put people back in the seats. Since Wayne Gretzky's retirement, the league has not had a single player on which it could hang its hat. Mario Lemieux came back after retiring with back problems and other ailments, but he is not the same player he once was, and his injury concerns make him an unsuitable candidate to be the NHL's post-lockout poster boy.

The new and improved NHL will need a player who is just hitting his prime, someone who can promote the league both to fans and corporations for years to come, someone who can transcend the game like Gretzky once did. If such a person exists, he may come from the group of 12 players profiled in this book. None of them were 30 years old when the 2005–06 NHL season began, and they are all stars.

Of course, there are many other players who also could have been included in this book, such as Boston Bruins centre Joe Thornton, Minnesota Wild sniper Marian Gaborik and Philadelphia Flyers winger Simon Gagné, to name a few.

But the ones selected here are the crème de la crème, the elite young NHL players who have the most potential to carry the league's fortunes into this new era of professional hockey, one that the NHL hopes will be its most prosperous ever.

Only time will tell if they are successful, but for the fans, watching them try will be a lot of fun.

Chapter One

Rick Nash

Rick Nash would have gladly waited his turn. Sitting at the 2002 NHL entry draft in the home arena of his beloved Toronto Maple Leafs, surrounded by 50 of his family and friends who made the short drive from his hometown of Brampton, Ontario, Nash thought he had it all figured out. He'd read the scouting lists and hockey pundits who said smooth-skating Medicine Hat Tigers defenceman Jay Bouwmeester was a lock to go to the Florida Panthers with the first pick, and he believed them. Why wouldn't he? He was, after all, only six days from his 18th birthday, barely even an adult. Who was he to question the experts?

But what Nash forgot while getting swept up in the pomp and pageantry of the biggest day of his hockey life was the interview he had with Columbus Blue Jackets general manager Doug MacLean, who held the third pick in the draft. "I'd love to have you," MacLean told Nash, "but I don't know if I'm going to get you at number three."

Nash, obviously flattered by MacLean's desire to have him on his team, paused a moment before coming up with what he felt was a perfectly reasonable solution to MacLean's dilemma. "Well," Nash said, "why don't you go get me."

Sitting in the stands of the Air Canada Centre at the draft a few days later, Nash didn't believe for a second that MacLean would take his brazen advice so seriously. But Nash's response had only confirmed what MacLean already knew—he'd do whatever it took to get Nash into a Blue Jackets uniform.

Panthers general manager Rick Dudley had openly coveted Bouwmeester but started wavering in the weeks leading up to the draft, enough to cause concern in Columbus. MacLean knew that Atlanta Thrashers general manager Don Waddell had essentially decided he needed a franchise goaltender and would take Finland's Kari Lehtonen. If Dudley was being more open about favouring Bouwmeester, MacLean could have sat back and waited for Nash to fall down to him. But with Dudley flirting with the idea of grabbing Nash, MacLean had to move.

Minutes before Dudley was to make his first pick, MacLean offered him the Blue Jackets pick at number three and the option to swap picks with

Columbus in 2003. Dudley snapped up the deal after sending Waddell a couple of late-round picks to ensure he didn't select Bouwmeester, and MacLean had his prize. While all this wheeling and dealing was transpiring, Nash was still thinking about all those scouting lists he'd read over the past weeks and months. "I was sitting there just thinking about Bouwmeester going first to Florida and the next thing you hear there's been a trade," Nash said. "My stomach just dropped...it was like going on a big roller coaster."

After consummating the most important trade in Columbus franchise history, MacLean walked to the podium and announced that Rick Nash was the number one pick in the 2002 NHL entry draft. The Nash clan, all 50 of them, went crazy with joy. All except for one.

"Everybody said he'd probably go third before the draft," recalled Nash's mother, Liz. "After he was picked number one, I didn't even cry because I was in such shock."

For MacLean, he saw his bold draft-day manoeuvring as a necessity if he wanted to get any sleep that night. "I haven't said it very often," MacLean said later, "but I would have been sick to my stomach leaving the draft without him."

❧◆☙

Although Nash wasn't aware of it that day, he was on the road to superstardom, a road that began on a tiny pond in Brampton. Nash's father, Jamie, and older brother, James, first got Nash into a pair of skates when he was only two years old, having barely learned how to walk.

"He was a good skater," Liz Nash said. "He was skating backwards before most of the other kids were skating forwards."

Nash has been on the fast track ever since. He dominated the Greater Toronto minor hockey ranks, and when a growth spurt hit at age 14, Nash's reputation grew as well. By the time he made it to his bantam draft year with the Toronto Marlboros in 1999, he was one of the top forwards in Ontario, if not in Canada. He scored a staggering 61 goals with 54 assists for 115 points in only 34 games that year, showing off his soft hands, long reach and deceptive speed for a gangly kid. But most of all, Nash displayed a wonderful sense of timing.

Dale Hunter, the 19-year NHL veteran and the owner, general manager and coach of the Ontario Hockey League's (OHL) London Knights, went to a prospects tournament to get a look at Nash in person to prepare for the bantam draft.

"He had two goals in the first five minutes we saw him" Hunter recalled. "But at the end of the game he had an empty-net breakaway [for a hat trick], and he unselfishly passed the puck." Hunter didn't need to think long to decide who he would take with the fourth pick in the 2000 bantam draft.

Nash continued the success he had known his whole hockey-playing life in London, posting 31 goals and 35 assists in 58 games in 2000–01 to finish second on the team in points and first in goals. That performance easily earned him the OHL's rookie of the year award, and he was placed on the Canadian Hockey League's first all-rookie team.

Nash also made his international debut that year, winning a bronze medal with Team Ontario at the 2001 Under-17 World Hockey Challenge in Nova Scotia. He finished second on the team in scoring with 5 goals and 2 assists in four games, and in one game he scored 2 goals in only 11 seconds. Detroit Red Wings scout Joe McDonnell was one of the roughly 10 scouts from various levels that watched Nash play in the tournament, and he was impressed with the teenager's skill set.

"He's a total package," McDonnell said. "Size, skill, hockey sense—whatever you look for in a player, he's got it all."

In August 2001, Nash won a gold medal with the Canadian under-18 team at the Six Nations Cup, leading the team in scoring with 5 goals and 5 assists in five games, including a hat trick and 2 assists in Canada's 9–4 win over Russia in the gold medal game. That set Nash up for his NHL draft year with the Knights, where he once again excelled with a team-high 32 goals and 40 assists playing on a lower-rung team.

Nash was also a source of comic relief in the dressing room, keeping the team loose, even when things weren't going so well on the ice. A favourite pastime of Nash and his teammates was going out to the local mall in London, gluing loonies to the floor and then laughing at the people trying to pick them up. One of his fellow Knights, Logan Hunter (the coach's nephew), remembers another one of Nash's favourite pranks.

"Rick does a pretty good impression of our assistant coach, Jacques Beaulieu, so right at the trade deadline, he was calling kids and telling them they'd been traded," Hunter recalled with a laugh. "Had some of them going pretty good."

Despite his great performances on and off the ice, what really set Nash apart and caught the eye of every NHL scout was his selection for the 2002 Canadian world junior team as a 17-year-old, making him the youngest player on the team. Barry Trapp, the Toronto Maple Leafs director of amateur scouting, Hockey Canada's director of scouting at the time, remembers giving Nash two strikes before he even stepped on the ice.

"At the world juniors, I made it clear I didn't want any 17-year-olds," Trapp said. "But anywhere we put him—at centre, right or left wing—he'd score a goal. He made us take him."

Nash began as a third or fourth liner on head coach Stan Butler's team but eventually worked his way to a regular shift, scoring a goal and adding an assist as Canada played Russia in the final to take the silver medal in the tournament held in the Czech Republic. His performance left a lasting impression on Butler. "I've never seen a player step in at such a young age and be able to dominate a game the way he has," Butler said. "He's a great player."

When Nash returned to the lowly Knights after playing with the best teenagers on the planet, he practically took on the OHL by himself. His Knights limped into the playoffs with the eighth and final seed, giving them a date with the league's best regular season squad in 2001–02, the Plymouth Whalers.

But Nash was a man possessed over the six game series. He led London to a 4–2 series upset with 6 goals and 4 assists. The superhuman performance made him a lock to be one of the first names called at the NHL draft later on that summer.

"He really matured in the postseason," Detroit Red Wings assistant general manager Jim Nill said in the weeks preceding the draft. "He became a leader. Everybody knows his skill level—he has a good feel for the ice, he sees the goal and the seams so well— but put that together with his leadership, and that's why he's going to be a top pick."

It was words like these that made the Blue Jackets MacLean so nervous at the draft, forcing him to swing the deal that had changed Nash's life forever. All of a sudden, the 18-year-old was no longer just a great hockey prospect, he was a number one NHL draft pick, one that led his team to mortgage the following year's draft to have a chance at landing him.

"I sure hope [MacLean] thinks he made the right choice," Nash said later. "He showed a lot of confidence in switching the draft picks and that put a lot of pressure on me to perform."

So Nash performed, and he didn't waste much time, either. In his first NHL game, suiting up as the youngest player in the NHL, he scored the game-tying goal in a 2–1 comeback win over the Chicago Blackhawks on October 10, 2002, making him only the eighth number one draft pick in NHL history to score a goal in his first game.

Although he said before the season began that he only wanted to stay in Columbus the whole year, Nash finished that rookie season with 17 goals and 22 assists in 74 games, coming second in the Calder Trophy balloting for NHL rookie of the year and taking part in the YoungStars Game during all-star weekend.

Nash grew up a lot that rookie year as well. He refused the Blue Jackets' offer to set him up with a billet family in favour of getting his own place. Most NHL teams don't allow an 18-year-old kid—especially one they had just signed for over $8.5 million—to live on his own in a strange town, but Columbus was confident that Nash was mature enough to handle it.

"Age is just a number," Nash said. "I didn't act like an 18-year-old and I couldn't be like a real 18-year-old, so why should I live like one?"

Nash, at 19, was still the youngest player in the NHL in 2003–04, but he definitely didn't play like it. He felt satisfied with his rookie year but was convinced he could have produced even more if he had some more muscle to fight off checks in front of the net. He played his rookie year at 6-foot-4 and 188 pounds, but by the time he came back to training camp in September, Nash weighed a solid 208 pounds. He put the 20 pounds of extra muscle to work immediately, going to the net harder and staying there longer. He scored 8 goals in his first 10 games and 15 in his first 23 games.

On December 6, 2003, Nash capped a five-game goal-scoring streak with his 18th of the season, surpassing the total for his entire rookie season in only his 26th game of the year. MacLean watched the spectacle with a certain degree of awe. "He's probably way ahead of where we expected him to be when we drafted him. When you draft an 18-year-old, you're always a little nervous," MacLean said in October of that year. "Our people felt he was going to be a star in the league but, I mean, he's on pace for 50 goals right now."

By late January 2004, Nash was the league's leading goal scorer and had scored 30.1 percent of the Blue Jackets' total, but the teenager didn't see carrying the fortunes of the entire franchise as anything to lose much sleep over. "I really don't feel too much pressure, and the club doesn't put too much pressure on me," Nash said. "I just know I am supposed to go out there and score every night."

He went back to all-star weekend that year, except this time he was suiting up in the main event. He became the youngest player to appear in an all-star game since Wendell Clark of the Toronto Maple Leafs in 1986. Nash's consistent pace continued in the second half of the season, but Atlanta Thrashers winger Ilya Kovalchuk and Calgary Flames captain Jarome Iginla poured it on after the all-star break, and the three young stars tied for the league lead in goals with 41 apiece.

With that, Nash became the youngest player to win the league goal-scoring crown—a year and a half younger than Wayne Gretzky was when he won it for the 1981–82 season. Nash also became the first teenager to score 40 in a season since Jimmy Carson in 1988, and Nash's 58 career goals before the age of 20 ranks eighth in NHL history.

His breakout performance should have granted Nash superstar status, but he still wasn't recognized as one of Canada's best players, let alone the NHL's. Nash was invited to play for Canada at the senior world championships after the 2003–04 regular season was over, but he was struck with a severe case of tonsillitis the day before his departure and had to undergo surgery.

When it came time to select Canada's entry in the World Cup of Hockey, Nash's name was mentioned as a possibility. He was, after all, the NHL's leading goal scorer. But when push came to shove, Nash was deemed expendable. "Obviously it was disappointing; I thought I had a chance," Nash said later. "But they took the best players in Canada, and if I was too young or my resume didn't fit their team, then I have many years to play."

Nash did not play in the NHL in the fall of 2004 due to the lockout that cost the league an entire season. Instead, he packed his bags for Davos, Switzerland, to join the Swiss Elite League, playing on a line with Boston Bruins star Joe Thornton. While Thornton led the team with 54 points in 44 games, Nash was a close second with 46, including 26 goals. Nash scored nine times in the playoffs to help lead Davos to the Swiss championship. Although few 20-year-olds have the option of moving to Switzerland to work, the excitement of the new cultural experience seemed to wear off for the young Nash.

"Well, there's not much to do in a little town of 17,000 people," said Nash. "No movie theatre, no mall, so there wasn't much to do other than stay at the rink and hang out with the guys, go eat dinner. But it was good, it was a real laid-back environment."

Shortly after his Swiss league season came to an end, Nash was summoned once again to play for Canada at the world championships after many big-name players like Mario Lemieux, Joe Sakic and Jarome Iginla declined invitations. The world championships turned out to be Nash's international coming-out party, with hockey-starved fans worldwide watching as the NHL lockout continued.

Nash was placed back on a line with his Davos teammate Thornton and Philadelphia Flyers forward Simon Gagné on the other wing. The line was easily the best of the tournament, with Thornton finishing first in scoring with 16 points in nine games and Nash finishing a close second with 15 points, including a tournament-leading 9 goals. That earned him a spot on the tournament all-star team as Canada won the silver medal.

But one goal in particular put the spotlight squarely on Nash as the NHL's next great scoring star. In Canada's third game of the tournament, a 3–1 win over the United States, Nash streaked down the ice on a partial breakaway with U.S. defenceman Aaron Miller in hot pursuit. Keeping Miller away from the puck with his body, Nash cut across the front of the net, waited for U.S. goaltender Rick DiPietro to commit, then coolly flipped the puck over the falling DiPietro and just under the crossbar. The Canadian bench was in a state of shock.

"If you'd have seen our bench when he scored that goal," Nash's Canadian teammate Shane Doan said. "Guys were looking at each other going, 'Oh man.' He led the whole NHL in goals—I think it was the first time a teenager led the NHL in scoring since Wayne Gretzky—and you didn't really hear that much about him. It was the funniest thing. It was so quiet it was ridiculous. The league should have...I mean, the kid's incredible. And not only a great hockey player, he's the nicest guy. So respectful. And the scary thing is that he's going to get bigger. He's going to fill out more, and he's going to get stronger. He already takes the puck to the net better than anyone else in the league. He's really remarkable, he really is."

Doan has no more reason to be concerned because Nash, before even being allowed to legally drink a beer after a home game in Columbus, became a bona fide NHL superstar at the world championships. And the best is yet to come.

Just Call Me Cash

Rick Nash didn't expect to be the first player selected in the 2002 NHL entry draft. But once he was, he wasn't about to let a golden opportunity pass him by. It took Nash and Columbus Blue Jackets general manager Doug MacLean some time before coming together on a contract for the new franchise player. The negotiations began in the summer of 2002 and continued through the Blue Jackets' training camp in Summerside, Prince Edward Island.

When Nash finally signed on the dotted line, mere days before he scored his first NHL goal in his first game, he agreed to a very personalized bonus package. On top of the base annual salary of $1.185 million (rookie salaries were capped at $1.2 million at the time), Nash received a bonus package worth $8.561 million over three years. Why the extra $61,000? It matched Nash's number 61 on the back of his jersey. From that point on, his new Columbus teammates took to calling the blue-chipper "Rick Cash."

Chapter Two

Sidney Crosby

When the phone rang, Sidney Crosby thought it was just another reporter calling for yet another interview. After all, the hockey prodigy had already handled hundreds of media interviews before he was even old enough to drive, and this one was probably no different. Crosby was in Los Angeles, California, at the time, training in preparation to be the youngest player—at only 15 years of age—to take part in Canada's under-18 national team training camp in Calgary a few days later.

Crosby answered the phone, and the voice on the other end of the line belonged to Donna Spencer, a reporter for The Canadian Press wire service, and she had some extraordinary news. A few days earlier, Wayne Gretzky—yes, The Great One—had given what he probably thought was an innocuous interview to a reporter with the *Arizona Republic* newspaper in Phoenix. When the reporter asked

Gretzky if there was anyone he thought could break some of the 61 NHL scoring records he either holds or shares, he didn't expect Gretzky to mention a specific name. But, surprisingly, Gretzky did.

"Yes, Sidney Crosby, he's dynamite," Gretzky responded. "He's the best player I've seen since Mario [Lemieux]...He's that good. I went to watch him play this year, and I actually got on the ice with him. He's got it all."

Upon hearing the news of Gretzky's anointment over the phone, Crosby couldn't utter a word in response. He was numb. Finally, after gathering his thoughts, the prodigy replied to Spencer. "Wow, I hadn't heard that. That's something else. That's pretty special for Wayne Gretzky to say that. I don't think his records will ever be broken. That's a compliment for him to say that for sure."

The young man, who hadn't even taken part in a major junior hockey game or in any international competition, didn't realize it at the time, but Gretzky's compliment was the official launch party for the hockey world's brand new travelling act: The Sidney Crosby Show. It was a hit with fans desperate for a dominant offensive superstar, and Crosby suddenly became a saviour for hockey at a time when it needed one the most.

Crosby had an agent by the time he was 14, was profiled in *Sports Illustrated*, became only the fifth player to be selected to Canada's junior national team at the age of 16 and signed a multi-million dollar endorsement deal at 17. All before suiting up in a single NHL game.

Crosby's story begins much earlier, in a dingy basement in the Halifax hamlet of Cole Harbour, Nova Scotia. Crosby's father, Troy, was a goaltender in the Québec Major Junior Hockey League (QMJHL) who was drafted in the 12th round of the 1984 draft by the Montréal Canadiens. Unfortunately for Troy, the Habs had selected another goalie in the third round of that very same draft, a chap by the name of Patrick Roy, and the elder Crosby never managed to make the jump to the NHL.

Troy and Trina Crosby's first child was born August 7, 1987, the reason Crosby wears number 87 today (8th month, 7th day, '87). Before he was even three years old, his parents put young Sidney in a pair of skates. Troy helped nurture his son's love of the game by converting their basement into a mini hockey rink and would regularly don his old goalie pads so that his son could shoot at him. But Troy was forced to stop when Sidney was only nine years old because the slap shots coming at him were leaving him battered and bruised.

"He was killing me," Troy said. "I told him, 'You don't need a goalie, just shoot at the net.'"

Crosby began playing minor hockey when he was only four years old, and by the time he was seven, he already had the first of what would soon be hundreds of newspaper interviews under his belt. While playing atom hockey at the age of 10, Crosby gave an idea of how good he would become by scoring a ridiculous 159 goals and 121 assists for 280 points in 55 games.

But when a youngster stands out that much, especially a youngster playing hockey in Canada, problems tend to follow. Crosby was the target of such nasty taunts and abuse from other hockey parents that he sometimes went home from the rink with tears streaming down his face. Troy admits that some of the abuse directed at his son was because of his own antics at the rink, but most of the taunts were fuelled by petty anger, pure and simple.

One time, as an eight-year-old, Crosby was playing in a provincial playoff game. As he celebrated one of the five goals he would score in that game, a parent leaned over the glass and yelled at Crosby, "Go home Crosby, you bum! You've got no skill!"

Another time, Crosby cried after a woman called him a "prima donna" in the arena lobby. It got so bad that Crosby took to skating in the pre-game warm-up without his jersey so he couldn't be identified.

"I don't know if jealousy is the right word, but there was definitely some resentment," Trina Crosby said. "Maybe not with the kids, but the parents. At one point, it was really hard to go to the rink if there had been a big article about Sidney in the newspaper."

Unfortunately for Crosby, his performance on the ice made the articles, and the negative attention that resulted from them, inevitable. But he never let the verbal jabs affect his game.

"He ignores it; he walks away from it," Troy Crosby said. "I've seen people with kids of their own hanging over the glass screaming and yelling things at him, unbelievable things, when he was just nine years old. But he doesn't lower himself to their level. He just worries about Sidney and playing hockey...Wayne Gretzky, Mario Lemieux, Eric Lindros, all those people had the same problems growing up. We just move forward."

Crosby's wild success in the minor hockey ranks made him the exception to almost every age-requirement rule in Nova Scotia. At 13 years old, still PeeWee age, he made the Dartmouth Subways midget AAA team—two age groups higher than his own. Even though there was no specific rule barring a PeeWee age player from playing midget hockey, the provincial hockey council ruled he was too young, which led Crosby's father to appeal the council's decision to the higher-ranking Nova Scotia Hockey Association. While the association weighed the decision, Crosby stayed off the ice for six weeks, making him probably the youngest hockey player ever to hold out.

The appeal, however, failed, and Crosby was sent to the Cole Harbour bantam AAA Wings.

"I would have been challenged in midget," Crosby said at the time. "I'm still going to get better, but I think I would have improved a lot more in midget."

Crosby proceeded to score 86 goals with 96 assists for 182 points with the Wings, winning the 2000–01 provincial championship tournament scoring title and Most Valuable Player (MVP) award. In the summer of 2001, he was drafted with the fifth pick of the second round by the Truro Bearcats—a team in the Maritime Junior A Hockey League—just two months before his 14th birthday. The Truro general manager at the time, Steve Crowell, couldn't resist taking a flier on the phenom, even though Crosby would be putting his slight 5-foot-7, 145-pound frame on the same ice as men who were up to 21 years of age.

"They don't come along very often this skilled, this young," Crowell said after the draft. "He's got the ability to play at our level. Obviously with his size, we'll have to have lots of protection for him."

Crosby didn't sound the least bit intimidated after hearing the news. "Yeah, I can adapt to it," he said, only after noting what a surprise it was to be drafted by a junior team at age 13. "I've been adapting to each level I've gone to each year. It's no different. It's a bigger step, but I think I can do it."

He was well on his way, sitting second on Truro's training camp scoring list, when the Crosby family decided that the two-hour round-trip commute from Cole Harbour to Truro four or five times a week was too much for a ninth-grader to bear. So Crosby went back to the midget AAA Dartmouth Subways and lit it up, scoring a staggering 106 goals with 111 assists in 81 league and tournament games. He was named MVP of the 2002 provincial and Canadian championships, leading the Subways to the national final with 24 points in seven games.

Then, during that summer in Los Angeles the fateful moment came: The Next One met The Great One. Gretzky and Crosby skated on a line together in a 3-on-3 drill, and that was all it took to convince the greatest hockey player ever that he had just seen his successor.

From that point on, it seemed as if some of Gretzky's magic had rubbed off on Crosby because his stock as a household name in the world of hockey began to skyrocket. Crosby's decision in the summer of 2002 to attend Minnesota prep school Shattuck-St. Mary's instead of playing his second year of midget or Junior A hockey made for banner headlines across Atlantic Canada.

The general manager of the Halifax Mooseheads, a team in the QMJHL, tried in vain to convince the league's other teams to allow Crosby into the league as a 15-year-old player on the condition he play for his hometown team—in this case the Mooseheads. The suggestion was voted down by 11 of the league's 16 teams.

Crosby went to Minnesota partly because Shattuck-St Mary's is widely recognized as one of the best hockey training institutions in North America, but it was also to get away from the heckling and scrutiny that came with being the best young hockey player in Canada.

After scoring 72 goals with 90 assists in 57 games and leading Shattuck to the United States national midget championship, Crosby decided to enter the QMJHL draft rather than wait a year and accept one of the hundreds of college scholarship offers he'd already received. For making that choice, he was publicly thanked by the Canadian junior hockey central scouting director, probably because it made naming the top prospect for the 2005 NHL draft a cinch. The first pick that year belonged to the Rimouski Océanic, and there was no question as to who they would select.

"Rimouski did their part," Crosby said on draft day, "now I think it's time to do mine."

He didn't waste any time.

In a pre-season game, Crosby racked up 8 points, leading his teammates to start calling him Darryl, after former Maple Leafs great Darryl Sittler, who once had an NHL record 10 points in one game. In his regular season debut Crosby dazzled the crowd in Rouyn-Noranda by scoring a third period natural hat trick that included the winning goal, leading Rimouski back from a 3–0 deficit to win 4–3.

In his home debut at the Colisée de Rimouski a few nights later, Crosby scored twice—including the winner in overtime—and added 3 assists in a 7–6 win over Moncton. If there had been any doubt about Crosby's status as a hockey prodigy, he successfully erased them in just over 120 minutes of hockey.

But later in the 2003–04 season, Crosby showed off one of his greatest talents, taking some of the best elements from other players and adding them to his own repertoire. He remembered watching a goal scored by University of Michigan centre Mike Legg during the 1996 National Collegiate Athletic Association (NCAA) tournament. In that game, Legg was behind his opponents' net, left alone by the two defencemen. So he decided to lay his stick flat on the ice against the puck, swing the puck up onto the blade of his stick and tuck it into the top corner of the net lacrosse-style over the shoulder of the unsuspecting goalie. That goal tied the national quarterfinal game 2–2 as Michigan went on to win the game 4–3, and eventually the championship.

Crosby tried the same move in November in a game the Océanic was already leading 5–0 over the Québec City Remparts. With Rimouski on a power play and having been left to his own devices behind the net, Crosby executed the copy-cat play to perfection before proceeding to skate full-tilt down the ice, waving his arms in celebration. That move earned Crosby the wrath of *Hockey Night in Canada*'s Don Cherry, who on national television called the phenom a "hot dog" and warned him that if he continued behaving this way someone would hurt him in retaliation. Two days later, Cherry was summoned to address the issue at a press conference in Halifax.

"It was like I'd said something about the Pope," Cherry said on the following week's broadcast. "It was unbelievable."

Just before Christmas in 2003, Crosby fulfilled a lifelong dream when he was named to the Canadian junior national team, joining Gretzky, Eric Lindros, Jason Spezza and Jay Bouwmeester as the only players ever selected as 16-year-olds. As soon as Crosby got the news, all he could think to do was look for a phone to tell his parents.

"It felt good to make that call," Crosby said afterwards. "They've made a lot of sacrifices for me to play hockey."

Although Crosby didn't dominate the tournament, he was no slouch either, picking up 5 points in six games and becoming the youngest Canadian to score a goal in the world juniors. Crosby went back to Rimouski with a disappointing silver medal after a tough 4–3 loss to the United States in the final, but he finished his rookie year of major junior hockey strong. His 54 goals and 81 assists in 59 games not only led the QMJHL in scoring that year, it was the highest point total in the entire Canadian Hockey League (CHL). For his efforts, Crosby was named national player of the year, a feat unheard of for a rookie who was not yet draft eligible.

Crosby got off to a sluggish start—by his lofty standards—in his second season with Rimouski. He had only 74 points in his first 35 games before joining Team Canada once again for the 2005 world junior championships. Crosby's performance at the world juniors this time around, however, was far more dominant than his first. His line with Boston Bruins product Patrice Bergeron and Corey Perry of the London Knights was the dominant trio of the tournament. Crosby registered 6 goals and 3 assists in six games to help a well-balanced Canadian team win its first world junior title in eight years.

When he returned to Rimouski, Crosby moved to a new level of greatness, even for him. In his 27 regular season games as a world junior gold medallist, he compiled unthinkable numbers of 40 goals and 54 assists for 94 points, an average of nearly 3.5 points per game. His performance in the second half of the 2004–05 season gave him 66 goals and 102 assists in 62 regular season games, meaning he either got a goal or an assist on more than half of Rimouski's league-high 333 goals scored that year.

By this point in his young life, Crosby's income from endorsements was already in six figures according to his agent Pat Brisson. But in March 2005, with his popularity in Canada higher than it had ever been thanks to the world junior gold medal, he signed a five-year endorsement deal with Reebok worth a reported $2.5 million.

Crosby led Rimouski to the 2004–05 QMJHL title to earn a berth in his first Memorial Cup, where he became the first player to win the CHL's player of the year award twice, cementing his status as one of the greatest juniors in hockey history.

"I just want to be known as a player who was honest every night, who shows up every night and never took anything for granted and played for the love of the game," Crosby said on awards night. "I have a passion for the game, and I try to show that every night I play."

Although Crosby dazzled the crowds for much of the tournament, he was effectively shut down by Perry's London Knights in the Memorial Cup final and wrapped up his Rimouski career with a second-place finish.

Crosby had arrived in Rimouski as an English-speaking kid who knew literally four words of French, but he left Rimouski two seasons later bilingual—handling French media interviews with ease—and fully prepared and determined to conquer the hockey world.

The NHL lockout soured a lot of people on the game, but Crosby's imminent arrival in the pros had all of the league's owners salivating that his star power would bring alienated fans back to their arenas. For the Pittsburgh Penguins—who won the right to select him by winning the lottery for the first pick in the 2005 draft—Crosby's arrival also gives them new hope of ending years of tumultuous financial problems. It remains to be seen if he has that ability, but it is certain that Crosby will enjoy every second he spends in the NHL, whether he turns into its greatest player or biggest bust. It's something his parents, and more specifically Troy, instilled in Crosby from day one.

"The minute you take things for granted," Crosby likes to say, "it can all be gone."

A Hall-of-Famer at 16

Ever since Sidney Crosby was a toddler, he dreamed of suiting up for Canada at the world junior hockey championships. When that dream finally came true in 2003, Crosby was only 16 years of age, still a toddler in hockey terms.

He came of age in Canada's second game of the tournament against an over-matched Swiss team. With the clock winding down in the third period of a game Canada was already leading 6–2, Crosby drove down the right wing with the puck, skipped over a diving Swiss defender, made a dramatic cut towards the net and roofed a sharp-angle wrist shot past Swiss goaltender Daniel Manzato with only 14 seconds left in regulation time. The meaningless goal made Crosby the youngest player—at 16 years, four months and 24 days—to score for Canada at the world juniors.

"It wasn't even anything I knew until after the game," Crosby said. "I never really think about age, but when they brought that up it was definitely pretty special."

It is widely believed Crosby became the youngest player to score for any team at the tournament, but the International Ice

Hockey Federation's statistics on the subject are not all that reliable. Hockey Canada public relations employee André Brin picked up the puck, just in case anyone wanted to hang on to the historic piece of rubber. And it's a good thing he did—today that puck sits in a display case at the Hockey Hall of Fame in Toronto.

Chapter Three

Marian Hossa

He was on the cusp of everything he had dreamed of. The start of a career in the NHL was at his fingertips; it was the completion of a difficult year where he had to battle homesickness and a language barrier, and there was nothing Marian Hossa wanted more than to score a goal.

It was the championship game of the 1998 Memorial Cup, and Hossa's Portland Winter Hawks and the Guelph Storm were tied 3–3 late in the third period with Canadian junior hockey supremacy riding on every shift. With just over five minutes left to play in regulation time, Winter Hawks coach Brent Peterson tapped the Western Hockey League's (WHL) rookie of the year on the shoulder, the player who had already given his team a goal and an assist in the game, and the 19-year-old Hossa jumped over the boards.

As Hossa crossed the ice, Guelph's Ryan Davis came out of nowhere and caught the talented winger with a vicious, and illegal, knee-on-knee hit. Hossa crumpled to the ice, writhing in pain. Although he didn't know it at the time, he had just torn the anterior cruciate ligament in his left knee, the one that controls forward motion, the one that controlled his future in the NHL.

He eventually got up, propped up on the shoulders of two teammates, and limped his way off the Spokane Arena ice. As Hossa received treatment from the team trainers, his teammates were in their dressing room getting ready to start overtime.

"The room was a little down without Hossa," Peterson said later. "He played wonderful and our guys just said, 'Let's do it for Marian.'"

At 6:21 of the extra frame, Portland's Bobby Russell put a rebound past Guelph goalie Chris Madden, and by the sound of the crowd, Hossa knew his team had just won the Memorial Cup. Although consumed by a combination of fear, doubt and pain, Hossa wasn't about to let this moment pass him by, not after everything he had gone through to get there. He limped his way back to the ice, sat down in an office chair and was carted around by his teammates to bask in the glory.

But as Hossa rested the historic Memorial Cup on his knee, he wasn't sure if he would ever get to compete at this level again, ever get to play the game he had loved essentially since birth, ever get to realize the lifelong dream of an NHL career. In a sense, his entire hockey-playing life flashed before his eyes.

Growing up in Trencin, a bustling textile town of 60,000 in the northeastern part of Slovakia, near the border of the present-day Czech Republic, Hossa and his younger brother, Marcel, were born into a family where only one thing mattered. "Hockey always came first," said their mother, Maria, "before everything else."

Their father, Frantisek, played defence for two years on the Czechoslovakian national team alongside the sibling trio of Peter, Anton and Marian Stastny—the first family of Slovakian hockey. Hossa first put on a pair of skates when he was about four years old, and whenever Frantisek's pro team had an optional skate, he took Marian and Marcel onto the ice with him.

Frantisek also helped his sons build a rink in the playground next to the family's two-bedroom apartment, using plywood stolen from a construction site to fashion a set of rudimentary boards. Building the makeshift rink was necessary because there was only one indoor arena in all of Trencin, and ice time was obviously hotly contested. Only the best and most promising young players were permitted on the ice, and it wasn't long before Hossa was one of those boys. From the beginning, Frantisek noticed his eldest son had extraordinary peripheral vision. He was able to find open teammates and spot oncoming defenders unusually well.

When Hossa was 10 years old, he sold his entire hockey card collection and used the money to buy a Wayne Gretzky instructional video for about $15. "A lot of money for a 10-year-old at that time," Hossa remarked. "You'd try some of his moves in practice, but then when you got in a game it was a different story."

Even if he was having trouble mastering The Great One's dekes right away, that video sowed the seeds of creativity and stickhandling that would become the strength of Hossa's game.

"Actually, I was not a great skater," Hossa admits. "[But] I was always able to score goals. I could stickhandle, but the skating was not as good as I want it to be."

Every year, between fifth and eighth grade, Hossa attended an elite hockey school with the best players in Trencin. At 16, he played for the Dukla Trencin junior team and racked up 42 goals and 49 assists. He played the next season on the first line for Dukla Trencin's senior team in the top Slovak professional league, skating against men in their 20s and 30s and scoring 25 goals with 19 assists in 44 games.

Hossa played in the 1997 world junior championships in Switzerland and scored 5 goals in six games for the sixth-place Slovakian squad. Ottawa Senators director of player personnel, Marshall Johnston, was scouting the tournament, and Hossa definitely caught his attention. Ottawa's head scout André Savard made several trips to Trencin that winter on Johnston's recommendation, and it wasn't long before he, too, became a Hossa fan.

At the 1997 NHL entry draft in June, Hossa was the second-rated European prospect behind Finland's Olli Jokinen. The Senators, sitting with the 12th pick, were elated to see that Hossa was still available when it came time for them to take the podium.

"He's talented," Savard said after drafting Hossa. "He has great hands, great vision. He's a very exciting hockey player."

That day marked the beginning of a challenging year for Hossa, one that saw him moving to a strange land at the age of 18 with only a few words of English in his vocabulary, but would also see his stock as a future NHL star shoot through the roof.

The media in Ottawa bombarded him with questions about his reputation for being a weak defensive player. But with his offensive display in his first NHL training camp, Hossa quickly made people forget about his supposed lapses on defence. In his first pre-season game, he got an assist and was a noticeable force all night. He finished the exhibition schedule with 7 points in seven games and, with star Senators winger Daniel Alfredsson holding out in a contract dispute, Hossa made the team to start the season.

"He's here to stay," head coach Jacques Martin said the day the final cuts were made. Martin's prediction barely lasted two weeks. Hossa managed just one assist in his first seven NHL games, and the Senators decided it was best if he played his first year in North America with the WHL's Portland Winter Hawks.

"The thing that I liked about Marian immediately was that he fit right into our team," Portland coach Brent Peterson said. "He's a very good hockey player, but even more than that he's a good personality. He works hard. He's not a crybaby and he doesn't worry about what's going wrong when he isn't playing well. He just comes back the next night and tries that much harder."

Junior hockey afforded Hossa a lot of time to learn English. With long bus rides a fact of life in junior hockey, Hossa slowly picked up the intricacies of English by watching movies and asking his teammates over and over again, "What did he say?"

"Some of our trips were 15 hours long," Hossa said. "You get to see a lot of movies."

On the ice, Hossa was learning another language as well, the North American hockey code. Although he had 9 points in his first 10 games with Portland, Hossa struggled to understand why players weren't getting penalties when they grabbed his arm or hooked his elbow. But most of all, for the life of him, Hossa couldn't understand why so many players refused to carry the puck into the offensive zone and opted instead for the safer dump-in. "It was like they didn't want to carry the puck and risk making a mistake," Hossa said.

In early December 1997, Hossa went back to Slovakia to try out for his home country's Olympic team that would go to Nagano, Japan. He then continued on to Finland for his second world junior championships where he notched 8 points in six games.

Hossa had been gone for almost a month, but when he returned to Portland, he picked up with the Winter Hawks exactly where he'd left off. He finished the 1997–98 season with 45 goals and 40 assists in 53 games to win the WHL's rookie of the year award and was named to the CHL's all-star team. It took Hossa a few games to adjust to playoff hockey in North America, where the line between legal and illegal play blurs even further than in the regular season.

"It was a new experience for him," Peterson said. "Instead of looking up at the referee, he had to learn how to fight through those checks."

He had only 6 goals in his first 12 playoff games, but in the league final, Hossa exploded for 7 goals in a four-game sweep of the Brandon Wheat Kings.

"He was just awesome," Brandon coach Bob Lowes said after the series. "Although he averaged almost two goals a game against us, he was getting seven and eight great scoring opportunities a game... When he saw a seam between two defencemen, he would plow through it. He's so strong on the puck. We couldn't handle him, and he killed us."

Hossa carried his momentum into the 1998 Memorial Cup, scoring 4 goals with 3 assists in Portland's three round-robin wins to help the Winter Hawks earn a bye directly into the final. And then, with just over five minutes to play in regulation time of a 3–3 hockey game, Guelph Storm winger Ryan Davis took out his knee and Hossa's whole career, everything he had worked for, was suddenly in peril. As soon as he was able to get to a phone after the 4–3 Portland overtime win, Hossa called his parents to give them the bittersweet news.

"We were here at home, in Trencin, waiting for Marian to call and tell us if his team won," Maria Hossa recalled. "He finally called, but his voice was different. I thought maybe he had lost. He said, 'No, we won, but I'm hurt.' I cried."

Three weeks later in Ottawa, with his parents with him at the hospital, Hossa underwent successful reconstructive surgery to repair the torn anterior cruciate ligament in his left knee. That was the good news. The bad news was that Hossa was staring at four months of arduous rehabilitation, at least. He attacked his rehab the same way he attacked opposing nets. Senators strength coach Randy Lee described Hossa's approach to his workouts as going "above and beyond what's normal."

While in Ottawa, Hossa befriended centre Radek Bonk, a Czech native, who helped him get further accustomed to life on this side of the Atlantic Ocean. "It was the first time I was living on my own," Hossa said. "I didn't know how to go to the bank and pay my bills. It doesn't sound like a big thing, maybe, but you need to have everything in your life [in order] so you can focus on your game."

Hossa wasn't allowed to step back on the ice until November, six months after the injury. "I have been in the gym so long," he said joyfully after the solo skate in Ottawa's Corel Centre. "I needed to feel cold." Finally, on December 5, 1998, he received permission from team doctors to play against the New York Rangers. Although he was held pointless on 16 shifts and 11:45 of ice time, Hossa's knee passed with flying colours. He was placed on the third line with Bonk and Magnus Arvedson almost immediately, and the trio quickly became regarded as the best third line in the league. "We went from a checking line to a checking line that could score," Bonk said. "That changed everything."

Hossa really turned it on in March, scoring 6 goals with 4 assists to be named NHL rookie of the month, giving him 15 goals and 15 assists on the year. He finished second to Colorado's Chris Drury in the 1998–99 Calder Trophy balloting despite missing 22 games while recovering from his surgery, and he was named to the league's all-rookie team.

During his first full season in the NHL the following year, Hossa finished third on the team in scoring with 29 goals and 27 assists, but a home game against the Toronto Maple Leafs on March 11, 2000, had a profound effect on the budding star's psyche. Hossa entered that game on a hot streak, with 9 goals in his previous 14 games, one of those zones where you feel everything you put on net will go in.

With less than five minutes to play in the second period, Hossa found a loose puck coming towards him in the Toronto end off a turnover and saw a scoring opportunity. Just as Maple Leafs captain Mats Sundin was slapping the puck out of the zone, Hossa spun around and wound up with a wild swing at the puck. Standing behind Hossa, unbeknownst to him, was Toronto defenceman Bryan Berard. As Hossa completed the follow-through on his ill-advised golf swing at the puck, the heel of his stick struck Berard directly in the right eye, rupturing it. Hossa went to the penalty box and sat there in a complete daze as trainers attended to Berard on the ice, wondering if he had just inadvertently blinded someone he had never even met. Berard was rushed to Ottawa General Hospital and was operated on for three and a half hours as doctors attempted to save the eye.

The following day, a nervous and repentant Hossa went to the hospital to see how Berard was doing and found his parents, Pam and Wally. They recognized him immediately. "He could hardly talk at the hospital," Wally Berard said. "He must have apologized to us four or five times."

As he walked up to Berard's hospital bed, Hossa's eyes welled up with tears as he struggled to find the appropriate words for the moment, if indeed there were any. Instead, he began to cry. If Berard had any resentment for Hossa, he didn't let it out then, or ever, for that matter.

"It was an accident, a freak accident. It could have been me doing it to you," Hossa remembers Berard saying. "He was a very strong man in the hospital. Very strong."

Despite getting Berard's gracious forgiveness, Hossa was not the same player he was before the accident. In the final 13 games of the 1999–2000 regular season Hossa scored only 2 goals, and he was kept completely off the scoresheet in Ottawa's six-game loss to the Maple Leafs in the first round of the playoffs. "I became less aggressive," Hossa said. "I was afraid to do something that might hurt someone. Hockey wasn't fun anymore."

Before leaving for Trencin that summer, Hossa phoned Berard, who told him again that he should get the accident out of his mind, that he needed to concentrate on hockey. In order to do that, Hossa decided it was best to get away from hockey.

He spent the summer playing tennis and hanging out with friends. It worked. Hossa came back for the 2000–01 season focused on hockey again, finishing second in team scoring with 32 goals and 43 assists. But, more importantly, he permanently shed his pre-draft reputation of being a one-dimensional player.

On November 18, 2000, Hossa was asked to kill a penalty for the first time in his Ottawa career. He not only killed off the penalty, he set a franchise record with two short-handed goals in the game, and his assist on another one by Bonk marked the first time the Senators had ever scored three times short-handed in one game. For good measure, Hossa added a power play goal in the same game for his first career hat trick. He was named to the all-star team that season, his first of three all-star selections over four seasons.

In 2002–03, Hossa set another Senators record with 45 goals, topping Alexei Yashin's 44-goal season of 1998–99. The bigger impact came with a goal he scored in the first game of Ottawa's second-round playoff series against the Philadelphia Flyers, where he dangled his way through the Flyers defence for an eternal 15 seconds before setting up centre Bryan Smolinski, which resulted in Hossa scoring on a rebound to tie the game 2–2. Flyers coach Ken Hitchcock said watching Hossa during that sequence made him dizzy.

Ottawa won that game and the series 4–2 before bowing out in game seven of the third round to the eventual Stanley Cup champion New Jersey Devils, marking an end to the Senators' deepest trip into the playoffs in modern team history.

That dizzying goal was more than just fodder for the sports highlight shows, it served notice to the league that Marian Hossa had overcome all the adversity that was strewn on his path and that he had officially arrived as an NHL star.

"It's year by year and step by step, a slow process, and the coach has to trust you," Hossa said. "And then, all of a sudden, you're in a game when you feel nobody can take anything from you, because you have the confidence to do it. That's what I had that game. I knew I could go around people and have control of the puck, and I felt I am able to do what I want to do."

And he's been doing it ever since.

The Sixth Sense

After watching Marian Hossa play for only one season, Ottawa Senators backup goaltender Ron Tugnutt thought he had the exciting Slovakian winger all figured out. Hossa was, quite obviously in Tugnutt's eyes, a psychic.

"You're tempted to say the puck follows him, but it doesn't," Tugnutt said before Hossa began his second year in Ottawa. "He knows where the puck is going to go. Talented players have a knack for that. They go to the open ice and find the puck. And if you give Hossa time with the puck, he's going to do some magnificent things with it. Who knows how good he can be? I'm just glad he doesn't read the papers so he doesn't see all the great things people say about him."

Those people have continued saying great things about him his entire career, just as Hossa keeps getting to the puck a half second before it gets there.

Chapter Four

Roberto Luongo

Florida Panthers general manager Bryan Murray was sitting at the 1997 NHL entry draft, biding his time until his team's 20th pick rolled around. He watched as one potential franchise player after another got snatched up by other teams. After the New York Islanders used the fourth selection on a lanky goaltender from Montréal by the name of Roberto Luongo, Murray longingly asked anyone within earshot, "Why can't we ever get players like that?"

Murray was not the only hockey type sitting in the Calgary Saddledome that day dreaming of Luongo guarding their net. By that point, all of 18 years old, Luongo had already established himself as a potential difference-maker, a goalie who could win games by himself. His reputation as an elite netminder at that age was certainly not misplaced; Luongo had accomplished more than enough to warrant the heavy praise. But it would certainly have been shocking to Luongo if anyone had told him when he began tending goal at the age of 11 that he'd one day have NHL general managers fawning over him seven years later.

Luongo, who grew up in the heavily Italian Montréal suburb of St-Leonard, was the eldest of Tony and Pasquelina Luongo's three sons. He was enrolled in the local minor hockey league when he was eight—very late for a Canadian kid. Although Luongo wanted desperately to play goal, his parents thought he should work on his skating as a forward first. He gave it a shot, playing on lower-level intercity teams for three years before being cut from his Atom CC team. It was only then, at the age of 11, that Luongo decided to take his shot between the pipes.

As the years went by, Luongo forgot the name of that coach who cut him in Atom, but he's grateful nonetheless. "It's thanks to him that I'm playing goalie," Luongo said.

It didn't take Luongo very long to climb into the upper echelon of up and coming Québec goalies, a status that is not easily attainable in a province that has produced more NHL goalies than any other place on earth. At the age of 15, Luongo went to play Midget AAA hockey for Montréal-Bourassa, a program that had already produced NHL netminders Martin Brodeur, Felix Potvin, Stéphane Fiset and Éric Fichaud, among others.

Luongo spent the 1994–95 season under the tutelage of Montréal-Bourassa goaltending coaches Mario Baril and François Allaire, the latter of which is widely credited with developing and fine-tuning the butterfly style made popular by Patrick Roy and copied by goalies worldwide. Luongo put together a solid rookie season with a 3.85 goals against average in 25 games in the high-scoring Québec midget AAA league, making him one of the most sought-after players for the 1995 Québec Major Junior Hockey League (QMJHL) draft.

Luongo's family didn't want to deprive their son of any opportunities, but they also didn't want him to completely depend on a hockey career. He was a strong student in high school, and U.S. colleges were already calling with scholarship offers. As the draft approached, Luongo and his parents came to an understanding. "We didn't think about hockey as a career then, I didn't know how far it could take him," Luongo's mother said. "We made a deal that if he was drafted in the first round, he'd go to juniors, and if he wasn't he'd wait for college. He was the second overall pick, so we didn't have a choice."

That pick was made by the Val D'Or Foreurs, making Luongo the highest-drafted goalie in QMJHL history, and it was quite possibly the best move in franchise history. Luongo was an instant success in Val D'Or, appearing in 23 games as a 16-year-old rookie and posting a solid 3.70 goals against with a 6–11–4 record.

Luongo set a franchise record in 1996–97 with 32 wins while allowing a scant average of 3.10 goals against in 60 games with a .901 save percentage, numbers nearly unheard of in the high-octane QMJHL. In the playoffs, he almost single-handedly led Val D'Or to a five-game playoff upset over the Memorial Cup champion Granby Prédateurs.

"He's the guy who has carried this team," Val D'Or general manager Michel Georges said during the playoffs. "He has been the inspiration for the rest of the guys. When we drafted him, we were looking for a guy who could carry the team in two years. He proved to everybody he could be that guy."

The most impressive asset of Luongo's game in the eyes of NHL scouts was his capacity to remain calm. Luongo never appeared the least bit bothered by anything, whether he allowed six goals or shut out the opposition. That calm was a result of all the responsibilities that Luongo had shouldered while growing up in St-Leonard.

"He's always been quiet, modest and mature," Luongo's mother said. "When he was young, his father and I owned a shoe store and there were many times when he had to leave him in charge of his two younger brothers or, with his father working so much, when he had to be the man of the house. He was very mature at a young age, he was almost like a second father."

Luongo was, and still is, a break from the conventional mold of elite goaltenders, almost exclusively smaller and therefore more agile and quick. But he was 6-foot-3, 180 pounds at the time, sporting size 15 feet. When he dropped down into his butterfly stance, it was almost as if he was casting an eclipse on the net, with just a thin outline of mesh visible to shooters.

"Roberto is the prototype goalie for the year 2000," Allaire said later. "He's got the perfect profile for today's NHL. He's different from a lot of the older goaltenders—he's got size, but for a big guy he's really athletic."

New York Islanders general manager Mike Milbury shared Allaire's assessment of the young Luongo, using his fourth overall pick to make him the highest-drafted goalie in NHL history in 1997, at the same time making Florida Panthers general manager Bryan Murray's mouth water.

Luongo was sent back to junior and had the best year of his young career. At the midpoint of the 1997–98 season, he was selected to serve as the backup goalie for Canada's entry to the world junior championships.

Canada finished a disappointing eighth at the worlds in 1998. After finishing Canada's 6–3 loss to lowly Kazakhstan in the seventh/eighth place game, Luongo sought out Hockey Canada director of scouting Barry Trapp, gave him a hug, and told him it would be a different story a year later.

"I knew right then and there who the number one goalie would be [in 1999]," Trapp said later.

Luongo returned to Val D'Or and led the Foreurs to the 1998 QMJHL championship and a berth in the Memorial Cup. In their opening game, Luongo was astounding, making 49 saves as Val D'Or lost 5–4 to the Spokane Chiefs. Even though his team didn't win a single game in the tournament, Luongo cemented his status as the next dominant product of the Québec goaltending factory.

At the 1999 national junior camp in Winnipeg, Luongo entered as the undisputed number one netminder, based largely on what he had told Trapp a year earlier. "This was his position to lose," Trapp said. "When he goes down into that butterfly, you tell me what part of the net you can see?"

Canada not only had the home-ice advantage in Winnipeg, they also had a decided advantage in nets. Luongo's play carried a pretty mediocre team—only by Canadian standards, mind you—to the championship final against Russia. He posted two shutouts, stopped a tournament-leading 94.2 per cent of the shots fired his way and allowed an average of 1.92 pucks to get past him per game.

Against Russia, Canada was smothered by a better-skating team, but thanks to Luongo, and a third period goal by Bryan Allen, they were able to finish regulation tied 2–2. But it didn't take the Russians long to claim the championship with a goal just

over five minutes into the overtime period, leading an exhausted and distraught Luongo to lie
motionless in his crease as the Russian team celebrated its victory right in front of the net.

As he skated up to centre ice to accept his award
as the tournament's top goaltender, Luongo had
tears in his eyes. "I'd trade the honours for the gold
medal," Luongo told reporters upon his arrival at
Montréal's Dorval Airport following the tournament. "I really wanted to win gold."

While Luongo was away with the national team,
the rebuilding Foreurs traded him to the Bathurst
Titan, and Luongo promptly led that team to the
1999 Memorial Cup.

The Islanders signed Luongo to a three-year contract shortly after watching him perform at the
world juniors, prompting Milbury to say, "In time,
we believe that he can be an elite goaltender."

Apparently, Luongo didn't progress fast enough
for Milbury's liking. Luongo spent the 1999–2000
season bouncing back and forth between the
Islanders and their American Hockey League affiliate, the Lowell Lock Monsters. Luongo's NHL
debut finally came on November 28, 1999, against
the Bruins in Boston, and it was one to remember.
Luongo stopped 43 shots that night to lead the
Islanders to a 2–1 win, providing a glimpse of what
he was capable of at the NHL level.

Yet Milbury continued antagonizing his young
star, once publicly questioning Luongo's decision to

spend the day looking for an apartment when he was supposed to play that night, and finally sending him back down to Lowell with Luongo one start short of earning a significant salary bonus.

A week before the 2000 draft, word spread that Milbury was looking to trade Luongo as he eyed Boston College standout Rick DiPietro to be the Islanders' new goalie of the future. Florida Panthers general manager, Bryan Murray, who had never forgotten watching Luongo step up to the podium in 1997, was quick to get Milbury on the phone. After a week of negotiations, Milbury selected DiPietro with the first pick overall, breaking his own record for the highest-drafted goalie in NHL history. Milbury then packaged Luongo and centre Olli Jokinen—who was drafted just before Luongo at third overall in 1997—to the Panthers for forwards Mark Parrish and Oleg Kvasha.

"As the draft progressed, it was clear that the value of Luongo was greater than the value of the first overall pick," Milbury explained to bewildered reporters. "We're rolling the dice a little bit. Roberto is going to be an excellent goaltender in this league. He's a class act and a kid we'd have been happy to ride with. But in our mind, if we could get DiPietro, he possessed an element that Roberto perhaps does not possess. He handles the puck as well as any goaltender in hockey today, not just any young prospect, anyone in any league anywhere."

For the Islanders, it went down as probably the worst trade in franchise history. For the Panthers, however, it was like winning the lottery without having to buy a ticket.

"Our scouts all know him, and they're all awfully excited right now," a beaming Murray said. "He's been excellent throughout his career...All I know is you don't get to the top level and win—or even compete—if you don't have a top goaltender."

Luongo was surprised at the move, considering he was never given a real shot at the number one job in Long Island, but he knew he would get that opportunity immediately in Florida. He took to his new spot on the Panthers roster with a new lease on his hockey life. He played in 47 games in 2000–01, compiled a 12–24–7 record for one of the worst teams in the league and had a sparkling 2.44 goals against average with five shutouts. His .920 save percentage was sixth best in the NHL that year and tied for second-best all-time for a rookie.

Luongo was selected to represent Canada at the 2001 world championships following the season, but his tournament was cut short when he broke the index finger on his right hand while stopping a slap shot. Armed with a new four-year contract, Luongo entered Panthers training camp in 2001 as the team's clear number one goalie. He put up the same kind of numbers, but his season ended in March after tearing a ligament in his right ankle.

In 2002–03, Luongo once again had a solid year for a bad Panthers team to earn another trip to the world championships. He never forgot his disappointment in losing the world junior final to Russia four years earlier. "That was a great experience, one of the best of my life," Luongo said at the start of the tournament. "If it wasn't for that goal in overtime, things would have been that much greater. I think about that a lot, especially when you're back here playing internationally. This is my chance to redeem myself and, hopefully, this year will be the one where I get the gold."

Luongo's words proved to be prophetic. Canadian starter Sean Burke pulled a groin in Canada's 8–4 semi-final win over the Czech Republic, so Luongo played the final against Sweden. After allowing two goals in the first period to fall behind 2–0, Canada rode Luongo's 37-save performance to a 3–2 win. Luongo had his redemption.

"After they scored their second goal I was a little mad, I told myself, 'I can't let any more in,'" Luongo said after receiving the gold medal. "Now I know what it feels like to be on the other side. It's a beautiful thing, a beautiful day for Canada."

Although the world championship gold medal proved Luongo could play in the big game, it wasn't until the 2003–04 season that his name was grouped with the best goalies in hockey. The Panthers were relying on a young and inexperienced defensive squad that year, and opposing forwards knew just how to take advantage. They peppered Luongo with a barrage of shots that season; they came from all angles and came in bunches.

Luongo played in his first all-star game that year, winning the goaltending portion of the all-star skills competition. By the end of the season, Luongo had faced 40 or more shots 15 times and had a 6–7–2 record in those games. His shutout total of 23 before his 25th birthday was one better than Martin Brodeur had at the same age. Even though Luongo set an NHL record with 2475 shots against and 2303 saves, his save percentage of .931 was still third best in the NHL.

"Not too many goalies make you have a meeting about the goalie, and he's one guy that you do," Philadelphia Flyers coach Ken Hitchcock said. "Psychologically, he can really get to people. He makes saves that border on unbelievable, and that becomes psychological after a while."

Luongo led Canada to another gold medal at the world championships in 2004, and his performance earned him a spot as the backup to Brodeur on Canada's entry in the World Cup of Hockey. Brodeur had sprained his left wrist in Canada's last round-robin game, which meant that Luongo would be in nets for the semi-final against the Czech Republic.

Luongo had been in the same situation two years earlier at the world championships, and the result this time was the same—Canada won

4–3 in overtime. Just like he did in the world championship gold medal game against Sweden, Luongo had a 37-save performance as Canada advanced to the final before dispatching Finland 3–2 to win the gold medal.

With those performances behind him, Luongo officially removed a tag that had followed him throughout his career. He was commonly known as the best young goalie in the NHL but that wasn't enough for Luongo.

"Forget young," Luongo once said. "Bottom line is, I want to be the best. That's it. I want to be the best in the world."

Hello, Bonjour, or Ciao—It's All the Same to Luongo

Roberto Luongo was born to an Italian immigrant father and an Irish-Canadian mother, so growing up he comfortably grasped French, English and Italian. Although Luongo left home at the age of 16 to play junior hockey, the Italian side of his heritage was never too far away.

In Val D'Or, Luongo spent two years as a billet with an Italian family there who he still keeps in touch with to this day. Once Luongo moved on to Miami, it didn't take him long to find another Italian family to take him in. A pizza restaurant in Coral Springs owned by Bobby Cerbone and Guy D'Aiuto quickly became Luongo's second home.

"They're my family," Luongo said. "I feel as comfortable with them as I do with my own family."

The gang at the Pizza Time Restaurant soon formed a fan club called Luongo's Legion, and they became well known as the rowdiest fans at Panthers games.

"There were about 30 of us, all Italian," Cerbone recalled. "One game we start singing this soccer song, 'Ole, ole, ole, ole,' and all of a sudden the whole arena joined with us, and it was beautiful. Then it flashed on the screen, 'Luongo's Legion is here.' So they named us."

Chapter Five

Jarome Iginla

Jarome Iginla has had his doubters for most of his life. There were the kids in his Alberta hometown of St. Albert who didn't believe a black player could ever make the NHL; the Western Hockey League (WHL) scouts who ignored him in the bantam draft; the Calgary media who questioned the Flames' wisdom of trading Joe Nieuwendyk for an unknown commodity still in junior; the NHL officials who left his name off the all-star ballot; the Hockey Canada officials who only invited him to the Olympic orientation camp as a last-minute injury replacement; and, most notably, Jarome Iginla himself.

But in the end, Iginla has proved them all wrong. He's become the world's most complete and intimidating forward, someone who can provide his team with the big goal, the big hit, or even the momentum-turning fight.

Jarome Arthur Leigh Adekunle Tig Junior Elvis Iginla—the official name on his birth certificate—was a Canada Day baby, born on July 1, 1977, in Edmonton, Alberta. His father, Elvis Iginla, immigrated to Canada from Lagos, Nigeria, three years earlier and married an Oregon-born woman named Susan Schuchard, but the two divorced before Jarome's second birthday.

Schuchard raised Iginla as a single mother, with a lot of help from her parents, in the lily-white Edmonton suburb of St. Albert, though Iginla remains close with his father, an Edmonton-based lawyer. From an early age, even though he was a talented athlete who was the starting catcher for the Canadian Junior Baseball Team, Iginla's ambitions were firmly rooted in hockey. But as the son of a black Nigerian father and white American mother, few gave the youngster much of a chance of realizing his dream.

"As soon as I started playing hockey at the age of seven, I wanted to be an NHL player," Iginla said. "Sometimes, kids might say, 'There aren't very many black people in the NHL,' and I was aware of it. There weren't very many, but I followed how they all did...It meant a lot to me to be able to see other black hockey players in the NHL."

Schuchard knew she had to prepare her son for all the taunts and racially motivated slurs that would be sent his way as he navigated the minor hockey ranks. She taught him very early on that there was no way he could control what other people said or did, but the one thing he could control was the way he reacted.

Schuchard remembered a moment where it became evident that her son had taken in all of the advice she had given him. "It was another player," she said. "He couldn't tell the difference when Jarome had his helmet on, but when he took it off, the kid said, 'You're just a nigger.' Jarome just shrugged and shook his head."

Iginla also had the advantage of growing up as a huge fan of the Edmonton Oilers during their glory days of the 1980s. One of the pillars of that dynasty was the Oilers netminder, Grant Fuhr. Fuhr shared Iginla's mixed bloodlines and tinted skin colour and served as a wonderful inspiration for the young Iginla. "I remember saying, 'Look, there are black players, and Fuhr's not just playing, he's starring,'" Iginla said.

Iginla took that inspiration and ran with it. Although WHL scouts passed him over in the bantam draft, 15-year-old Iginla opened some eyes in Alberta by scoring 34 goals in 36 games for the St. Albert Saints in 1993. Later that fall he moved to Kamloops, BC, to play for the WHL's Blazers. The team's decision makers tried to ease the rookie into the system so he ended up languishing on the bench, or some nights, in the press box.

"I was on a very good team," Iginla says. "I felt I was as good as or better than some of the other young players in the league who were playing more on worse teams. It worked out in the long run, but it was difficult to take then."

Iginla posted 9 points in 19 playoff games for Kamloops that year as they won the WHL title before going on to win the 1994 Memorial Cup, the Blazers' first of two in a row. In 1995, after a 71-point season playing on a Memorial Cup–winning team that featured future NHLers Shane Doan, Darcy Tucker, Tyson Nash and others, Iginla was selected 11th overall in the NHL entry draft by the Dallas Stars. As if that wasn't sweet enough, the draft was held in Iginla's hometown of Edmonton, within earshot of all those kids who years earlier had told him there wasn't room for a black player in the NHL.

Iginla was on his way to the best season of his career with Kamloops when, on December 19, 1995, Dallas traded his rights along with goaltender Corey Millen to the Calgary Flames for star centre Joe Nieuwendyk. The day after the trade, a Calgary newspaper ran the headline "Jarome Who?" But it didn't take long for Flames fans to figure out exactly who Iginla was. He was their new franchise player.

A few weeks after the big trade, Iginla set about building his legend. He was named MVP for notching a tournament-leading 12 points in six games to lead Canada to the 1996 world junior championship in Boston, scoring the eventual game-winner against Russia in the gold medal game. Upon his return to Kamloops, he put the finishing touches on a dominant season of 63 goals and 73 assists for 136 points in only 63 games to earn a spot on the Canadian Hockey League's first all-star team. But the Blazers got knocked out in the WHL playoffs, denying Iginla a third straight trip to the Memorial Cup.

The same night that the Kamloops' season ended, the Flames requested Iginla's presence in Calgary the next morning, where they were playing game three of their first-round playoff series with the Chicago Blackhawks. Iginla woke up early the next day and boarded a flight for Calgary, having no idea what to expect, or why he was even going. He had a quick meeting with Flames general manager Al Coates and signed his first NHL contract about an hour before the game. He then headed down to the dressing room to join his new teammates, whom only a day earlier he considered his heroes. The whole process had happened so quickly that he didn't even have time to get nervous.

Iginla was placed on the first line centring the Flames' star winger Theoren Fleury and German Titov, and he thrived almost instantly. He set up a goal by Fleury and dropped the Blackhawks' perennial all-star defenceman Chris Chelios with a hard check, not once, but twice.

"The biggest thing is you go from watching the NHL playoffs the night before, seeing the highlights, cheering for Calgary, watching Theo and

Trevor Kidd and Titov, cheering against Chelios and Ed Belfour. These are guys I'm looking up to one night wondering, 'Wouldn't it be awesome to play?'" Iginla said. "Because I don't know if I'm going to play an NHL game, ever. I want to. I'm planning on it. I'm dreaming of it. But you don't know when that day's going to be. Then, all of a sudden, it's literally overnight."

Although the Flames lost that game 7–5 to fall behind 3–0 in the series, Iginla had left his impression on his Flames teammates. "I remember after that game," Coates said, "Fleury coming over to me and telling me, 'That kid can play on my line any time.'"

Iginla scored the Flames lone goal in his second game on a low snap shot from the slot at 5:53 of the second period, but Calgary lost a triple-overtime marathon 2–1 as Chicago completed the sweep.

A few months later, on October 5, 1996, Iginla played his first regular season game in Vancouver and scored his first career goal, a great first step towards a solid rookie season of 21 goals and 50 points to finish second in the Calder Trophy balloting for rookie of the year honours. But what Iginla didn't know then was that game four against Chicago a year earlier was the last playoff game he would play for a long time, as the Flames embarked on a rebuilding program that kept them out of the post-season seven years in a row.

Iginla was the centrepiece of the Flames' youth movement, but his progression towards NHL stardom moved a little slower than Calgary would have liked. His goal total dropped to 13 in 70 games his sophomore season, but he rebounded with 28 goals in 82 games in 1998–99. Iginla's breakthrough came the following year when he posted career highs of 29 goals and 34 assists for 63 points, enjoying a 16-game point streak along the way. He improved slightly on those career marks in the 2000–01 season, but Iginla's best was yet to come.

In the late summer of 2001, Canada's best hockey players were converging on Calgary for the Olympic team's orientation camp. Iginla wasn't on the list of invitees, but since he didn't particularly feel he deserved to be there, he didn't take it as a slight. Then, Philadelphia Flyers forward Simon Gagné hurt his shoulder, and a spot suddenly opened up. Team Canada's executive director Wayne Gretzky—one of Iginla's boyhood idols—extended an invitation to the up-and-coming Flames forward. Gretzky called Iginla's then-fiancée Kara Kirkland (they were married in 2003) with the news, and when she told Iginla, he figured it was his Flames teammate Marc Savard pulling a prank. "I can just imagine pulling in there with all my equipment, and have them say, 'What does this guy think he's doing here?'" Iginla said.

Iginla's presence at the camp not only endeared him to the Team Canada executives in charge of selecting the team, it also erased any doubts he may have had about his place among the NHL's elite. "It's funny how things work out," Iginla said. "I'm sure one of the reasons I got to go to the camp at all was because it was in Calgary and I was in Calgary. Gagné got hurt and I was there, pretty handy, to fill in. And I can't tell you how much being there did for my confidence, seeing that I could keep up with all those stars. That really helped launch my season."

Iginla began the 2001–02 season with his second career "Gordie Howe Hat Trick"—one goal, one assist and one fight—in a 4–2 road win over the daunting Red Wings at Detroit. In fact, Iginla had 2 assists in that game.

Then in October, in a 3–1 win over the Florida Panthers, Iginla embarked on a 15-game points streak during which he scored a whopping 18 goals with 13 assists for 31 points to take a stranglehold on the league scoring race that he would never relinquish.

Although Iginla's performance that season— 52 goals and 96 points—earned him the Lester B. Pearson MVP Trophy as voted by the players, his breakthrough moment came at the Salt Lake City Olympics in February 2002. He scored his first goal of the tournament in Canada's 7–1 whipping of Belarus in the semi-final. But in the gold medal game against the host United States, Iginla's line with Joe Sakic and Gagné was easily the most dominant on the ice.

Iginla gave Canada a 2–1 lead in the first period, driving hard to the net and fighting off a Brian Leetch check to convert a beautiful cross-ice feed from Sakic. The U.S. tied it 2–2 in the second, but Sakic restored Canada's lead before the end of the period with a power play goal from the point. The third period was some of the best hockey ever played, as the Americans tried desperately to tie the contest as the clock continued to tick down towards a Canadian victory.

Iginla iced the game for Canada with just under four minutes left when his shot from the slot bounced off the trapper of U.S. goalie Mike Richter and flew up in the air, eventually bouncing behind Richter and slowly trickling across the goal line.

The line combined for 8 points between them to lead the charge in a 5–2 victory that broke a 50-year Olympic drought for the Canadian hockey program and sent Iginla on the road to superstardom.

"Looking back, it's the final game that I'll remember the most," Iginla said on the one-year anniversary of the gold medal win. "The game was so intense. I didn't think about winning or losing until the last three minutes. That's when I thought, 'We're going to have this.' It was just the best feeling."

As great as that feeling was, Iginla experienced more success in the 2003–04 season that would rival his Olympic euphoria. His Calgary Flames— who still hadn't played a playoff game since Iginla was a teenager—finally squeaked their way into the post-season tourney in 2004 despite a subpar second half of the season. Iginla started that season very slowly, but he rebounded to finish the year tied for the league-lead in goals with 41. In the playoffs, however, Iginla took his game to new heights. Every time Calgary needed a big goal, Iginla answered the call. He scored twice in game seven of Calgary's first-round series against the Vancouver Canucks and set up Martin Gelinas' series-winning goal in overtime.

In the second round against the high-powered Red Wings, Iginla helped create Calgary's only goals in a pair of 1–0 wins that gave the Flames the series in six games. Against the San Jose Sharks in round three, he scored the first goals in Calgary's 3–0 win in game five and its 3–1 series-clinching win in game six.

By the time the Flames had reached the Stanley Cup final against the Tampa Bay Lightning, Iginla had game-winning points in half of Calgary's 12 playoff wins. In game five of the final, with the series tied 2–2, Iginla had what his centreman Craig Conroy called "the greatest shift I've ever seen." With just over five minutes to play in the first overtime of a 2–2 hockey game, Iginla lost his helmet early in the shift, nearly set up a goal with a backhand pass, backchecked to win the puck back for Calgary, motored back up ice and unleashed a mammoth slap shot on Lightning goalie Nikolai Khabibulin. The rebound was too much for Khabibulin to handle, and Oleg Saprykin banged home the rebound to give Calgary the win and a 3–2 series lead.

Even though the Flames lost the next two games and the series, Iginla cemented his status as one of the NHL's next great poster boys. He can light up the scoresheet, drop the gloves, drive you into the boards, give a great interview and still sign every autograph requested of him afterwards. In short, his doubters have been silenced for good.

Need a Room?

Jarome Iginla's strengths are well documented, but if he has one weakness, it may be that he is too nice. Iginla was dining at a Salt Lake City eatery with his extended family during the Olympics when his waitress told him there were four men from Calgary sitting at another table. Iginla got up, walked over to their table and sat down for a little 10-minute powwow. The four men had driven down from Calgary to Utah and bought some tickets from a scalper to watch Canada play the Czech Republic during the round-robin portion of the tournament.

Since hotel rooms in Salt Lake City were completely non-existent, the four men were sleeping in their car in the parking lot of a local hotel. Having heard their tale, Iginla got up and went back to his family. A few minutes later, he returned to tell the guys he had booked them in the local Marriott Courtyard, and he even wrote down some directions to the hotel. When the fans from Calgary checked out of the hotel the next day, they found out that Iginla had not only secured the reservation, he had paid the $250 for the room as well.

Chapter Six

Zdeno Chara

Z deno Chara was considered a throw-in, an appendage to a trade that was bigger than him, even though he was the biggest player in NHL history. The main attractions of the draft-day deal on June 23, 2001, were Alexei Yashin, who sat out the entire year in a contract dispute with the Ottawa Senators, and Jason Spezza, a heavily-hyped super-prospect with franchise player potential.

Chara, to that point in his career with the New York Islanders, was considered by most hockey fans as a novelty act, a 6-foot-9, 255-pound Goliath on skates. That reputation was perpetuated by the Islanders' coaching staff, who insisted Chara concentrate only on playing mistake-free and clearing bodies away from the front of his net. Rushing up ice, or carrying the puck for that matter, was extremely frowned upon. So Chara's inclusion in the blockbuster trade that sent Yashin to the

Islanders for winger Bill Muckalt and the second pick in the draft, which the Senators used to get Spezza, was hardly headline material.

But what nobody knew then—and what everybody knows now—was that the throw-in would be the most valuable piece of that deal.

"When I compare Yashin and Chara," said the engineer of that trade, former Senators general manager Marshall Johnston, less than two years later, "I like that deal one-for-one."

It was never easy for Chara to shed the label of simply being a big defenceman. Of course, when you're seven feet tall in skates and use a stick that's six feet long, it's not an easy reputation to shake. His parents, Zdenek and Viktoria Chara, were hardly short at 6-foot-2 and 5-foot-9, respectively, but they weren't exactly ducking to get through doors.

❦

As a boy growing up under communism in the Slovakian textile town of Trencin, Chara helped his family tend to their animals, but he was also being groomed to become an elite athlete.

Chara's father, a Greco-Roman wrestler who represented the former Czechoslovakia at the 1976 Montréal Olympics, put the 13-year-old Chara under a training regimen. The boy worked out three times a day; he ran before breakfast, lifted weights after breakfast and cycled at night. "Many times, he pushed me so hard that I ended up crying," Chara said years later. "I would wonder why he was so mean to me, but I didn't understand what he was trying to do. He meant it in a good way."

Chara was a reasonably big teenager for his age, but when he was 16 years old he shot up six inches to 6-foot-6. All of a sudden he was unusually huge. "I remember one night," his father said, "he called me into his room and told me that he could feel his thighs growing."

Chara didn't adapt very quickly to his new stature, and it showed on the ice. "It was a very tough time for me," he said. "I was growing so fast my coordination couldn't keep up."

Hockey coaches in Slovakia, most particularly in Trencin, were accustomed to players who had speed and skill. Trencin is home to such NHL snipers as Marian Hossa, Marian Gaborik and Pavol Demitra, among others. Faced with such a unique case as Chara, Trencin's hockey coaches didn't really know what to make of the gangly teenager, or what to do with him. Players with size were less coveted in Europe because the large international ice surface—about 3000 square feet bigger than a North American rink—made speed a more valuable trait than brute force. Almost every Slovakian player that made the NHL played forward, and the country had never produced a single star defenceman.

Most everyone encouraged Chara to forget hockey and concentrate on a sport where his height would be more useful—basketball. But when Chara ripped down the rim while dunking a ball at his neighbourhood school, he was no longer welcome to play that either. So Chara continued playing hockey, despite all his detractors.

At 17, Chara played Junior B hockey for Trencin, but by then he was so big that finding equipment that fit him became a real challenge. Chara's shin pads were too short and his shoulder pads so small they were almost useless. Worse still, Chara played the second half of that season with one skate blade separated from the boot. Since he was playing such a low level of hockey, he wasn't a priority case for new equipment in Trencin, so Chara used duct tape to hold his skate together. "It wasn't too bad," Chara recalls. "I wanted to play, so I made the best of the situation. It was no big deal."

The Islanders, despite Chara's lack of experience, were impressed enough with his size to take him with the 56th pick of the 1996 NHL entry draft. All of a sudden, Chara, never even selected to play on his own junior national team, was being given a chance. But he couldn't see himself taking full advantage of that opportunity playing at home, where no one believed he should be playing hockey in the first place, so Chara moved to Canada to play with the Prince George Cougars of the Western Hockey League (WHL).

"If I had stayed [in Slovakia], I probably wouldn't be playing hockey today, I'm sure," Chara later said. "It was probably the best thing that happened to me."

Although Trencin's coaches had no idea how to take advantage of Chara's dimensions, he was a coach's dream in the rough and tumble WHL. Chara still needed to work on his mobility, but there was no one who could challenge him physically and get away with it.

"Zee was a lot different than other guys, so if you tried to measure him using all the usual standards, you could think this guy could never play," said Stan Butler, Chara's coach in Prince George. "But he would do things that wouldn't just surprise you, they'd shock you."

The smaller North American rinks suited Chara's game to perfection, allowing him to better use his reach and sparing him the chore of having to chase darty forwards when he could just drill them into the boards instead. He also gained a reputation as one of the league's best fighters, using his leverage to throw tough guys around like rag dolls. "Because my dad was a wrestler, he taught me very early how to protect myself, to stand up for myself," Chara said. "He knew how to prepare me."

After helping the Cougars make a decent run in the 1996–97 WHL playoffs, Chara signed a three-year contract with the Islanders and, after some grooming in the minors, made his NHL debut in Detroit on November 19, 1997.

Over the following two seasons Chara showed significant improvement. The Islanders preached simplicity to their new defenceman, and he followed their every word, chipping the puck off the glass and out of his zone whenever he got the chance. In 1998–99, officially his rookie season, Chara averaged 18:54 of ice time per game while leading the Islanders in hits and finishing fourth on the team in blocked shots. At the end of the season Chara's talent was finally validated by the Slovakian national hockey program when he was invited to play in the world championships, the first time he represented his country in international competition. It soon became a habit.

Chara played for Slovakia again in the 2000 world championships and helped lead the team to a silver medal, the best result ever for the tiny country of about 5.5 million people. The team's performance caused such a frenzy that Slovakian Prime Minister Mikulas Dzurinda made a surprise trip to St. Petersburg, Russia, to watch the final—a 5–3 loss to their Czech rivals—and the country hired two private jets to fly the team home, where their adoring public awaited them.

Chara appeared to have gained confidence with Slovakia's performance and showed up for training camp in the fall of 2000 ready to make his mark in the NHL. Although the Islanders were still curtailing Chara's burgeoning offensive abilities, he displayed improved consistency. He averaged 22:20 of ice time in playing all 82 games that year, one of only three Islanders players to do so, and he led the NHL with 373 hits.

The next spring, as Chara was relaxing at home in Trencin after his third straight world championship appearance, he got a phone call informing him that he had been traded to the Ottawa Senators. Although he didn't know it at the time, the trade would give his hockey career a massive boost.

The Senators had just suffered their third straight elimination in the first round of the playoffs. It was the second year in a row the Toronto Maple Leafs had knocked Ottawa out in the first round, and the second time in three years the Senators failed to win a single playoff game. In short, the Senators were widely seen as the softest team in the NHL.

Chara was perfectly suited to toughen the Senators up, while Ottawa also managed to get some offensive talent in return for Yashin by drafting Spezza. In essence, Ottawa got the top North American prospect in the draft and the biggest player in NHL history in exchange for someone who didn't play a single game for the Senators all season. Although the general public wasn't making much of Chara's move to the Senators, his new teammates couldn't have been happier to welcome their hulking new defenceman. For Marian Hossa, who grew up a few blocks away in Trencin, being boyhood friends didn't change the fact that Chara made his life painful whenever he attempted to go anywhere near the net.

"I'm a lot happier that he's on my team," Hossa said in the weeks following the deal. "I've talked to Marty [Havlat] and Radek [Bonk] too, and they're pleased they don't have to go against him anymore."

Chara thought he knew exactly why Ottawa traded for him, and as soon as he arrived he began talking up his strength. "I like to play physical, to make it really uncomfortable for the other team's top players to play against me," he said. "That's my game."

Except that Ottawa's front office had seen something in Chara that the Islanders never did: a major offensive weapon. Head coach Jacques Martin emancipated Chara from his chains, encouraging him to rush the puck if he saw an opening, and eventually moving him onto the power play to act as a gargantuan screen in front of the goalie. The first time Chara filled that role for Ottawa, he scored a goal to end a five-game string where Ottawa went 1-for-17 with the man advantage.

Chara thrived on all the new responsibility. In his first season in Ottawa he scored 10 goals, four more than in his 231 previous NHL games combined. He also set new career marks with 13 assists, 23 points, 4 power play goals, 2 game-winning goals and a plus-30 defensive rating, the best on the team and fifth best in the NHL.

"When we saw him before with the Islanders, we knew that what he brought was the physical dimension," said Senators captain Daniel Alfredsson, after about half a season playing with Chara.

"But he's mobile, he's good with the puck and he doesn't panic. I think we've really been surprised with his skill."

Finally, for the first time in his life, let alone his career, Chara was being judged on something other than just his size.

But in February 2002 Chara had one of the biggest disappointments of his life at the Olympics in Salt Lake City. Because Slovakia was a relative newcomer on the international scene, and despite their silver medal at the 2000 world championships, they had to play in a tournament to qualify for the Games. The problem was that the qualification tournament took place while the NHL schedule was still on, so nearly all of the Slovakian players had to miss at least one of their NHL games if they wanted to play in all the Olympic qualifiers, something none of their teams would allow.

Hossa and Chara were released by the Ottawa Senators to play in Slovakia's second qualification game against Latvia. With a 3–0 loss to Germany already in the books, the Slovakians had to beat Latvia and then Austria if they wanted any shot at the main draw.

Hossa and Chara played a game against the Detroit Red Wings, then got on an overnight flight to arrive in Salt Lake City at 6 AM, the morning of the Latvia game. The two players went straight to their hotel room and slept until noon when they heard a knock on the door. Chara opened the door and saw Slovakian general manager Peter Stastny standing there with head coach Jan Filc. They had bad news.

Because Washington Capitals star Peter Bondra was available for Slovakia's game against Austria, Stastny and Filc needed to keep a roster spot open for him to play. Since neither Chara nor Hossa were released by the Senators to play against Austria, one of them would have to sit out against Latvia, and it was deemed Hossa would be more valuable in the game than Chara.

Once again Chara was being left out because he did not fit the mold of the ideal Slovakian player. It was akin to being left at an Olympic altar. But Chara took the snub, only the latest in a long line of them from his native country, like a man. A bigger man than most.

"There's nothing I can do about it," Chara said hours after hearing the bad news. "We can only have so many players, and because we lost [against Germany], we have to win the next two games... I wanted to attend the Olympics, to do the best for my country. On the other hand, sometimes you have to sacrifice. They made the decision. I respect it. It's fine."

Upon his arrival back in Ottawa, Chara prepared for the biggest test of his hockey life—playing in the first playoff game of his career. Senators fans couldn't wait. For years they had watched as their hockey team got pushed around like little boys being bullied at recess, and they were all counting on Chara to make that a thing of the past. But it wasn't only the fans; having Chara wearing their jersey gave the Senators a newfound sense of physical confidence. It was as if each of the players had put on 10 pounds by his mere presence.

"He's going to enjoy this, he's a playoff type of guy," Hossa said just before the Senators were to take on the big and tough Philadelphia Flyers. "You don't have to be afraid with him at your back."

The Flyers weren't particularly concerned about the Senators, relying on the old perception of how to eliminate Ottawa in the first round. "All we have to do," Flyers enforcer Donald Brashear said before the series, "is play them physical."

But Chara made some of Philadelphia's biggest forwards eat Brashear's words. Ottawa lost the first game of the series, but then went on to win the next three by identical 3–0 scores, and Chara's presence started to wear on the Flyers stars. "Oh my God," Philadelphia centreman Jeremy Roenick said, "with his wingspan and size, it's like he's about 13 feet long."

The Senators took game five 2–1 in overtime to make it past the first round for the first time in four years, earning them a date with their annual spring dance partners—the hated Toronto Maple Leafs. The Senators were really going to find out if their off-season deal would bear fruit. Ottawa won 5–0 on the road in game one, but the Maple

Leafs came back to knot the series at one with a 3–2 win. The two teams then split the next two games in Ottawa to send it back to Toronto tied two games apiece.

The winner of game five would take a stranglehold on the series. If the Senators could pull it off, they would have a chance to win the series back at the Corel Centre in front of their fans who had been subject to much heartache at the hands of the Leafs.

The Senators jumped out to a 2–1 lead going into the third period but allowed the tying goal with just under eight minutes to play. Moments before Alfredsson scored the game-winning goal for Ottawa, Chara attempted what looked to be a very casual play by pinching in off the blue line to keep the puck in the Toronto zone. Just after making the play, however, Chara was hit by the Maple Leafs Alyn McCauley and immediately left the ice.

The next morning, what had been a jubilant team was suddenly downtrodden with the news that Chara had a strained medial collateral ligament in his knee and would miss the final two games. The single most dominant factor in the series would no longer be with them out on the ice. If Chara's importance to the Senators was ever questioned, it was quickly answered when Ottawa lost game six at home 4–3 and fell completely flat in getting shut out 3–0 in Toronto in game seven, marking the third straight year the Leafs knocked the Senators out of the playoffs.

Although the series was negative for the Senators as a team, it was a coming-out party for Chara. The next season he was named to the 2002–03 Eastern Conference all-star team, and the following year he was named an NHL first-team all-star and finished second to New Jersey's Scott Niedermayer in the Norris Trophy voting for the league's best defenceman.

This was the kid who wasn't meant to play hockey, who was supposedly better off on a basketball court, who was apparently too slow and goofy to ever master the game.

But he has done just that.

A Prince George Van-Owner's Dream

When Zdeno Chara, all 6-foot-9 and 255 pounds of him, first arrived in Prince George, BC, to play major junior hockey with the Cougars, he didn't have a whole lot of money. Cougars coach Stan Butler was an influential figure in Prince George, and he persuaded a local car wash owner to give the young Chara a job.

"I went by a week later and asked the owner how he was making out," Butler recalled. "He says [Chara] was the best employee he ever had. He was the only guy who ever worked there who didn't need a ladder to clean the roof of a van."

Chara's size, however, wasn't always as appreciated by the town folk. Chara was placed with a billet family in Prince George. Before long, Butler received a phone call from Chara's hosts. "They said they were open to having another player," Butler said, "but on the allowance that we were giving billets, they could not afford to feed Zee."

Chara admits that his appetite is bigger than most, but that's only natural seeing as the man's *everything* is bigger than most. But he insists his stomach was not the only one driving a hole in his hosts' wallets. "I was there with another player who was about 220 pounds," Chara said in his defence. "We both ate a lot."

Chapter Seven

Dany Heatley and Ilya Kovalchuk

Dany Heatley and Ilya Kovalchuk both insist they hit it off as soon as they met at their first rookie camp in 2001 with the Atlanta Thrashers. But the first time they met on the ice at the 2000 World Junior Hockey Championships in Moscow, Heatley was not one of Kovalchuk's biggest fans.

With Russia clinging to a 2–1 lead late in the third period of a preliminary round game, and the Canadian net empty in favour of an extra skater, Kovalchuk picked up the puck at his own blue line with an unfettered path to the net at the other end of the ice. Heatley, playing for Canada, was a few metres behind Kovalchuk, trying in vain to catch up to the speedy winger. Heatley's position provided him with a great view of Kovalchuk who, after crossing the Canadian blue line, took one hand off his stick and pumped his fist in celebration *before* calmly sliding the puck into the gaping net to give Russia an insurmountable 3–1 lead over their biggest hockey rivals.

Although the loss was a disappointment to a nation of hockey fans, it was Kovalchuk's hasty celebration that caught the ire of the Canadian players and those who were supporting them back home. As Kovalchuk continued to dance around the ice in ecstasy, Heatley didn't find the move particularly amusing. "Not at the time," a smiling Heatley said about a year after the tournament. "Some guys obviously were a little mad."

But by this point, Heatley had half a season under his belt playing on the same line as Kovalchuk with the Thrashers, giving him a front-row seat for his linemate's animated goal celebrations. "If you're on the other team, you don't want to see that," Heatley continued, "but when he's on your team, that's what you want."

Heatley's and Kovalchuk's simultaneous arrival to the Thrashers in 2001 was like hockey's version of the perfect storm—two powerful forces converging on the same place at the same time. Heatley was Atlanta's first-round pick in the 2000 draft, going second overall after the New York Islanders selected goaltender Rick DiPietro. But the Calgary native went back to the University of Wisconsin for his sophomore season, where he was nominated for the Hobey Baker Award as U.S. college player of the year in 2001, but lost out to another goaltender, Buffalo Sabres prospect Ryan Miller of

Michigan State University. Kovalchuk came to Atlanta as a hot-headed 18-year-old who had just finished two seasons playing in the Russian Elite League and was the first Russian to be selected with the number one overall pick in the NHL draft.

Although their two personas seemed completely incompatible, Heatley and Kovalchuk became fast friends after rooming together at the Thrashers rookie camp in Michigan.

The pair of young stars came from similar sports environments. Heatley's father, Murray, played professionally in the World Hockey Association and in Germany, where he met Heatley's mother, Karin. Heatley was born in Freiburg, Germany, in 1981. Murray had his son in skates by the age of three, and Heatley often tagged along to his dad's practices and games. By the time Heatley and his family moved to Calgary just after his fourth birthday, he was already bitten by the hockey bug.

Kovalchuk's father, Valeri, played professional basketball in Russia's first division in the city of Tver, not far from Moscow. Kovalchuk was taken to the gym by the time he was three years old to work on stretching and coordination. When he was five years old, his dad looked out the window and watched as his son played ball hockey. He saw it right then and there. His son would be a hockey player.

So both of the youngsters had been groomed for this moment almost since birth, and therefore all eyes were on Heatley and Kovalchuk as the Thrashers real training camp began in the fall of 2001. Kovalchuk had blazing speed, enough size to play a rugged game and an incredible knack for being able to shoot a puck while skating at top speed without having to glide to line up his shot. Heatley was a physical presence with good ice vision and pillow-like hands, who was at his best between the faceoff circles and the net.

Heatley and Kovalchuk didn't wait very long to give Atlanta fans a taste of their potential, each of them scoring two goals in their first pre-season game. Kovalchuk finished that exhibition season as the team's top scorer with 6 goals and 4 assists in six games, and Heatley grabbed 3 goals and 1 assist playing on the opposite wing.

Once the regular season began, however, it was Heatley who was most at ease among the pros. It was to be expected, since Heatley played two years in college, but he still exceeded the Thrashers hopes by getting at least a point in 9 of his first 13 games.

Kovalchuk, on the other hand, was having trouble grasping the North American hockey code. The first three penalties of his NHL career were for diving. His play in his end of the rink, an area he almost never ventured to in Russia, was a liability in the NHL. Thrashers coach Curt Fraser didn't want to limit his young star's obvious offensive talents, but he also couldn't have one of his players floating around outside the blue line while the rest of his team was pinned in their zone.

In early November of the 2001–02 season, Fraser benched Kovalchuk one game for missing two crucial defensive assignments that led to 2 goals in a 4–1 loss. "He has habits from other places, and we work with him every day to break those," Fraser said in explaining his move. "I'm not going to turn this kid into a third-line checker. As he plays, we can teach him defense."

By this point, however, Kovalchuk's offensive flair was beginning to show, while Heatley was consistently producing at an alarming rate. The league took notice of them at the YoungStars game during all-star weekend when Kovalchuk pumped in six goals and added an assist to win the game's MVP award. It became increasingly obvious that the NHL Calder Trophy for rookie of the year was going to one of the two Thrashers rookies. Heatley and Kovalchuk were riding one-two in the rookie scoring race when, with 16 games left in the season, Kovalchuk dislocated his right shoulder and was out for the rest of the year.

Although he still finished in first place among NHL rookies with 29 goals, missing the end of the season cost Kovalchuk any shot at winning the award, as Heatley was on his way to a 26-goal, 41-assist campaign. Heatley received 48 of the 62 first-place votes in the balloting, while Kovalchuk received the other 14 to finish second. The following year Heatley and Kovalchuk didn't skip a beat, improving their play after the arrival of new head coach Bob Hartley midway through the 2002–03 season.

During all-star weekend, it was Heatley's turn to make a statement. Playing with the big boys this time, Heatley scored 4 goals through two periods to tie the record for most goals in an all-star game. During the second period, Heatley was paid a visit by one of the holders of that record, Wayne Gretzky. "Don't stop at four," Gretzky told him. "Get six or seven, something you'll be proud of for a long time."

Heatley did get one more goal, but it didn't officially count as it came during a shootout, but he was still a no-brainer pick as the game's MVP even though his Eastern Conference team lost. Heatley finished the season with a team-best 41 goals and 48 assists while Kovalchuk had 38 goals and 29 assists.

Kovalchuk was still struggling with his defensive responsibilities and Hartley treated his lapses with tough love, letting him steam on the bench any time he had a miscue in his own end. But Hartley didn't mind as much as it seemed. Defence can be taught, but Kovalchuk's skills are not covered by any chapter in the coaching manual. "Kovy and I are like father and son," Hartley said soon after another Kovalchuk benching. "I'd rather try to slow down a thoroughbred than try to kick a donkey to get going."

The Thrashers were improving at the same rate as the two young superstars, and Hartley's arrival as coach actually triggered a late-season run to the playoffs in 2003 that came up just short. But the momentum at the end of the season was a source of great optimism in the Thrashers' front office for the first time in the franchise's short history.

Just before the start of the 2003–04 season that hope was shattered by a tragic accident. While Heatley was driving teammate Dan Snyder home from a team function in suburban Atlanta in his black Ferrari sports car, he came upon a winding road with a stone wall bordering one side of it. Travelling more than double the speed limit at about 130 kilometres per hour, Heatley crashed the car into the stone wall, thrusting his friend from the vehicle. Snyder succumbed to the massive brain injuries six days later. Heatley survived the accident, suffering torn anterior cruciate and medial collateral ligaments in his right knee, breaking his jaw, bruising a kidney and damaging his left shoulder. But more painful than any of those wounds was the guilt he felt for the loss of his dear friend Snyder.

"I'm going to deal with this forever," he said months later. "Every time I go to sleep I think about Dan. It'll be with me for the rest of my life...As a person, I'll never be the same."

Heatley was already in line to face a number of criminal charges, but when Snyder died, one count of first-degree vehicular homicide was added. Snyder's parents, however, did not want Heatley to go to jail and immediately came out in support of their son's good friend. The Snyders' support and compassion went a long way towards Heatley's eventual plea agreement to serve three years probation with 750 hours of community service.

From the standpoint of the Atlanta Thrashers, the accident was an emotional blow, but it also suddenly increased Kovalchuk's importance in the team's success. Starting his first season without Heatley, Kovalchuk got off to a torrid start, being named NHL player of the month for October with 11 goals and 6 assists as Atlanta lost only three of its first 11 games of the season.

While Kovalchuk was ripping up the NHL, Heatley was attempting to recover from his physical and, most importantly, emotional scars. The reconstructive knee surgery Heatley underwent usually takes four to six months of recovery time, but less than three months later he was back on his skates. On January 28, 2004, close to four months after the accident, Heatley played his first game with the Thrashers, returning to a standing ovation from the fans at Philips Arena. As Heatley lined up to take the opening faceoff, St. Louis Blues forward Keith Tkachuk lined up opposite him and whispered a few words. "I told him we were thinking about him—me, our entire team, the league," Tkachuk said. "[I] just wanted to give him support. He's an exceptional person...and it's important that he was just out there."

Although it took him a few games to shake off the rust, Heatley finished the season strongly with points in 18 of his final 24 games to finish with 13 goals and 12 assists in 31 games.

Kovalchuk, meanwhile, put the finishing touches on his best season yet, tying the Columbus Blue Jackets Rick Nash and Calgary Flames Jarome Iginla for the league-lead with 41 goals. Heatley continued his season playing for Canada at the 2004 world championships and proved that the horrible accident was behind him, leading the tournament with 8 goals and 11 points to claim MVP honours and lead Canada to its second straight gold medal.

But Heatley faltered somewhat in the subsequent World Cup of Hockey and 2005 world championships, and before the start of the 2005-06 season he ended his dream partnership with Kovalchuk.

Heatley asked the Thrashers for a trade so he could give himself a fresh start as he continued to recover from the emotional scars of the accident, and Waddell obliged by sending him to the Ottawa Senators for star winger Marian Hossa and defenceman Greg DeVries.

Just like that, the perfect storm had been calmed.

~♨~

Chapter Eight

Jose Theodore

It was the blocker-save heard around the world. The Montréal Canadiens were desperately clinging to a 2–1 lead with just under half a period left to play in the sixth game of their 2002 opening-round playoff series with the Boston Bruins. The Canadiens had no business even being in the playoffs, let alone in a position to oust the top-seeded Bruins. But here they were on the verge of advancing to the second round thanks solely to the brilliant play of their man in nets, the local kid made good, Jose Theodore.

Boston, however, wasn't about to go away quietly. They had taken the play to Montréal throughout the third period of game six, if not the entire series, and were buzzing around Theodore's net looking for the tying goal that could salvage their season. Boston's formidable bookends, power wingers Glen Murray and Bill Guerin, had posted themselves so close to Theodore they could smell him. Meanwhile, their Bruins teammates feverishly tried to get anything and everything at the net.

Suddenly, Murray was all alone in front of Theodore, but his shot got stopped by a lightning quick pad shooting out to intercept it. Moments later, a Bruins shot got through a crowd and past Theodore but clanged off the post. The puck lay in the crease, a little tap away from the Montréal goal line, and Guerin's eyes lit up in anticipation as he saw it sitting there within his reach. Theodore, who had stepped up in his crease a little to challenge the original shot, wasn't sure where the puck was, but he had a hunch. In an instant, as Guerin thought he was scoring the game-tying goal, Theodore spun around, sent his stick flying and blindly whipped his blocker hand behind him with his head turned the other way in a desperate move towards the goal line. Guerin's shot struck the blocker fractions of a second before it entered the net, and a star was born.

That save was played, and replayed, on every sports telecast in the hockey-playing world that night. Although the Canadiens went on to lose in the second round to the Carolina Hurricanes, the save vaulted Theodore into the upper stratosphere of hockey stardom. And it officially put an end to a rocky ascension where his ability to be a starting goalie in the NHL was constantly put into question.

That ascension essentially began when Theodore was born as the youngest of Ted and Marie-France Theodore's five sons in the Montréal suburb of Laval, Québec. When Jose was seven years old, his older brothers needed someone to play in nets. They put Jose into a set of goalie pads, and he hasn't taken them off since.

The beginning of Theodore's junior hockey career with the St-Jean Lynx of the Québec Major Junior Hockey League (QMJHL) was solid, but not spectacular in any sense. Although no one doubted that Theodore possessed talent, he wasn't seen to have any more talent than a number of other goaltending prospects from the Canadian Hockey League. At least that's what the Montréal Canadiens thought when they prepared their list for the 1994 draft.

The Canadiens had four goalies—Éric Fichaud, Jamie Storr, Dan Cloutier and Theodore—who they were happy to take with their second-round pick. As it turned out, the rest of the league made the decision easy for them because Theodore was the only one out of the four still available when the Canadiens selected him 44th overall.

For a kid who grew up in the suburbs of Montréal, it couldn't have turned out any better. "This has been my dream since I was young," Theodore said a week after the draft, "to play for or against the Canadiens."

Theodore led his new team, the Hull Olympiques, to the 1994–95 QMJHL championship and a berth in the Memorial Cup the following season before attending his first training camp with the Montréal Canadiens in 1995. Of course, Theodore had no illusions of making the team, and even if he did, they were instantly erased as soon as he saw Patrick Roy skating on the same ice as he was. The number one goalie's job with the Canadiens was secure, but at some point Roy had to retire. Roy was already verging on 30 during that training camp, and Theodore, at 19, looked to have the perfect timing. When Roy retires six or seven years down the road, Theodore would be primed to take his place.

Or so it seemed.

In December 1995, the foundations of the entire Canadiens franchise crumbled around them when Roy—after a very public stare-down with coach Mario Tremblay—vowed he would never play another game for Montréal. Canadiens general manager Réjean Houle didn't need long to find a taker for Roy's services, and within days of Roy's demand, he and Mike Keane were traded to the Colorado Avalanche.

In return, Houle got two wingers and a goaltender, Jocelyn Thibault. Thibault was only 20 years old and he already had two years of NHL experience behind him, which Theodore didn't. It appeared to everyone that Houle had just acquired the Canadiens goaltender of the future, the exact position Theodore thought he could fill.

"What can I do? I have no control over it. I'm not with the Canadiens, we'll see next season," Theodore said after the trade. "If I play well, everything will fall into place. If we play for the same team, we'll make a great duo. A goalie doesn't have to play 75 games a season. All I want to do is play in the NHL, preferably with Montréal. You never know what can happen."

Theodore apparently drew some inspiration from the trade and began playing the best hockey of his life. His numbers for Hull improved dramatically and earned him an invitation to join Canada's national junior team for the 1996 world championships. Although he platooned with Marc Denis throughout the early stages of the tournament, it was Theodore who got the call to start against the powerful Russians in the semi-final game.

Theodore rallied his overmatched Canadian teammates to a 4–3 victory with 46 saves, and he followed that up with a 33-save performance in Canada's 4–1 gold medal win over Sweden. He was named the tournament's, and thereby the world's, top goaltender.

"We're an emotional people and that spills over into our hockey," Theodore said in the jubilance of the Canadian dressing room. "We don't accept second place."

Theodore had a fantastic training camp with the Canadiens that September, allowing only two power play goals on 89 shots in two exhibition game victories. But Montréal felt it was unfair for Theodore to stay with the big club and sit on the bench behind Thibault, so he was sent to the Canadiens' American Hockey League (AHL) affiliate in Fredericton, New Brunswick, where he was the number one goalie.

When Thibault broke his finger in late October, Theodore was back in Montréal, and in the first NHL start of his career against the San Jose Sharks on November 2, 1996, he made 31 saves in a 4–3 overtime loss. The next night in Phoenix against the Coyotes, Theodore made a strong case for remaining with the big club with 46 saves in a 4–4 tie. "We can't send Theodore back down if he keeps playing like this," Tremblay said after the Phoenix game. "He's forcing our hand."

Theodore continued his strong play while Thibault recovered from his injury, so much so that Montréal decided to keep three goaltenders when Thibault was ready to return.

"I feel I'm good enough to play in the NHL," Theodore said once Tremblay announced he would stay in Montréal. "Two weeks ago, I wasn't sure because I didn't know what to expect...Every day, I feel I'm improving."

The bubble burst for Theodore less than a week later when he was sent back to the AHL after allowing three goals on 12 shots in a game against Florida. In Montréal, meanwhile, the locals were becoming restless with the tandem of Thibault and his backup Pat Jablonski as both of them faltered. In February, the Canadiens called Theodore back up from Fredericton and announced Jablonski was on the trade block.

Theodore played so well the rest of the year that many began to question whether he should be the starter instead of Thibault. But it was in the 1997 playoffs that Theodore made his mark on the notoriously fickle Montréal fans. The Canadiens were overmatched against the New Jersey Devils in the first round and it showed; Thibault allowed an average of five goals a game in three straight lopsided defeats. A desperate Tremblay called on Theodore to stop the bleeding, and he got the start at home in an effort to avoid a humiliating sweep. Theodore was up to the challenge, stopping 56 shots—including 28 after regulation time had ended—to lead Montréal to a 4–3 triple overtime win.

"I'll never forget it, that's for sure," Theodore said of his playoff debut. "Thirty years from now, I'll remember that game."

Theodore had to think he had proven his worth to the Canadiens brass. But that off-season, after the Devils beat Theodore and the Canadiens in game five, Montréal signed veteran goalie Andy Moog to share the load with Thibault. Before training camp had even begun, Theodore had practically no chance of making the team. Sure enough, near the end of training camp, Theodore was cut and sent to Fredericton.

He didn't play a single regular season game for Montréal in 1997–98, but for the second year in a row Theodore did finish the Canadiens final playoff game when he relieved Moog in Montréal's 3–1 loss to Buffalo in game four of the opening round. Moog retired that off-season, opening the door for Theodore to vie for a job in the NHL. This time, finally, he got his shot as the Canadiens went with a combination of him and Thibault. But both goalies played poorly to start the year, and the Canadiens lost their patience. Thibault was shipped off to the Chicago Blackhawks for veteran goalie Jeff Hackett, and Theodore was back in Fredericton by January.

Theodore and his agents, Bob Perno and Don Meehan, were beginning to lose patience with the Canadiens. "If we feel he has no future in Montréal," Perno said shortly after Theodore was demoted, "we'll do something over the summer."

It never got that far, as Theodore became the primary backup to Hackett in Montréal for the 1999–2000 season. Theodore played in 30 games while staying with Montréal the entire season for the first time since he was drafted five years earlier. His solid play led to the birth of a goaltending controversy in Montréal, as the media and fans wanted to see the hometown kid play more often.

They got what they wanted the following year when Hackett suffered a broken hand early in the season. This opened the door for Theodore, and he walked right through it, playing in a career-high 57 games, getting five shutouts and posting a 2.57 goals against average. But the highlight of the season came on January 3, 2001, in Long Island, New York.

The Canadiens had a 2–0 lead and the New York Islanders had pulled their goalie in the dying seconds of the game. The puck came behind the net, Theodore stopped it and sent a backhand skywards and down the ice. Although he was only attempting to clear his own zone while avoiding a potential penalty for shooting it out of play, Theodore's shot landed at centre ice and slowly meandered its way into the empty Islanders net.

"It was awesome," a beaming Theodore said after the game. "I was jumping all over the place. We got the win and the shutout, and I got a goal. It was a pretty good night for me."

Theodore became only the sixth goalie in NHL history to be credited for a goal, but in fact he was only the fourth goalie to actually shoot a puck into the net. The other two got credit for being the last player to touch a puck before an opponent put it in their own net.

Theodore solidified his status as the team's top goalie in 2000–01, winning the team's Molson Cup for the most three-star selections over the course of the season. But Hackett was still on the team come training camp, and the Canadiens wouldn't anoint either one of them as the starter because they both had great training camps.

But Hackett was 33 years old at this point, and he suffered an early-season injury for the second year in a row, this time a separated shoulder. Theodore was handed the reins. He played in 20 of the team's first 27 games in 2001–02 and was lights out, posting a 2.03 goals against average with a .931 save percentage over that time. "I've waited a long time for this, so I might as well take advantage," Theodore said then. "I'm at a young age. I'm only 25; to play this much is a bonus."

In January, as he was putting the finishing touches on his fourth shutout of the season in a 2–0 win over the Washington Capitals, Theodore was named to his first NHL all-star team. It was at around the same time that Canadiens head coach Michel Therrien announced that even though Hackett was healthy enough to play, Theodore was his number one for the rest of the season.

With 19 games left in the regular season, Hackett suffered an injury to the same shoulder, ending his campaign. The pressure now fell on Theodore to lead the team to the playoffs for the first time in four years, the Canadiens' longest playoff drought ever.

"Jose has to find a way for our team to get to the playoffs, nothing else will be accepted after three years [out of the playoffs]," Canadiens goaltending coach Roland Melanson said bluntly. "Jose might play every game, a lot is riding on his shoulders."

Theodore did everything that was asked of him, and more. He played in 21 of the Canadiens' last

22 games, including 17 in a row that culminated in a seven-game winning streak to clinch a Canadiens playoff berth. The Canadiens met the Bruins in the first round as huge underdogs, but Theodore proved to be the equalizer. Although he struggled through the first four games of the series, his Canadiens teammates picked him up by scoring enough goals to earn a 2–2 split. That's when Theodore took over, stopping 43 shots in Boston to hand the Canadiens a 2–1 win, even though they were outshot 44–13. Then came game six, and Theodore's miraculous blocker save on Bill Guerin that preserved the Canadiens' series victory.

After the Canadiens were eliminated by the Carolina Hurricanes, Theodore's summer of love began. He had already earned the Roger Crozier Saving Grace Award for posting the league's best save percentage at .931, but at the 2002 NHL awards that summer Theodore cleaned up. He beat out his boyhood idol Patrick Roy to win the Vezina Trophy as the league's top goalie, and then, with the final award of the night, Wayne Gretzky announced Theodore as the recipient of the Hart Trophy for the league's MVP.

"My legs are weak," an astounded Theodore said after the ceremony. "I couldn't believe it when Gretzky pronounced my name. I still can't believe it."

Theodore's instant stardom was a little difficult for him to handle. That summer, he accepted nearly every invitation sent to him, filming commercials and playing in a rock concert with Québec star Éric Lapointe. He was also embroiled in a summer of contract negotiations with the Canadiens that stretched into September. Theodore finally agreed to a three-year deal that paid him $5.5 million a year, making him the highest-paid Canadiens' player in the team's storied history.

The summer whirlwind was a little too much. Theodore was not properly prepared for the 2002–03 season, and his play suffered as a result. The Canadiens missed the playoffs again, largely because Theodore's numbers had ballooned into the realm of mediocrity. "I never had the time to clear my head," Theodore said after the 2002–03 season was over. "Our [2001–02] season ended May 15, I got the [Hart and Vezina] trophies on June 20 and a wave of events followed. Even my parents were complaining that they never got to see me. When camp began, I still wasn't hungry to strap on the pads. It felt like camp came quickly."

Theodore kept a lower profile in the summer of 2003, due largely to the arrests of his father and brothers in connection with a loan-sharking ring operating out of the Montréal Casino. There were also published photos of Theodore hanging out with members of the criminal biker gang the Hells Angels. Although police made it clear Theodore was not a target of their loan-sharking investigation and that the photos proved nothing, some people in Montréal began to wonder if it might be a good idea to trade him. It was a good thing for the Canadiens that they didn't.

Theodore reverted to his Hart Trophy form in 2003–04, posting a 33–28 record with a 2.18 goals against average and .919 save percentage to lead the Canadiens back to the playoffs to once again meet, and beat, the Boston Bruins in the first round of the playoffs. But Theodore, even after his dream season in 2002, and even though he has achieved star status in the NHL, will never be satisfied.

"I wasn't happy just to be drafted," Theodore once said. "I wanted to be a starter, I wanted to go to the All-Star game. I haven't won the Stanley Cup yet, so it's important to aim high, and you have to be ready to make the sacrifices to achieve your goals because it doesn't happen by chance. You create your own luck, and your own destiny."

He's created himself a pretty good destiny in Montréal.

One Shot, One Goal

Although Jose Theodore has proved to be one of the best goaltenders in the NHL, his career didn't get off to such a rollicking start. On February 21, 1996, in Hartford, Connecticut, Canadiens goalie Pat Jablonski had been shelled in nets, and a nervous 19-year-old Theodore was sent in to finish the game.

"I remember it wasn't a good start," Theodore said. "On my first shot, Sami Kapanen scored on a 2-on-1. But at least it was a nice goal, and not one from centre ice."

Chapter Nine

Vincent Lecavalier and Brad Richards

Vincent Lecavalier is a large man, so it stands to reason that he casts a pretty imposing shadow. Just ask Brad Richards, the man who has lived in that shadow most of his hockey-playing life. The Tampa Bay Lightning forwards—born only 11 days apart in 1980—have been joined at the hip ever since they were 14 years old. They played at the same high school in Saskatchewan, the same major junior team in Québec and the same team in the pros.

But long before the two became NHL stars and Stanley Cup champions, it was always Lecavalier who attracted all the scouts, all the attention, all the praise, and nearly all the credit for anything Richards did. Lecavalier was ordained as the best forward to come out of Québec since Mario Lemieux and as the "Michael Jordan of hockey" by Tampa Bay Lightning owner Arthur Williams after the Lightning took Lecavalier with the first overall pick in the 1998 draft.

Basically, Lecavalier was expected to duplicate the exploits of two of the biggest superstars in sports, and he was barely 18 years old. But if Lecavalier was the chosen one, Richards was the overlooked one. Even though he always put up numbers similar to Lecavalier's as they were made their way through bantam, midget and finally major junior hockey, Richards was constantly being slighted because he did not possess his good buddy's impressive stature. But by the spring of 2004, just before the Lightning made a run at the Stanley Cup, Richards and Lecavalier had each gone to the opposite ends of the spectrum.

Richards was the consistent offensive producer who never failed to reach 60 points in his four years with the Lightning, a pleasant surprise for a third-round NHL draft pick. On the other end there was Lecavalier, the franchise's supposed saviour whose six-year career to that point had been marked by inconsistent play, feuding with coaches, unmet expectations and having his team captaincy removed. All of a sudden, Richards was the proven commodity and Lecavalier the one with something to prove. But the playoffs finished with Lecavalier putting to rest any doubts about his character, and Richards officially entering the brotherhood of NHL stars.

It was exactly how Lecavalier and Richards dreamed it would turn out when they were 14 years old and bunked next to each other at Athol Murray College of Notre Dame in tiny Wilcox, Saskatchewan. The boys were both intimidated by being so far away from home at such a young age and took an instant liking to each other.

Lecavalier, who came from the Montréal suburb of Île Bizard, was the youngest of Yves and Christiane Lecavalier's three children. Yves, a firefighter and former junior hockey player, took his son to the rink when he was only two and a half years old. Lecavalier played organized hockey at the age of four against kids twice his age, and by the time he was six years old, locals were already coming to the rink just to watch him play.

Lecavalier's older brother Philippe had attended Notre Dame and had a full hockey scholarship to play defence at Clarkson University in Potsdam, New York. When the younger Lecavalier left home to play at Notre Dame, he hoped to follow the path his brother marked for him.

Richards came to Saskatchewan from the tiny fishing hamlet of Murray Harbor, Prince Edward Island, and was the eldest child of Glen and Delite Richards. Richards' father was a lobster fisherman, like his grandfather and great-grandfather were. Similar to Lecavalier, Richards was first taken out on the ice by his father when he was two and a half years old. Although Richards had all the respect in the world for the difficult work his parents endured in order to put food on the table, lobster fishing wasn't something he wanted to do for a living.

"I guess if I wasn't playing hockey, I'd be fishing and playing hockey in the senior league back home," Richards said during the 2003–04 playoffs. "I just didn't want to get up every morning and go fishing with my mom and dad. My brother likes it, but I couldn't do it. I had to be a hockey player, because I wasn't going to be a fisherman."

Richards and his family decided the best way to do that was to go to Saskatchewan and Notre Dame, where he would have a chance to play a higher calibre of hockey than what he was exposed to in tiny Prince Edward Island. The coach at Notre Dame at the time, Terry O'Malley, knew he had a stud in Lecavalier, but he wasn't positive Richards could overcome being only 5-foot-6 as a 14-year-old. "Lecavalier was tall, even then, and Richards was a lot shorter," O'Malley recalled. "Lecavalier was an obvious shoo-in to make our top bantam team, but Richards went down to the wire."

Richards' uncanny knack for making things happen offensively with his superior ice vision and passing skills eventually won over the coaches at Notre Dame, and the pair were the only grade nine students to play on the school's top bantam team in 1994–95.

The following year the good buddies dominated the bantam league, with Lecavalier notching 104 points and Richards getting 99 points. Both were invited to join the Notre Dame midget team for their playoff run and finished one-two in post-season scoring.

Even though Lecavalier had come to Saskatche-wan with hopes of getting a college scholarship, he couldn't resist the lure of junior hockey after the Rimouski Océanic of the Québec Major Junior Hockey League (QMJHL) selected him with the fourth overall pick in the 1996 midget draft.

Richards, however, was looked over in the QMJHL draft and stayed behind at Notre Dame for another year of seasoning. He played for the Notre Dame Junior A team in 1996–97 despite only being the age of a first-year midget player.

Lecavalier's arrival in Rimouski, meanwhile, took the QMJHL by storm. It didn't take long for the Québec media to compare him to other great French-Canadian stars, and by the end of the year he was widely considered the province's best hockey prospect since Lemieux was shattering the league's scoring records.

Before the 1997 QMJHL draft, Lecavalier encour-aged his bosses in Rimouski to go have a look at Richards, who was on his way to scoring 87 points and being named the Saskatchewan Junior Hockey League's rookie of the year. The Rimouski scouts were sold, and the Océanic used their first-round pick in the draft to reunite the friends. Richards adapted to the major junior level remarkably well, tying Lecavalier for the team-scoring lead with

115 points in 1997–98 and being named a QMJHL all-star.

But, once again, it was Lecavalier who drew all the attention, being named to the Canadian national team while Richards watched the world junior tournament at home. Lecavalier was the consensus number one prospect for the 1998 NHL entry draft, and Richards, it was believed by some, was simply riding the coat tails of his talented friend and linemate, reaping the benefits of playing with such a can't-miss prospect.

After Lecavalier went, as everyone expected, number one to Tampa Bay at the 1998 draft, he began talking up his friend to the Lightning staff, who didn't pick again until the third round, 64 picks away. Richards was still available when the 65th pick came up, and the Lightning grabbed him. Once Richards was through getting his jersey at the podium and doing his interviews, Lecavalier was waiting to greet him.

"I can't get rid of him," Richards joked to a reporter after the draft.

The Lightning said his relationship with Lecavalier was a factor in their decision to pick Richards, but it wasn't the only factor. "I'd be lying if I didn't tell you it helped that they've been together and they're friends," Lightning head scout Don Murdoch said after the draft. "But we didn't just take him because he's [Lecavalier's] linemate. We took

Brad Richards because Brad Richards is a heck of a hockey player."

He just wasn't as good of a hockey player as Lecavalier, not then anyway. At training camp, Richards was hardly given a sniff before being shipped back to Rimouski, but Lecavalier was instantly installed as a centrepiece of the Lightning attack at the ripe age of 18.

With Lecavalier being fed to the NHL wolves in Tampa Bay, Richards became the undisputed leader of the Océanic in Rimouski. He piled up 131 points and passed Lecavalier to become Rimouski's all-time leading scorer (though he was passed six years later by another kid from the Maritimes, Sidney Crosby), but he still wasn't invited by Canada to play for the national junior team. "I've been having the best season of my life," said the 18-year-old Richards upon hearing news of the snub. "But it's a 19-year-old tournament and that's the way it is."

That wasn't the end of Richards' disappointment. At Lightning training camp before the 1999–2000 season, he was determined to earn a spot on the team and join Lecavalier, who had a decent rookie season the year before with 13 goals and 15 assists while playing on the third line and in all 82 games. But Richards didn't stick and went back to Rimouski for his third season of major junior while Lecavalier prepared for his second year in the NHL.

It was the widest gap in the two friends' careers since they met, and it was also the best years either of them had ever had. Lecavalier led the team in goals with 25 and in assists with 42, living up to all the hype that had surrounded him a year earlier. On March 11, 2000, Lightning head coach Steve Ludzik, following the trade of team captain Chris Gratton, named Lecavalier to take his place. He became the youngest full-time captain in NHL history at 19 years of age, two years younger than his hockey idol Steve Yzerman was when he was named captain of the Detroit Red Wings.

Tampa Bay general manager Rick Dudley saw nothing wrong with thrusting a teenager into such an important leadership role, largely because he had the support of his teammates. "He sets the example," Dudley said of the decision. "He's not loud, but he has a presence. The day we traded Gratton, 10 players called me to say they wanted Vinny as captain."

One of those players who supported the decision was goaltender Dan Cloutier, who remembered a time he was feeling down after a couple of bad games while sitting next to Lecavalier on the plane. "He started telling me about how things were going to get better, and he suggested a couple of things to turn my game around," Cloutier remembered. "It was weird. He's a 19-year-old kid, right? But the way Vinny carries himself, it's as if he's been in the league 10 years."

Richards, meanwhile, was doing everything in his power to prove to the Lightning that they made a mistake cutting him. He led all Canadian Hockey

League (CHL) scorers with 71 goals and 115 assists for Rimouski in 1999–2000, posting the highest point total in the QMJHL in 11 years. He also had a ridiculous plus/minus rating of plus-80, by far the best in the country.

Richards was finally selected to represent Canada at the 2000 world junior championships, posting 6 points in seven games for the bronze-medal winning squad. But it was in the playoffs that Richards showed everyone what he could do with a puck. He scored 37 points in only 12 games as Rimouski romped its way to the 2000 QMJHL title to earn a berth in the Memorial Cup in Halifax.

A few days before Rimouski played in the tournament final, Dudley told reporters in Tampa that he felt it was unlikely the Lightning would sign Richards before the June 1 deadline, at which point he could re-enter the NHL draft as the CHL player of the year and scoring leader. "He's a kid we'd love to have," Dudley said at the time, "but if it doesn't work out, it's not the end of the world for the Tampa Bay Lightning."

Lecavalier was aware of his friend's predicament, and called Richards for a little pep talk. "He told me to keep believing I was the best player on the ice," Richards said, "not to let the contract talk get to me."

Richards was having a pretty mediocre tournament—only by his lofty standards—leading into the Memorial Cup final with 6 points in three games. As the Barrie Colts prepared to face Rimouski in the final, Colts forward Mike Jefferson (who later changed his name to Mike Danton) told reporters that Richards "wouldn't last five games" in the rougher Ontario Hockey League.

Richards responded with actions rather than words as he got 2 goals and 2 assists to lead Rimouski to a 6–2 win in the final for the first Memorial Cup championship in franchise history. Richards, just after being crowned the tournament's MVP, couldn't help but gloat a little over Jefferson's comments, especially after he refused to shake Richards' hand after the game.

"What can he say?" Richards asked after the game. "We won 6–2, I had a great game and we won the Memorial Cup. There's nothing he can say."

Richards, all of a sudden and just a few days before the deadline, found himself with a lot of leverage in his contract negotiations with Dudley. Fearing he would lose the top player in Canadian junior hockey, Dudley agreed to Richards' demand that he receive the maximum salary allowable to a rookie, signing him to a three-year contract laden with bonus clauses.

"I haven't slept a whole lot lately and I'm unbelievably happy to get this done," Richards said after signing on the dotted line.

The following fall, there was no way Tampa Bay could justify cutting Richards from the 2000–01 team, and he was once again on the same team with Lecavalier. Richards thrived almost immediately, being named the NHL's rookie of the month for October and finishing with 62 points in 82 games to come second in the Calder Trophy voting for rookie of the year.

But that season was the beginning of Lecavalier's fall from grace. Halfway through the year, Lightning coach Ludzik was replaced by John Tortorella, a brash disciplinarian from Boston. Tortorella and Lecavalier clashed almost immediately. The following season, Tortorella stripped Lecavalier of his captaincy and asked Dudley if it was possible to trade Lecavalier, who he called "Lazy Vinny."

Dudley began accepting offers for his disgruntled centre, but it was Dudley who was shown the door by upper Lightning management. Incoming general manager Jay Feaster immediately went about repairing the damage done, assuring Lecavalier he was still important to the franchise. "I told Vincent, straight up, I would not be the answer to the trivia question, 'Which stupid general manager traded Vincent Lecavalier?'" Feaster said.

It was a good thing for the Lightning that Feaster felt that way, because Lecavalier soon combined with Richards to lead the franchise to the NHL promised land. Lecavalier had a career-best 78 points in 2002–03 while Richards had his best season with 74 points. But it was in the 2003–04 playoffs that the two really shone.

Richards had outscored Lecavalier during the regular season with yet another career-high of

79 points to Lecavalier's 66. He had become, in the eyes of many observers, the Lightning's most reliable performer and brightest young star at the age of 24, supplanting Lecavalier in that role after years of comparisons and slights.

When the playoffs hit, Richards continued his incredible season, but this time it was Lecavalier who was out to prove his doubters wrong. The Lightning beat the New York Islanders in five games in round one, but Lecavalier failed to register so much as a point. In round two, Tampa Bay was to face Lecavalier's hometown Montréal Canadiens, and that's when the kid from Île Bizard came into his own. With just 17 seconds to play in game three, Lecavalier somehow managed to put his stick between his legs to tip a shot into the Montréal net for the game-tying goal, which was then followed by Richards' goal just over a minute into overtime. The Lightning won and gained a 3–0 stranglehold in a series they went on to sweep.

During the series, the chemistry in the Lightning dressing room was nearly derailed when Hockey Canada announced its team for the upcoming World Cup of Hockey. The Lightning's and the league's leading scorer, Martin St-Louis, was obviously named to the team, but so was Richards, finally giving him the validation as being one of the best players in hockey, something that he had sought for so long. Except that Richards couldn't be as happy as he wanted because, for the first time in his life, he had beaten out Lecavalier for a spot on the team. Shortly after the Canadian team was announced, the two went out for brunch.

"Brad didn't want to bring it up because he had been named and I hadn't and it was not talked about until I brought it up," Lecavalier said. "Finally I congratulated him on making the team and he said 'You should have been there too.' Of course I thought so too. I was upset. I admit it but I kept it to myself."

Lecavalier used the slight as motivation and revealed a side of his game no one had ever seen. Although Tampa beat the Flyers in seven games to advance to the Stanley Cup final, the only reason Philadelphia was even in that position was thanks to the bruising play of centre Keith Primeau, and his physical style rubbed off on Lecavalier. In the final series against the Calgary Flames, Lecavalier was seeking out people to hit and, in game three of the Cup finals, went toe-to-toe with Flames power forward Jarome Iginla in one of the most memorable fights in finals history.

"I've been trying to play more physical in the last five or six games," said Lecavalier during the Cup series. "I saw what [Keith] Primeau did [for Philadelphia] in our last series and how he was hitting everybody and I tried to do some of that. It gets you in the game."

Lecavalier's improved aggressiveness, and an NHL record of seven game-winning goals in the playoffs from Richards, led the Lightning to the Stanley Cup, beating Calgary in seven games with Richards awarded the Conn Smythe Trophy as playoff MVP.

Shortly after the playoffs, Hockey Canada was informed that Yzerman was unable to play in the World Cup. Team Canada executive director Wayne Gretzky immediately called Lecavalier to take his hero's place. There was no doubt who would be the first person Lecavalier called as soon as he hung up the phone with Gretzky. "I called Brad right after," Lecavalier told reporters after his selection. "He was really happy. We've been great friends for so long and we've been through so much together."

While Richards got his shot at redemption in the NHL playoffs, fulfilling a lifelong dream to bring the Stanley Cup back to his sleepy fishing village of Murray Harbor, Lecavalier breathed new life into his career and solidified his status as one of the world's best players in the World Cup. He scored 2 goals, including the dramatic game-winner in overtime of the semi-final against the Czech Republic, and added 5 assists to be named World Cup MVP after Canada downed Finland 3–2 in the tournament final.

The performance put forth by Richards and Lecavalier over the previous six months completed the coronation of the NHL's newest one-two punch, one that should be feared by every team in the league for the next decade.

~❦~

Chapter Ten

Jay Bouwmeester

The seasoned hockey scout walked into the arena completely unprepared for what he was about to see, probably because he had never seen anything like it. Barry Trapp had come to watch the Alberta under-17 team's camp in Calgary, conveniently close to Trapp's office at Hockey Canada where he was the director of scouting. When Trapp looked out on the ice, his eye was immediately drawn to a man-sized defenceman with a buttery stride effortlessly skating faster than the best 17-year-old players in the province.

Trapp's natural conclusion was that this was an older player, someone just coming out for a skate, maybe even needing some work coming back from an injury. But he had to make sure. So he walked over to a group of scouts who had been watching the proceedings on the ice to look for an answer.

"Who's the major junior guy out there skating with the kids?" Trapp asked them.

"That's 14-year-old Jay Bouwmeester," one of the scouts replied.

Trapp was stunned. "I sat down and watched him the entire hour and a half," Trapp recalled years after that first encounter. "I was mesmerized."

Any time Jay Bouwmeester put on a pair of skates, he tended to have this similar effect on anyone who happened to be watching him. Throughout his childhood dominating the Alberta minor hockey ranks, right up to his growing role with the NHL's Florida Panthers, Bouwmeester's fluid skating stride has led hockey people to extend the boundaries of hyperbole.

"This boy glides better than most people skate," Columbus Blue Jackets general manager Doug MacLean once said after watching a 16-year-old Bouwmeester become the youngest player to play for Canada at the world junior hockey championships in 2000.

The general manager of the Tampa Bay Lightning at the time, Rick Dudley, took it one step farther after watching Bouwmeester at the same tournament. "He's got size, poise and he skates as fast backwards as most guys do forwards," he noted.

Bouwmeester was born to skate. A tried cliché, perhaps, but in this case it couldn't describe the situation any better. He had begun walking when he was just nine months old, so Bouwmeester was quicker than most kids to look for new challenges.

When he was one and a half years old, his mother Gena went downstairs to find that her infant son had somehow managed to get his older sister Jill's roller skates on and was going for a leisurely skate in the basement.

Not too long after that, when Bouwmeester was about three, his father Dan—who played defence for the University of Alberta hockey team from 1968–72—decided it was time for his son to try the real thing. Every winter, Dan flooded the backyard of the family's Edmonton home to encourage his kids to skate. But Bouwmeester didn't need any encouragement.

"I'll always remember the first time I put him on skates," his father recalled. "I was holding on to him and it was just, 'Get away from me Dad! I want to go on my own.' That was from day one."

But that was as close to a hockey rink as Bouwmeester would get for the next three years, as his father wanted him to perfect his skating before playing in organized games. "The better you skate backward," his father told him as he made his way around the backyard, "the better you skate forward."

Bouwmeester was instantly hooked, spending every available winter moment in the backyard mastering the powerful stride that would one day have NHL scouts drooling. But his natural athletic ability did not only apply to hockey. He was a skilled basketball and volleyball player as well as an eight-handicap golfer by the time he was 14. He also excelled in track and field, once claiming the city long jump championship. But hockey always came first, and Bouwmeester was determined to become the best.

"A lot of kids don't have Jay's work ethic," Dan said. "I never had to push him. Since he was very little, he had a stick in his hand. He was bashing a ball around from the time he could pick it up."

Bouwmeester began playing organized hockey at age six, and by the time he was nine he was already well known in Edmonton hockey circles for his skating ability. His father was his coach every year until he turned 14, by which point Bouwmeester was the best minor hockey defenceman in Alberta. He was already 6-foot-2 when he completed his first year of bantam with 13 goals and 36 assists in 35 games to be named the Alberta Bantam Hockey Association's most outstanding defenceman and rookie of the year.

Bouwmeester was a no-brainer top choice for the Medicine Hat Tigers in the Western Hockey League's (WHL) 1997 bantam draft, and a year later he played in the Tigers' last eight games of the season as a 15-year-old, scoring two goals and adding an assist. His official arrival to the major junior ranks in 1999–2000 was met with huge anticipation. Bouwmeester, now 6-foot-4 and 200 pounds at 16 years of age, was instantly one of the top defencemen, not only for the Tigers, but in all of Canadian junior hockey.

Trapp never forgot watching Bouwmeester two years earlier at the under-17 camp in Calgary. So when it came time to send out the invitations to the 2000 Canadian junior team's selection camp in December, Bouwmeester's name was on the mailing list.

"It's a big honour for me to get an invite," Bouwmeester said after hearing the big news. "I can't remember how long I've been watching the tournament. Every Christmas we would watch the world junior tournament."

Bouwmeester was one of two 16-year-olds invited to the camp in Kitchener, Ontario, that year, joining Mississauga Ice Dogs centre Jason Spezza. It was the first time Hockey Canada had invited two 16-year-olds to try out for the national junior team, which is usually composed of 18- and 19-year-old players. The unprecedented move made for a media frenzy surrounding the two phenoms. "At the world junior training camp in Kitchener there was a huge media gathering," Trapp recalled. "[Bouwmeester] took one spin around the ice, and you could hear a pin drop in that arena."

While Spezza appeared at ease handling the mass of reporters covering the camp, Bouwmeester wasn't. Many words have been used to describe Bouwmeester, but no one ever accused him of being chatty. Shy, mild-mannered, soft-spoken, reserved, demure and just plain quiet are far better terms to describe Bouwmeester's demeanor.

"When you're with Jay, it's like you've got your own room on the road," Bouwmeester's future roommate with the Florida Panthers, Lance Ward, said during his rookie season in the NHL. "I look over and I'm not sure he's breathing. He doesn't snore. He sits so still. The kid is so quiet, he tiptoes to the bathroom at night."

Dealing with the new distractions probably contributed to Bouwmeester getting off to a slow start at the selection camp, and it didn't help that he was uncomfortable wearing the full face cage that is mandatory for 16 year olds at the international level. "I know he doesn't like it," Dan Bouwmeester said during the camp. "I told Jay, 'Tell them you'll wear a tutu if it will help you get on the team.'"

When it came time to make the cuts, Bouwmeester had played his way into a good position to make the team without having to make like a ballerina. The Canadian junior team's tradition was to inform the players who had been cut with a phone call at the crack of dawn. "I went to bed and just hoped I wouldn't get woken by a ringing," Bouwmeester said. "When I opened my eyes and it was morning, I was about happy as I can be."

With Bouwmeester and Spezza both being selected to play for Canada, they joined Wayne Gretzky and Eric Lindros as the only 16-year-olds to make the cut. Bouwmeester, at 16 years and three months, became the youngest player to suit up for

Canada when he took to the ice for the world junior championships in Sweden.

Bouwmeester saw limited minutes when the tournament began, but by the end he was in the team's four-man rotation on defence, and his play had left a major impression on NHL types in attendance. He finished his first full season of major junior with 13 goals and 21 assists in 64 games, and in 2001 he was one of Canada's top defencemen at the world juniors despite still being the youngest player on the team.

"He's like ready-mix cake, just add water," said Brian Burke, general manager of the Vancouver Canucks at the time, while watching the 2001 tournament in Moscow. "The only question I have for him is what [jersey] number he would want."

While Bouwmeester was away in Moscow, Bob Loucks took over as the head coach in Medicine Hat. Although Loucks had heard nothing but good things about his top defenceman, he remained somewhat skeptical that Bouwmeester was indeed as good as people said he was. His doubts were very quickly put to rest. "Everybody was telling me how good he was but I couldn't quite believe that, nobody is that good," Loucks said. "The very first time I saw him step on the ice, well, he took two or three strides and I was giggling. He's that good, and you see it that quick."

Just days after his 18th birthday early in the 2001–02 season, Bouwmeester was named the top prospect for the 2002 NHL entry draft by Red Line Report, a status he would never relinquish. Bouwmeester was almost single-handedly responsible for the Tigers defence in 2001–02, sometimes logging up to 35 minutes of ice time for a losing team that missed the WHL playoffs for a third year in a row. He was also counted upon to anchor the Canadian junior team's defensive corps in 2002, his third year on the national squad.

After two straight bronze medals at the tournament, the Canadians finally reached the final against Russia but lost 5–4. Bouwmeester was at his dominant best, however, leading the tournament in plus/minus rating and being named a first team all-star, though the accolades did nothing to quell the sting of losing what was probably his last shot at world junior gold. "This is really disappointing because the game was just so close," Bouwmeester said after returning home. "But over the years, it will become something we can be proud of."

Bouwmeester finished his year for Medicine Hat with 11 goals and 50 assists in 61 games to earn a spot on the WHL's 2001–02 first all-star team. His coach Loucks knew that was the last time he would see Bouwmeester in a Tigers uniform. "I'd give up two of my own kids to have him back," Loucks had said, only half joking. "Jay will be one of the best NHL defensemen of all time."

By the time the 2002 NHL draft rolled around in June, it became obvious to most observers that

Bouwmeester would go first overall to the Florida Panthers.

"We have guys on our staff who have been scouting for 17 years, and he's probably the best skating defenseman any of us have ever seen," Panthers director of scouting Tim Murray said. "He's special. It's so rare that a guy that size is so agile and has such great speed."

But Dudley, who had been hired by the Panthers a month before the draft to be their general manager, played coy when reporters asked him if he was selecting Bouwmeester with the first pick. This act made MacLean, whose Columbus Blue Jackets had the third pick, very nervous. MacLean coveted London Knights winger Rick Nash, and while he was pretty sure Florida would take Bouwmeester, he didn't want to run the risk of losing Nash to either the Panthers or the Atlanta Thrashers, who had the second pick.

As Bouwmeester sat with his family in the stands of the Air Canada Centre in Toronto, completely prepared to be the first pick as everyone was telling him he would be, MacLean made a bold move just minutes before the draft began. MacLean offered Dudley the Blue Jackets' pick at number three, and the option to switch picks with Columbus in the 2003 draft in exchange for the first pick. Dudley, after sending a couple of late-round picks to Atlanta to make sure they didn't pick Bouwmeester, seized the opportunity to improve his club's draft status for the following year and pulled the trigger on the deal.

When it was Florida's time to pick third, Bouwmeester was still sitting in the stands, and Dudley got the guy he wanted all along. Although everyone assumed Bouwmeester would feel cheated out of a once-in-a-lifetime chance to be the first pick in the draft, the cool-headed defenceman insisted he couldn't care less. "I wound up with the team I thought I was going to anyway," he said after the draft. "It doesn't matter if you're number one or number three...a few years down the road, nobody remembers who went where."

The Panthers, a rebuilding team with very little established talent, inserted Bouwmeester straight into their top-four defensive rotation after his first NHL training camp showed that he could handle the jump from junior hockey to the pro ranks.

"I'd say he looks a lot closer to a four-year NHLer than a raw rookie," Dudley said before Bouwmeester's first regular season NHL game. "He's done wonderfully well so far. He's shown absolutely no intimidation at all. He makes the same crisp passes, still has the same vision and the wonderful feet he showed in junior."

On October 7, 2002, just 10 days after his 19th birthday, Bouwmeester signed a three-year contract with incentive clauses that could make it worth up to $11 million. He was worth the investment, playing over 20 minutes a night on the

Panthers' second defence pairing and taking part in all 82 of Florida's games as a rookie.

"The skating, that's what everybody obviously talks about because it's so wonderful," Dudley said. "But it's his vision and his thinking; that to me separates him from any other rookie. He sees the ice as well as any player on our team. His vacating of the zone is certainly, in my opinion, the best on our team already."

Although his transition to NHL life on the ice was a smooth one, adapting to life off the ice was a little rougher on Bouwmeester. It was the first time he had ever lived alone, and there were certain things he couldn't handle. For instance, when the Panthers rookies took the rest of the team out for dinner, a standard initiation ritual for first-year players, Bouwmeester brought enough cash to cover his portion of the $4000 tab. No credit cards or bank accounts for this rookie.

"He had trouble getting a social security number down here for a long time, so he couldn't get a bank account," said Ward, his roommate on the road. "He had three paycheques in his hotel room. I'm sure if he'd gone in to see the bank manager he could have got one, but he didn't want to bother him, I guess."

Although Bouwmeester was chosen to play in the 2002–03 YoungStars game during all-star weekend, he wasn't considered for rookie of the year honours largely because of his minus-29 defensive rating. The statistic is somewhat unfair in that it doesn't take into account that the Panthers often put Bouwmeester on the ice against the opposition's best forwards.

His play that season was good enough to persuade Hockey Canada to invite him to play on the senior men's team at the 2003 world championships, where he was once again the youngest player on the team. The 20-year-old Bouwmeester was a rock on the Canadian blue line, and he helped lead the team to its first world championship victory in six years.

As Bouwmeester stood on the blue line basking in his first championship victory, he heard the public address announcer call his name. Although he wasn't sure why he was doing it, Bouwmeester skated to centre ice and accepted a glass vase. It was only when he returned to join his teammates on the blue line that they told him he had been selected as the tournament's top defenceman.

His confidence strengthened by the world championships, Bouwmeester had an even better season on the Panthers blue line in 2003–04. He was second on the team in ice time, with over 23 minutes a game, and improved on his previous year's point total with 20 despite missing 18 games with a broken foot.

Bouwmeester returned to the world championships after that season and scored the game-winning goal in the gold medal final against

Sweden as Canada won consecutive championships for the first time since 1959. His strong play at the 2004 championships and his obvious potential as one of the burgeoning stars of the NHL got Bouwmeester a spot on Canada's team for the World Cup of Hockey, a best-on-best tournament where every NHL player was available to represent his country.

He inherited the spot of St. Louis Blues stalwart Chris Pronger, to whom Bouwmeester was most often compared, but it was clear that the youngster was only there as a spare part in case one of the team's top-six were to succumb to an injury. When Ed Jovanovski and Wade Redden were both injured in Canada's first two games, Bouwmeester stepped in and had an extraordinary tournament, not looking the least bit out of place among the best hockey players in the world as Canada went undefeated to win the World Cup.

Although everybody who had ever seen him play predicted Bouwmeester would be this good, no one could have predicted it would happen so soon. At the ripe age of 20, Bouwmeester was atop the hockey world, and he has no intention of coming down any time soon.

Finding Inspiration

Even though Jay Bouwmeester grew up in Edmonton, he was never a part of Oiler nation. Born in 1983, Bouwmeester has no memories of watching Wayne Gretzky feeding Jari Kurri for yet another goal, Grant Fuhr stoning someone on a breakaway, or Glen Sather chewing gum at a feverish pace behind the Oilers bench. Paul Coffey, the player whose skating stride Bouwmeester was constantly said to have copied, was out of Edmonton by the time Bouwmeester was three years old.

So where did he look for his hockey inspiration? To Michigan, where another quiet leader plied his trade in unassuming fashion: Steve Yzerman.

"He's my favourite player and always has been," Bouwmeester said. "I always liked the way he worked and played the game both ways."

As far as role models go, Bouwmeester could have done far worse.

NOTES ON SOURCES

Literally thousands of newspaper and magazine articles were used to shape the material found in this book. But those articles would simply be blank pages if it weren't for the dedicated work of NHL beat reporters across Canada and the United States who provided daily accounts of the players profiled here.

With youth being the common element in each of these players, there are very few books that have been written about most of them. One of the few, Jeff Rud's *Hockey's Young Superstars: The 25 Hottest Players on Ice* published by Raincoast Books (Vancouver, 2003), was a valuable source of background facts.

But most of the information and quotes came courtesy of the following news outlets and publications: *Atlanta Journal-Constitution, Associated Press, Boston Globe, Boston Herald, Calgary Herald, Calgary Sun, Canadian Press, Canwest News Service, The* (Wisconsin) *Capital Times, The* (Charlottetown) *Guardian, The* (Chatham) *Daily News, Chicago Tribune, Columbus Dispatch, Dallas Morning News, Edmonton Journal, Edmonton Sun, Financial Post, Globe and Mail, Halifax Daily News, Halifax Chronicle Herald,* Hockeydb.com, *Hockey Digest, The Hockey News, Le Journal de Montréal, The* (Kamloops) *Daily News, Kingston Whig-Standard, Knight-Ridder Newspapers, Miami Herald, Minneapolis Star Tribune, The* (Montréal) *Gazette, National Hockey League Official Guide & Record Book,*